Praise for the novels of Caprice Crane

Family Affair

"Perceptive, touching, and always hilarious, this is Caprice Crane's best work yet. It's an irresistible story with equal parts humor and heart."

—EMILY GIFFIN

"The phrase 'You don't marry the man; you marry his family' has never rung so true. *Family Affair* is so full of heart and humor, you'll want to squeeze into the family station wagon and sit shotgun for the ride."

—STEPHANIE KLEIN, *New York Times* bestselling author of *Moose*

"With a finely tuned ear for dialogue and a biting sense of humor, *Family Affair* is another winner. Crane is masterful at creating lovably flawed characters and placing them in hilariously relatable predicaments. I simply adored this book because no one does fiction funnier than Caprice Crane."

—JEN LANCASTER, *New York Times* bestselling author

"This is a clever and unique take on the romantic comedy—witty, touching, and often laugh-out-loud funny. I loved it."

—ALISON PACE, author of *City Dog*

Forget About It

"So funny and wise, I forgot about my own problems while reading it."

—VALERIE FRANKEL, author of *Thin Is the New Happy*

"So much fun . . . snappy dialogue . . . Crane's giddy, playful prose feels fresh."

—*Publishers Weekly*

"Caprice Crane's writing is so cool, I feel like the geek girl stalking her locker, trying to slide a mix CD through the slats before she spots me. *Stupid and Contagious* is hilarious and insightful. A book with its own soundtrack, this is one not to miss."

—Pamela Ribon, author of *Why Moms Are Weird*

ALSO BY CAPRICE CRANE

Stupid and Contagious

Forget About It

Family Affair

With a Little Luck

With a Little
Luck

a novel

Caprice Crane

Bantam Books Trade Paperbacks

New York

A Bantam Books Trade Paperback Original

Copyright © 2011 by Caprice Crane

All rights reserved.

Published in the United States by Bantam Books, an imprint of The Random House Publishing Group, a division of Random House, Inc., New York.

BANTAM BOOKS and the rooster colophon are registered trademarks of Random House, Inc.

Library of Congress Cataloging-in-Publication Data

Crane, Caprice
With a little luck : a novel / Caprice Crane.
p. cm.
ISBN 978-0-553-38624-0
eBook ISBN 978-0-440-42342-3
1. Superstition—Fiction. 2. Disc jockeys—Fiction. 3. Chick lit. I. Title.
PS3603.R379W58 2011
813'.6—dc22   2010053287

Printed in the United States of America

www.bantamdell.com

2 4 6 8 9 7 5 3 1

Book designed by Diane Hobbing

This one's for the fans. I am profoundly grateful for every single one of you. Every time I get an email from a reader it makes my day. *You* are the reason I do this.

With a Little Luck

Let a smile be your umbrella, and you'll end up with a face full of rain.

—GEORGE CARLIN

Chapter One

In this life, you could grow old sitting around waiting to get lucky.

That didn't come out right. What I meant is that waiting to accidentally run into Richard Branson in line to buy a burger at the very moment he's desperately looking for a new Executive Vice President of Adventure and Party Planning ("You'll just have to do," he says as he whisks you away in the limo), or waiting for that falling safe to just miss hitting you before it smashes through the sidewalk and plummets into a sewer tunnel, or waiting for a wealthy, athletic, artistic, wise, unpretentious, multilingual, manly, sensitive contradiction of impossible handsomeness to lean over and say, "Excuse me—I believe I left my stethoscope here on the way to the children's hospital" . . . Well, let's just agree you're going to be waiting awhile.

Me? I don't tempt fate. I don't dare destiny.

I may talk about hitting the lottery, but the truth is I never play because deep inside—on some level that's so far down it's beneath where I keep the memory of the time I walked in on my parents showering—I know there's no such thing as luck.

But I also have learned that believing there's no such thing as luck is very unlucky. Like, the worst. Beyond stealing someone's lucky four-leaf clover. (I know someone who did that and died. Seriously. Three years after doing it, he had a heart attack. And his great-granddaughter never forgave him—but I guess in some perverse way she got justice.)

If that sounds like a contradiction, I suppose maybe it is. But maybe not. Maybe I just don't believe in *good* luck. *Bad* luck—particularly of the sort arising from ignoring intuition and superstitions—that's another thing altogether.

The history of superstition is also a history of timing. We'll never know whether a lone sober Trojan looked across the courtyard on that fateful night and said, "I don't like the look of that horse thing. Bad luck." But if he or she had, the protest would have fallen on deaf ears: The masses were completely tickled pink by the offering. History has shown that it pays to be suspicious of large, seemingly useless gifts from one's sworn enemy. And that includes your aunt's sketchy second husband.

Consider: If the captain of the *Titanic* had pulled out his tin bullhorn and announced, "Someone in first class just threw a shoe into a mirror and broke it, so I've got a bad feeling about this route—let's slow down and head south," then as a purely scientific matter, superstition would have saved that ship. I'm just saying.

And if I had only listened to my intuition—that socially acceptable term for what is really superstition—I'd never have followed Emily Ottinger through that third yellow light (I swear it was still yellow) on the way to the mall and never would have ended up wrapping my mom's new Audi around Mr. Pitrelli's pickup truck when I was sixteen. Mean, old, grouchy, kid-hating Mr. Pitrelli, I might add.

One moment follows another. Next comes from previous. So you have to stay on your toes. Protect yourself. Listen to that little voice inside you that says, "Don't do that! You won't like the consequences." Look at all the stuff that's happened to you along the twisting road of your life—good and bad. Still think that all those seemingly disconnected, random events that have no interrelation, not even a simple correlation, have absolutely nothing to do with those best-laid plans crashing and burning in the face of your destiny? Tell my dad that. In a career spent chasing the elusive lucky score, he's come up empty more times than a fashion model's lunchbox.

Better yet, tell my mom that. She was the one unlucky enough to end up married to him.

U

I know that by now you're thinking I sound like I know the score. But I don't want to give you the wrong impression. I may know the score, but half the time I'm not sure I know the teams or even what game we're playing.

Most of the time, I feel like a total fraud. Like I have no idea how I've made it this far without the world figuring out that I have no idea what I'm doing or that I'm relying on some sign or the fact that I glanced at the clock at 11:11 or the fact that Paul McCartney's "With a Little Luck" was playing on the radio when my alarm woke me up to give me a little extra confidence that "we can make this whole damn thing work out." This "whole damn thing" being my life.

You'd think admitting to feeling like a fraud is the kind of thing that would qualify as an innermost thought. The very kind of thing that gives rise to the term "innermost thoughts," in fact—because they're born and live and die inside you, never seeing the light of day (unless you're the type who regularly drunk-dials an ex and starts a horrifyingly ill-advised confession with, "You know, I've never told anybody this before, but . . ."). You'd think someone with any semblance of self-awareness or a good enough filter or enough *Real World: Miami*s under her belt would know better by now than to confess these types of things to another living breathing person. But you'd be wrong.

U

Here I am in this outward cloak of certainty covering extreme self-doubt, walking into Game Night with a bottle of chilled champagne and an outfit that says, "I'm definitely stylish but comfortable enough in my own skin that I don't have to try that hard." What I'm really thinking is that I tried *really* hard to look like I'm not trying hard; in fact, trying to look like you didn't try hard is downright exhausting. Mind you, I'm not feeling terribly stylish. Especially since it's raining. Rain is never good luck. Just ask my hair. I feel pretty good about myself, though—all things being relative. Me feeling good about myself means my up-three-pounds, down-three-pounds existence was leaning toward the down side this morning, I don't have a golf-ball-sized zit screaming for attention on my cheek, and amazingly enough, tonight's rain hair doesn't have me looking like a brunette, Caucasian, female version of Don King. Definitely a good sign.

It's hard enough being a normal girl these days. Sure, I've just described a few wacky characteristics, but I'm not talking mentality here—I'm talking normal as in "not enhanced." More and more, everywhere I turn there's some girl, some naturally beautiful girl, who is determined to turn herself into a Barbie doll. It's frightening. Plus, with global warming and the sun getting hotter and hotter, isn't there a good chance that one day all of these gals will just start to melt? I vowed to myself that I will grow old gracefully—granted, I'm only twenty-eight years old, so I'm gonna reserve the right to change my mind at some point, but for now, I'll stick with what I've got.

Which, mind you, is pretty okay on most days. I have medium brown hair that's a couple of inches below my shoulders. I put highlights and lowlights in to make it a little more exciting, but the only thing that really does is set me back a couple hundred bucks every few weeks. I have brown eyes that are fairly boring, and I've been told I have a "perfect" nose, but I don't even know what that means. That said, nothing else about me is "perfect," so I'll take it. My teeth are straight (thanks, Dr. Edelstein!), and I have dimples when I smile, which I hate. Anyway, that's me. Nothing spectacular, but I did manage to have the cutest boyfriend in school in the sixth grade, so I'm not entirely hopeless.

I walk into the party behind a guy who is wearing a T-shirt that says "Everybody Dies." Oh, and that's not the best part. See, the *i* in "Dies" is shaped like a gun, and it's pointing upward, toward his face. Heartwarming. Hang on, it gets better. As he closes the door behind us, this dude's small black umbrella pops open and blooms in front of him. Then he spins around to close it, and the umbrella catches my favorite sweater and claws a huge hole in it. It seems to be happening in slow motion, the umbrella opening, my eyes widening, the menacing tip moving toward me like a sword thrust. This is suddenly like the shittiest version of *The Three Musketeers* ever. And, yes, I've seen the one with Charlie Sheen.

"Sorry," T-shirt Guy says with a shrug, nonchalantly unhinging his evil, renegade umbrella from my poor, sweet, now horribly disfigured sweater.

I exhale and swallow deeply. What can I say to him? What do you say when a complete stranger has not only just destroyed your sweater but also dragged you into his blatant violation of the "umbrella opened indoors" superstition, thus almost certainly setting off a downward spiral of unfortunate future events in your life?

"It's okay," I carefully respond, anger receding from DefCon 5 to a more reasonable 2. "But . . . aren't you worried about bad luck?"

"Aw, I don't believe in any of that," he says and laughs, as if my concern is silly.

I'll show him silly. "Well," I say, and I think about it before I say it and decide not to say it and then say it anyway. "I would be if I were you. Bad luck for both of us."

He turns and looks me square in the eye. I'd been too transfixed on his death threat of a T-shirt to look beyond it. His eyes are hazel. The kind of hazel in which, if you liked the guy, you'd notice the specks of green and gold, but if you despised him, you'd see murky brown, despite his desperately grasping at the hazel of it all.

"I promise you," he says, "you will not have bad luck because of this. It will be my bad luck, and mine alone. I'm owning the bad luck on this one." He seems amused, making air quotes every time he says "bad luck."

"Fine," I say. "I hope you're right."

"So you're wishing bad luck on me?" he asks, smiling.

"No," I correct. "Of course not. I'm just wishing it not on me."

"Right . . ." he says, and then looks around the party.

I get self-conscious and think he's bored of me, and why wouldn't he be? I'm the crazy person telling him his umbrella is going to ruin his life and possibly mine. I'd run for the hills, too.

"Well, nice meeting you," I say, even though we didn't really meet, no names were exchanged (although I'm calling him "Everybody Dies" in my head and I'm hoping he's calling me "Sweater Girl" in his because, hell, you know men, it could be a lot worse than that, like "Crazy Chick Who Thinks I've Doomed Us Both but at Least She's Kinda Hot"), and I wonder if he does think I'm kinda hot—men dig torn clothing, right?—but now I'm even regretting saying "Nice meeting you," so I rush off to blend into the party and leave this brutal, sadistic Eviscerator of Sweaters, his not-at-all brutal, wonderfully hazel eyes, and his inarguably bad luck behind me.

I haven't been to Jason's in a while because my work schedule rarely allows it, but also, I just don't love parties. I always feel like I'm being forced to have a good time. It's kind of like having your boss over for dinner. It's supposed to be fun but it just ends up being more work. Jason is known around town for having these super-elaborate game-themed parties, and invites are coveted. He has them catered by top-notch L.A. restaurants, sometimes multiple restaurants with tents stationed in various rooms in his house, and he always has two rooms of games going simultaneously. Still, I find them awkward at best. But I try to force myself out of my isolated shell every now and then and Jason's parties are as good an opportunity as any.

Jason is a script doctor who's pretty well known around L.A. He gets paid a lot of money to rewrite scripts that were written by people who were also paid a lot of money but didn't quite achieve what the producers wanted. Or they achieved what the producers wanted but not what the studio wanted. Or what they really failed to achieve was what the star wanted. Or what the star that replaced the original star wanted. And so on. So Jason comes in and "punches up" the script with new dialogue and jokes, and the big scenes that will usually end up in the trailer and quite often be the only funny parts of the movie. You know how sometimes you'll catch a movie and you've already seen all the best parts in the trailer? That was done on purpose. The movie sucked, so they hired a guy to come in and build five "trailer moments" into the script. These moments trick gullible viewers into the theater, helping the studio to recoup at least some of the money it spent. You know, like in *Point Break* when Keanu Reeves's boss says, "Do you think that taxpayers would like it, Utah, if they knew that they were paying a federal agent to surf and pick up girls?" And Keanu says, "Babes," to which the boss replies, "I beg your pardon?" And Keanu says, "The correct term is 'babes.'" Best line in the movie. Except it wasn't in the movie. It was only in the trailer. (And, yes, Keanu's name in the movie was Johnny Utah. You just can't make this stuff up.)

I didn't know any of this until Jason explained it to me. He also explained that he never gets any credit on the movies, which seemed kind of unfair, but he assured me he was crying all the way to the bank. Personally, I cry at the bank, too, most often after viewing my account balance.

But getting back to the party: Jason is wearing a bandana on his head, a sweatshirt, short shorts, and kneesocks—the kind with the colored bands at the top. He looks like a character from a Wes Anderson film, which presumably is what he was going for. Jason always encourages people to come to Game Night dressed as a recognizable character from a movie, and the best costume wins a prize. He's not strictly recognizable, but the shamelessness wins in my book, anyway. I didn't dress as anyone but me, because even that can be a challenge and it's not Halloween. Then again, with my newly ripped sweater maybe I'm a homeless person or a survivor in one of those post-nuclear-holocaust movies. Or maybe I'm a Freddy Krueger victim. Or—even worse—I'm Freddy Krueger! He wears a sweater, right?

I swallow my concerns and put on my game face as Jason kisses me on the cheek, takes the champagne, and subtly spins me around—forcing me into a face-to-face with, you guessed it: Everybody Eyes—I mean Dies. The (kinda adorable) bastard stands before me, smirking. I find myself glancing back and forth between his eyes and the gun on his chest.

"Like my shirt?" he asks.

"It's quite uplifting," I say.

"Everybody dies," he says, with a knowing nod.

"Yes," I reply. "I believe that was the original title of that R.E.M. song. But it seemed like a downer, so Michael Stipe went with 'Everybody Hurts' instead."

"We didn't actually meet before," he says, and extends his hand. "I'm Dustin."

"Hi, Justin," I reply.

"Dustin," he says.

"I'm sorry. I'm Berry."

"Well, which is it—you're sorry, or you're Berry?"

"I'm Berry. With an *e*."

"She means she's berry sorry," Jason says.

"Berry like the fruit," I overexplain. "Not with an *a*, like Barry Williams from *The Brady Bunch*." How many times have I said that? Enough to want to never hear myself say it again. Yet there it was. Does anyone even know who Barry Williams is? Do I watch too much Nick at Nite? While I'm lost in my thoughts, is Justin/Dustin saying something else?

He is: "Or bury. Like, with a *u*."

I smile. "You know, everybody dies, but not everyone is buried."

He smiles. My, that's a nice smile. "Berry."

"Berry," I confirm.

"Good," Jason says. "Now that you both know her name so well, you can be on the same team."

"Great," I say.

"Berry's single," Jason adds, immediately walking away in a supreme act of assitude, leaving Justin (no . . . Dustin) and me to stew in that teeming vat of awkward.

I'm going to ask that we pause for a moment here. Yes, I'm single. But was that necessary? Did Jason need to point it out like some yenta matchmaker? And on a scale of one to totally desperate, how did I just rate? So what if I haven't had a boyfriend in . . . um . . . a very long time? It hasn't been strictly my fault. I've had bad luck. Case in point: People are opening umbrellas indoors, right into me. How's a person supposed to find love with that kind of thing going on all around her?

"I don't know why he said that," I tell Dustin. (Yes. Dustin.) "That was . . . really unnecessary."

"Not necessarily unnecessary," Dustin says, grinning. Dustin is undeniably good-looking. And charming. My mood lightens as together we move into Game Room One.

"Hey, man!" some guy says to Dustin, raising a hand for a high-five. "Congrats on the Grammy!"

I watch Dustin carefully in this moment—partially because I'm wondering what this Grammy business is (he won a Grammy?), but more important, I'm wondering how he'll respond to a high-five. This is far more critical than it might sound. I myself am not a high-fiver. I suppose it's sort of a "dude" thing, but still, it gives me pause.

Dustin responds to the high-five in kind. I suppose it would be rude to leave the guy hanging . . . but anyway, what's this Grammy business?

"You won a Grammy?" I ask. "That's huge."

"Yeah, thanks," he says.

"Should I know who you are? You're not Kanye West, are you?"

"Yes, I am."

"Wow. You're all kinds of famous. And, well . . . occasionally hated."

"Only by friends, acquaintances, and immediate family," he corrects. "I'm actually a record producer. And I haven't ever worked with Kanye, but I'd love to."

"We all have our own crosses to bear," I say, taking a sip from my drink.

"That's what Jesus said."

That's when I spit on him. No, let me clarify: My drink suddenly came spraying out of my mouth, all over Dustin's completely-ridiculous-but-man-it-sure-is-growing-on-me T-shirt.

"Oh, my," I say, attempting to dab his shirt dry.

"You're trying to get me back for ruining your sweater, aren't you?"

"Yes, that's it," I say. "I was locked and loaded. Thank God you cracked a joke. I was about to drown." I look away in embarrassment.

"So what do your days entail?" he asks, sensing that I'm horrified and generously trying to change the subject.

"Eating, mostly," I say. "Errands. Taking my dog to the dog park."

"Okay, let's get back to the dog in a minute. No job, huh? Trust-fund baby? Wow, I knew I liked you. Come to Poppa. . . ."

"Ha! I wish. I work nights. In radio, actually. KKCR."

Dustin steps backward and smacks himself on the head. I didn't know people actually did that in real life. "Classic rock! Shit, you're Berry Lambert!"

"I am." He's heard of me? Wasn't the "Berry" part a giveaway? How many Berrys does he know? Chuck Berry? Fred Berry? Franken Berry?

"I should have recognized your voice," he says, and I must admit, I never get tired of hearing that. And now we have even more to talk about, and it seems my luck is changing.

Things progress famously from there. We've just won our seventh round of charades, with Dustin acting out the iconic scene in *Saved by the Bell* when Jessie gets hooked on caffeine pills and has a major meltdown: "I'm so excited, I'm so excited, I'm so, I'm so . . . scared!"

I turn to Dustin: "Do you ever feel like a total fraud? Like you have no idea how you've even scraped by this far without the whole world finding out? Sometimes I can't believe they pay me to do what I do."

"Every day," he says.

"Really?" I implore. Maybe it's the fact that I drank a whole beer (don't believe what you hear about radio folk—I'm a total lightweight), or maybe it's because I really feel the need to connect, but it seems like I can really talk to this guy.

"Shit, yes," he says. "I get paid to turn knobs and listen to music all day. The truth is, it's all the artist. Remember when Don Was hit the scene and everyone said he was a genius producer? Well, he produced Bob Dylan and the Rolling Stones! Give me Kobe and Shaq, and I'll be a Phil Jackson 'genius,' too. Half the time, I ask someone in the room, 'How's this?' And they say, 'It needs something— maybe more compression on the rhythm guitar or gate it a little.'

So I pretend to turn a knob and ask, 'What about now?' And they say, 'Yeah, that's better,' even though nothing's changed. So yeah, I hear ya. I'm in constant fear of being found out and forced to grow up."

"Oh my God," I say and laugh. "You kinda jumped metaphors with Kobe and Shaq, but I get it. I so get it. That's me. On the radio. Wondering when the other shoe is going to drop. Or when I'm gonna walk in and find out that they've hired someone even younger and cheaper than me, or someone with some kind of formal training, or even worse—our station's gone completely sans DJs and they're having everything done via computer. After all, it's classic rock as in 'classic.' All the songs are good by definition, so how hard is it to pick 'em? I mean, if I was a DJ for a 'mediocre rock' station and everyone listened to my show, now that would be talent."

We talk like this the whole time we're not acting out an animal, event, or movie title (Dustin would have been arrested in the Middle East for how he mimed *Cocktail*), and together we win first prize for our team. We decide to celebrate by going out for a drink, which turns into an all-night make-out session on my couch. I never take guys home with me—stop it, I know what you're thinking; it's true—but Dustin and I really seemed to click. We got each other's jokes and seemed to have everything in common, from a love of churros (delicious) to almost identical scars on our right arms (his from a broken wrist, mine from an unruly toaster oven) to having the same favorite *I Love Lucy* episode (you know the one: "Slowly I turned . . .").

When you barely know a guy and you take him home with you, I guess it's pretty much a given that you're gonna sleep with him. So I don't. I figure all the girls in the music industry probably just sleep with him at the drop of a hat. More specifically, the drop of his pants. (Or whatever. Something usually drops; that's my point.) Regardless, I draw the line at not-so-heavy petting. I want to stand out. Not be like all the other girls.

"This is super-fun and all," I say, gently pushing him away and sliding his fingers out of the all-too-convenient hole in my sweater. I look into his now-most-definitely hazel eyes. "But I don't want to give you the wrong idea."

"That you like me?"

"That I'm a whore."

"Sweet. So I don't have to pay you?"

"I'm serious," I say. "I kind of like you. And I never like anyone, so I don't want to screw this up by being a total slutbag."

"What if I like slutbags?"

He kisses me again, and it's a major effort to pull away, but I do. My thinking is this: Maybe the umbrella wasn't bad luck at all. Maybe it was good luck. Maybe all of my silly fears have been just that. You don't know how big this could be for me. This could be huge. Maybe his umbrella was meant to snag my sweater just so we would meet. I am definitely not going to ruin this.

I sigh and mentally dig in my heels. "I . . . think you should take off."

"My clothes?"

He's all smiles. It is increasingly hard to say no. So I don't.

"Yes," I say. "Most definitely yes. But some other time."

"Okay . . ." he says, rising from my couch. The word "rising" sticks in my mind, and I almost reconsider. But no. I'm going to do this one the right way.

I walk him to the door and store my number in his iPhone. He kisses me on my forehead and pulls me in for a hug. He says he'll call me tomorrow, and I feel almost giddy as I close the door behind him.

Oh, Dustin. Dustin. My adorable, hilarious, clumsy, poorly dressed Dustin.

It was Dustin, right?

It would be so nice if something made sense for a change.
—ALICE, FROM *ALICE'S ADVENTURES*
IN WONDERLAND

Chapter Two

Five days have passed since the Night of the Dustin, and it's painfully clear that my choosing to be "less easy" has inspired his choosing to "not call me again."

I'm disappointed but resigned to my fate. Such is life. "School" by Nirvana should be my theme song. "Won't you believe it? It's just my luck."

Who has time for relationships, anyway? (Is what people who aren't in relationships tell themselves.) Honestly, though, my hours really do make it tough. And I have other kinds of relationships. For instance, the Chinese restaurant around the corner knows my order without me having to say word one. (Or #52.) I don't even need to tell them my name most of the time. You know you're a regular customer when they answer the phone and say, "Hi, Berry. Same thing?" The diner across the street? Same. Granted, I like things the way I like them, and I take comfort in rituals. You might even say that sometimes I feel like if I don't order the exact same thing, the space-time continuum will be thrown off, and if I'm having a good week it will suddenly turn to shit. And of course, like all things, it could be a coincidence, but the proof is in the pudding. Especially if I order custard instead.

One change in my routine can set off a bunch of reactive dominoes that start with there being nothing left in the perpetually stale pot of coffee at work and end with one of my usual unusual listeners threatening suicide if I don't play "Sara Smile" by Hall & Oates. (I still think Oates got too much credit, but if he played a role in saving a life, I'm almost willing to forgive him anything. Except the mustache.) I only wish I was making that up. Regular radio listeners are a very special animal. They tend to call in, well, regularly. They tend to think they know you. They tend to be insane.

Remember, these are not new songs. These people can buy and listen to the CD or download the songs from the Internet anytime they want. But I get it. There's just something magical about requests on the radio. It brings back memories for "Mike from the Valley" of that night twenty years ago when he lost his virginity in the back of his parents' Dodge Dart. You know the story. "Whole Lotta Love" by Led Zeppelin came on the radio right when he was getting a "whole lotta love," and now he just needs to hear that song again tonight. But for every sad sack reliving his glory days and each crazy calling you from his tinfoil hat to tell you that his pet parakeet wants to warn the world that the end is near, there will be some nice person who heard you mention a pounded chicken dish three weeks earlier and will track down the recipe and send it in so you can try it out.

Of course, then there are the people who will actually cook the chicken and bring it to you. Like I'm gonna eat that? Twenty percent of all listeners hate the DJs they listen to—it's a fact; you can look it up—and nobody's looking for a cyanide surprise to brighten up their day—or put an end to it. So you have to assume that these people know you won't eat their food, as nice a gesture as it may be. And of course I feel bad when it's some little old lady who bakes chocolate-chip cookies and you just know they're not poisoned. But do you really know? Everyone has briefly, if mostly innocently, fantasized about killing someone at some point. I sure have. In fact, that little old lady is just like me. Except a lot older. And kinda shriveled up. Also, she smells kinda weird. And she has shifty wee old-lady eyes. Come to think of it, I'm calling the police.

So like everything, my audience is a mixed bag. But I tend to think the good outweighs the bad. Then again, I try to be a glass-half-full person. Although I stand by my theory that if you measure your happiness by the amount of liquid you have in your glass, you are either a cliché or an alcoholic.

Brace yourself: I'm going to come clean. My actual first name is Beryl. Quite possibly the ugliest name you've ever heard for a girl, right? Don't be shy. It is. I accept it. (Well, I accept it to the point of never going by it, at least.) Nobody's ever called me that—I've always gone by Berry—but it does say Beryl on my birth certificate. It's pronounced like "barrel," as in Cracker Barrel or Crate & Barrel or "barrel of monkeys." The name is of Greek origin, and it means light green semiprecious stone. I'd argue that I am entirely precious as opposed to semi, but if I had any bargaining power to begin with, I would have chosen a different name altogether. The word "beryl" is actually taken from the Sanskrit term "verulia," and the beryl was biblically considered a token of good luck.

So now you are fully up to speed on the etymology of my first name. I hope you appreciate this little detour through ancient languages, but there is a point—the reason my dad was so insistent on my name. The minute someone told him Beryl meant "luck," there was no changing his mind, because my dad, for better or worse (but almost always for worse), is a gambler. It's what makes him who he is. It's why my mom fell in love with him and why she ultimately left him.

So the superstition thing—I know it's kind of stupid. I know a lot of people don't buy into it, and that's fine for them. Or you, if you fall into that category. Me? If I hit two red lights in a row on my way to work I might as well just turn around and go home, because I know it's going to be a bad day.

Sadly, I can't do that because I work at a radio station, and if I don't show up two things will happen simultaneously: a) they'll have dead air, and b) I'll be fired. But the fact remains that it will be a bad day. That could mean that my board-op will be in a mood, and that happens more often than I'd like, or it could mean that my boss is on a tear because our competitor station is beating us in the ratings, or it could simply mean that I will have a bad hair day, fight with my mom, or get mayo on a sandwich after I expressly state "no mayo." And really, what is with that? Why the seemingly compulsive need to force mayo, folks? When will it be universally banned unless being used to make something beginning and ending with tuna? Because that is the only acceptable use, and even then—please use sparingly.

I wouldn't buy into it if nine times out of ten my superstitions weren't confirmed. But they are. They say that everything happens in threes. . . . It's true. One famous person dies and two more will follow. You get a paper cut and stub your toe? Count on biting your lip the next time you eat a piece of fruit. But fear not, it works in the reverse as well. You meet a great guy and get a promotion at work. . . . You're bound to find that pair of jeans that's been missing since October of two years ago.

To understand why I believe these things and not think I'm entirely off my rocker, I guess you need to know a little something about my dad, Brian Lambert. To this day, my father will insist that every superstition he has ever passed down to me is fact, not hypothetical—that luck is achieved by following a "code," and luck is, well, kind of like my dad's religion.

My dad was a professional gambler for my whole childhood. His game of choice was poker, and he was good. He would explain at length that poker is a skill and it has nothing to do with luck. But he could turn on a dime and tell you everything in life has to do with luck, so it would get confusing. Regardless, he had about sixteen thousand superstitions that I had to honor and live by or there would be hell to pay in the form of guilt, blame, and shame.

My dad always told me that the world was "my oyster." For one thing, I'm allergic to shellfish. That makes the analogy bad enough to begin with. But have you ever looked at an oyster? I mean, really stopped to give it a close examination? There's that curving, cloudy-gray shelf of shellfish fleshiness, topped by a dirty-brown ruffled disk, all swimming under a layer of glossy slime, the whole thing looking like a pile of washed-up sea vomit, or something you pull out of your sink drain when it's clogged.

So that's what my world is?

Bottoms up!

If Dad had only said, "The world is your fudge-mocha latte with caramel shavings," I'd have been on my way.

So now I'm just as superstitious as my dad—and not in a good way. Not even in an "isn't that adorable" way. I believe giving certain gifts can have catastrophic effects. For example, giving someone a watch is basically telling that person that it's time for them to go. Ditto for shoes. Give someone a pair of shoes and they will walk right out of your life in them. Seeing an ambulance is very unlucky, unless you pinch your nose. I won't step on cracks, walk under ladders, or say goodbye to someone on a bridge.

Oh, it goes on. I don't mind Friday the thirteenth, oddly enough, but I refuse to travel on a Tuesday if it's the twenty-second. I believe that everything happens for a reason, and one misstep can have disastrous consequences. And don't get me started on snakes, owls, black cats, the number four, or broken mirrors.

If you ask my best friend, Natalie, she'll tell you I am insane and that none of this stuff is true. But she secretly quasi–buys into it, too. Yet she'll say that I waste so much time and energy worrying about if I'm doing the wrong thing, stepping on a superstition, or paving the way for disaster that I don't have enough time to actually enjoy my life. Which a) is not true, and b) is a total contradiction, since anytime I'm out of earshot she'll say that she's had bad luck for the past four years because she broke a mirror and now she just has to suffer through the next three.

Now, if I'd known about her broken mirror I could have solved the problem when it happened, but because she doesn't want to encourage my craziness, she kept it from me. Too bad, because I would have told her she simply had to wait seven hours before picking up the broken pieces (one for each year of potential bad luck) and then bury them outside in the moonlight. But she didn't tell me. So now she suffers.

Poor thing. It's sad, really.

When I was little I thought that we were extremely fancy people. We'd drive up to Vegas every weekend and stay in hotels where they'd treat us like royalty. My mom and I practically lived on room service, and all of our meals would be comped.

My older brother, Peter, would usually stay at home or crash with friends. He was already a teenager when I was still carrying around stuffed animals. I loved him, of course, but he was always a bit of a stranger to me growing up. Once I was in high school and he was in his twenties we finally bonded, but by the time I hit my twenties he was in his thirties and living in Chicago.

So Peter missed out on our Vegas trips, and I always wondered if he knew what he was missing. I guess when you're a teenager you definitely have better things to do—at least you think you do. To me, Vegas was like Disneyland. Minus the rides, of course, but I don't much care for roller coasters, anyway. Between all the different hotels and themed casinos, it was my own version of an amusement park. I knew the names of all of the dealers at Dad's favorite tables in town, and they all knew me. It made me feel special. Looking back, I think they felt sorry for me and that's why they were so nice—what little girl wants to spend all of her time in smoke-filled rooms with no windows or clocks, watching her dad go through the crazy highs and lows that go with serious gambling? If the little girl doesn't know anything different, then it's not so bad. Until she grows up and realizes that nobody else lived that way, that smiles from people taking your money don't always mean friendship, and that although you can specifically seek out a magic show . . . everything in Vegas is pretty much smoke and mirrors. A guy can lose his mortgage money in an instant, but a buffet and a prostitute can make him still somehow end up feeling like he won something. Until the sun comes up, anyway.

That's the one thing my dad never did, though—cheat on my

mom. Through all of their drama, and there was plenty of it, he always thought the sun rose and set with her. The problem was that he spent so much time in casinos he never actually knew if the sun was rising or setting.

Nor did he care. He'd get lost in the games, and he'd be lost to us.

One time I took the elevator downstairs into Harrah's, wearing my footie pajamas, in the middle of the night, hoping I could drag my dad back upstairs because I knew how upset Mom was that he still hadn't come to bed. But my dad had an excuse that I know he believed with all his heart: Tommy Lee Jones was eating in the Oyster Bar, and when Tommy Lee walked in, he "nodded" at my dad. My dad took that as a sign that he was gonna win big that night. Because how often do you see a real live movie star, and how often does that star make eye contact with you? Dad's craps table was suddenly, miraculously "hot" within moments.

The problem with this particular night, aside from the obvious problems associated with a five-year-old wandering around in a casino, was twofold: One, I didn't tell my mom I was leaving our room and managed to sneak out when she was asleep, so when she woke up and found me gone, she thought I'd been kidnapped. She stormed into the casino, looking for me, wearing only her nightgown, sobbing to the point of barely being able to breathe. And two, when after almost an hour Mom finally found me, I tried to explain that I'd gone downstairs to bring Dad back for the night, but he couldn't come back right then because he got a "sign" from Tommy Lee Jones. But the words "Tommy Lee Jones" never actually emerged from my mouth. The words that emerged from my mouth were "Kathie Lee Gifford." See, I couldn't remember what name he said. I knew it was someone famous, and I knew it had "Lee" in the middle, and my mom watched *Regis and Kathie Lee* every morning and my dad would always comment about how cute she was, "if she'd just maybe stop talking," so Mom already had a tiny jealous streak when it came to Kathie Lee.

"What do you mean he can't come home because of Kathie Lee Gifford?" Mom said through a smile that I knew wasn't a real smile because of how her teeth were clenched. The bad smile turned into a worse smile seconds later when I replied, "He said she made him suddenly 'hot.' "

"Oh, *did she now?*" More teeth. More clenching. This was not good.

"I said he should come back upstairs, but he said something about 'crap' and Kathie Lee being hot—"

"That's it," my mom cut me off. "I've heard enough. And I've had enough."

That was pretty much the point of no return. My mom lost it. She packed up our bags and said we were done with Vegas . . . and my father. At least she was.

There were a good number of years when I felt guilty about it. Like if I'd only gotten Tommy Lee Jones's name right, my parents would still be together and we'd have been a happy family. But I know better. It could have been anything. Or nothing. And it wasn't even the Kathie Lee debacle that was the last proverbial roll of the dice. It was the fact that her child was wandering in a casino, in footie pajamas, at three a.m. That did it.

I'm pretty sure my mom hasn't been back to Vegas since that night. My parents divorced six months later. Even so, my dad never stopped loving my mom, nor did he stop loving Vegas. I'd spend every third weekend with him in his rented apartment in the Valley—the less cool (and predominantly less expensive) part of Los Angeles—watching him bet on sports games and play online poker, once that became "a thing."

I actually loved our weekends. And I love my dad, but then

again, I didn't have to be married to him. I could see how frustrating the gambling thing could be. Aren't poker players complete liars by virtue of the game? That could complicate things and blur trust in even the most trusting and trustworthy parties. Especially in a marriage. But in his defense, it wasn't like my dad had a job and quit it to play poker full-time, risking their financial security. They met when they were just out of college and he hadn't really even figured out what he was going to do with his life. He was playing a lot of poker at the time, and one day he kind of realized that he was making a decent living at it. He was being referred to as a "pro" poker player before he even knew he was one. And suddenly he was ranked and winning tournaments left and right. I asked him what happened, years after he'd stopped playing professionally—what really happened that forced him out of the tournament circuit— and the look he gave me was a combination of frustration, righteousness, and sorrow.

"You know," he said.

"I don't, Dad," I pressed. "I really don't actually know what happened."

What I did know was that he had been accused of cheating, but I knew my dad, and he wasn't a cheater. There was some big controversy that was at once public and private. Public enough to have shamed his name and forced him off the national circuit and into a life of low-level sports gambling with bottom-feeder bookies and guys you don't want to screw over. And private enough that nobody ever knew the story behind the story.

There was a long pause. I'd never asked my dad point-blank, and he knew that it was time to tell me, if only to finally get it off his chest.

"You remember your uncle Lou, right?" he said, eyebrows raised, lines gathering on his forehead.

He knew I did. Lou was a character. Lou was one of those hon-
orary uncles who's not related to you by blood but who you know
would give you his kidney if you needed it. Of course, fortunately
for Lou, since he's not actually a blood relative, his kidney is un-
likely to be a match. . . .

"Lou got into some trouble," Dad said, and looked away. It was
clear that he didn't want to tell me what kind of trouble, and I
didn't know if it was crucial to the story, so I sat silently, waiting for
whatever was going to come out next. "Lou's a good man . . . with
a good heart. But he'd buy his friends into tournaments. He had a
system going with some of the dealers, marked cards, that sort of
thing. He didn't tell me, wanted to keep me out of it."

"Okay . . ."

"That night, I was one of five players in, but I didn't know what
BS he had going on. I only found out after he got busted. He did
everything he could to keep my name clear, but you know how it is.
His word was no good anymore. I hit a lot of hands that night,
thanks to Lou. I just thought I was hot. The reality was very different. In hindsight, hell, I would have been better off being part of
the whole racket."

"No, you wouldn't have, Dad," I said. "You're more honorable
than that."

And he was. This was the guy who once went back into Ralphs
supermarket in the pouring rain because he noticed the cashier had
given him too much change.

"What's my life now?" he asked, and looked at me like I might
have an answer other than the obvious, and if I did, he hoped we
could somehow will it into a reality.

"You're not a cheater," I reassured him, but it didn't seem to matter. And I understood why. If you do the time, you may as well get
to do the crime. He'd been so shamed that his life spiraled down-

ward into a pretty depressing existence. He went from being a pro poker player, nationally known, playing televised games, the real deal . . . to being an online poker player with a side habit of sports betting. Weekends with high rollers in Vegas turned into weekends with degenerates at the Los Alamitos Race Course. Or worse . . . the OTB. Have you ever been to the OTB? I'm half surprised he doesn't shoot himself. What a difference a day makes.

I try to spend as much time as I can with my dad, but it tends to feel more like an obligation than a choice these days. And that's not because I don't want to see him. It's because he considers me his "good-luck charm," so if I don't see him and he loses a game or his horse comes in fourth, it's somehow my fault.

And I don't have time to be somebody's "genie." The hours I put in at the radio station are kind of chaotic. When I first started at the station, I took overnights because they told me everyone works their way up. Knowing that I'd have to start somewhere, I was happy to have any slot that was actually on-air. Five years in, I'm now on the night shift, which is seven p.m. to midnight. The truth is, aside from talk radio, there really aren't any overnight shifts anymore. Radio can't afford to pay people to stay awake. And if we're being really honest, I can go in and tape my shows when need be, and it takes just three hours of tape to fill five hours of programming. But I like being there. I like doing it live. The thought of everything being automated depresses me.

I also work Saturday nights now, which you'd think would make dating hard—you'd be right—and is maybe the reason Jason felt the need to flash the "She's single!" neon sign at Dustin. He was just trying to help. I wouldn't know what "date night" was if it showed up with a dozen long-stemmed roses and made out with me for three hours on the couch while we completely ignored whatever movie we'd thrown on. Or something.

I don't mind, though. Honestly, I don't. Music has been such an epic part of my life. Not to sound like "Mike from the Valley" or anything—I'm not longing to hear the soundtrack to my lost virginity. ("Everything You Want" by Vertical Horizon, in case you're wondering. And no, he did not turn out to be everything I wanted.) But like most people, I can hear a song and be taken back to an exact moment in my life, a certain experience that's frozen in time with that song as its soundtrack, and it's magical. The five senses aren't specific enough. Hearing, sure. But how about hearing a song that changed your life? Either by virtue of the lyrics having a profound impact on you or the song simply playing in the background at some incredibly significant moment. That is absolutely a sense—at least one of mine. It's the sense of connectedness. The words of a song expressing exactly how you're feeling, so you somehow don't feel so alone.

And I get to play music and be paid for it. How many people can say they get to do their dream job—speak into a mic and have their voices, their thoughts, their song selections, broadcast to millions of listeners? It's pretty cool. It's something I've wanted to do since I was in junior high and used to call the radio station to have them dedicate love songs to Greg Dinofrio. Just hearing them say "This one goes out from Berry to Greg" would give me hours of satisfaction. The next few days were dedicated to wondering whether Greg heard it. Most of June and July were consumed wondering why Greg didn't ask me to the end-of-the-year dance. The satisfaction of seeing Greg, his husband, and their adopted Chinese babies on their Facebook page would almost erase the shame of me actually taking the time to look him up nine years later. But rejections die hard. I would know.

Which brings me back to Bad Luck Chuck. When you rarely hook up with guys as it is, and then the one time you think you connect with someone you get slapped in the face/ego by reality, you tend to want to hibernate. Or eat pie. Or do whatever you do when you feel like crap.

In my case, I vent. Small problem? I'm on the radio. So my lack of a filter and occasional inability to keep my innermost thoughts "inner" sometimes leads to moments of regret.

"I mean, really," I hiss into the mic. "Is this what it's come to, fellas? Your lady doesn't put out on the first date, so you never call again?"

The board lights up, and instead of going into a song, I open the lines.

"Maybe he just didn't like you," says the mean female voice on the other end. "I don't like you. I've never liked you. You sound like an Aries. Maybe he hates anyone who's an Aries. He has good taste if he does. Filthy, filthy Aries—"

"You're right," I say, cutting her off mid-crazy. "He spent the night making out with me and staring into my eyes because he hated me."

I hang up on her, but I have four more blinking lines to choose from. One caller is maternal: "You're too good for him." The next is a girl who's recently experienced something similar, and once I've established that we're not talking about the same guy, I move on to the third caller, who is a guy offering to take me home tonight and definitely call me tomorrow.

As I politely decline and hang up with him, I notice my cell-phone ringing, so I start a song and answer. It's Natalie.

"Have you lost your mind?" she asks.

"No more so than usual," I answer.

"You're complaining about this guy on the radio? Because that doesn't seem desperate at all."

"I'm not trying to woo him at this point, so I don't care what it seems like. I think it's a valid point. It used to be women had to wait three dates before having sex or they'd look like sluts and the guy would never call again. Now if you don't look like a slut the guy will never call again? Who can keep up?"

"It was one guy. One instance. Not statistically significant. Not a reason to shout it from the rooftops. Or the airwaves, as it were."

"Oh, God." I exhale. She's right. "I got a little carried away, huh?"

"Little bit," she says. "But I caught you in enough time to just put it behind you and move on. Play some more music. Breathe."

"On it," I say. I throw on "Beast of Burden" by the Rolling Stones and take a few breaths.

These are the things that happen when you let your emotions take control of you. And I rarely do. Or I try not to. Having closely calculated moves at all times pretty much ensures that these lapses don't happen too often, but when they do I can usually trace it back to an unfortunate event, and if I were to look back at the night I met Dustin, it's so obvious. The freakin' umbrella. Duh. If that wasn't a sign of bad news to come, then I don't know what is. One of the most famous superstitions of all. Yet I shrugged it off because he said it was "his" umbrella. "His" bad luck. So I chose to live in the fantasy. I took his word that just being in close proximity to such an event wouldn't cause me any strife, but apparently I was wrong. Fine, he may get some bad luck coming his way, but it was a clear sign that I should have stayed away from him, and I didn't pay attention. Not to mention he ruined my sweater! Anyway . . . you live, you learn, you stay away from people with un-wieldy umbrellas and lame emo T-shirts.

The only sure thing about luck is that it will change.

—BRET HARTE

Chapter Three

As much as my name means "luck," I sure haven't seen much of it in my life. At least as far as matters of the heart are concerned. My longest relationship with a man has been with Moose, my seven-year-old Wheaten Terrier/Golden Lab/Tasmanian Devil mutt of a dog.

I got Moose when I was with Natalie, shopping for her fifty-two-year-old cat, Dudley. Okay, the cat's not fifty-two, but she's had him forever, and he was already old when she got him. He's probably only fifty-one. The pet store had an adjunct rescue set up in front of the glass doors, daring all who entered to pass by the seven cages full of unwanted dogs without completely crumbling. I tried to stare at the floor, but Moose's enormous head caught my eye just as I walked into the store. Sadness . . . guilt for not stopping . . . a connection? I couldn't stop thinking about him while we walked through the store, looking for a toy to add to the collection of sixteen thousand un-played-with cat toys Natalie already had. Her cat, mind you, doesn't play with a toy for more than a nanosecond before Natalie gives him a new one. At most, he'll sniff it. I think Nat once saw that bumper sticker that said "He who dies with the most toys wins" and took it to heart. She really wants Dudley to win. Sadly, she may never see him win, because it is practically guaranteed that that cat will outlive her.

I found myself drifting down to the dog aisle, drawn to a big rawhide bone. I thought, *That moose of a dog might like something to chew on while he sits in his cage and hopes that someone will take him home.*

So I bought the bone.

I explained to Natalie that I was just getting him a gift, but I think she knew better from the minute I walked up to the register.

"Do you think it would be okay if I gave one of those dogs this bone?" I asked the emotionless cashier as I motioned to the cages outside.

"Sure, I think it would be fine," she replied in a monotone. "But we're separate from them, so you'd have to ask the people running the rescue."

"Fair enough," I said. "If they say no, I'll just chew on it myself. Probably good for the teeth."

And . . . nothing. Not a smile to note that I was just making a joke. Not even a twitch. She just looked at me like I needed to move on and let the next person go ahead. Which I suppose I did. Seeking validation from pet-store cashiers wasn't on my checklist for the day, but it would have been a nice bonus.

I stepped outside, and Moose's tail started to wag like he was already my dog, happy to see me coming back outside to clear up this whole misunderstanding of him being in a cage. I felt a tug at my heart and willed myself to look away. As I walked to one of the two people running the show, I sneaked a glimpse back to see if he was still looking at me even though my back was turned. He was. And his tail was still wagging. *Perfect.*

"Hi," said the woman with the clipboard. Her hair looked like it hadn't been brushed since 2004.

"Hello," I said, and awkwardly held out my bone. "Would it be okay if I gave one of your dogs this rawhide?"

"You just bought that inside?"

"Sure did," I said, resisting the urge for an I-just-happen-to-carry-chew-bones-around joke.

"I suppose it's okay, then. Who's the lucky dog?"

"That one," I said, and pointed to Moose, who wasn't named Moose. Yet.

"Would you like to play with him?"

Yes. "No, that's okay," I said.

"You should. He'd love it."

Twist my arm, then. I walked over to his cage, and the woman unhinged the latch and slid the door open. You know the rest without me having to say anything. We got into my car, and he lay down on the passenger seat. He craned his neck over to my side and rested his head on my leg. I truly believe I was meant to happen across Moose that day. It was fate or luck or whatever you want to call it, but Moose and I were meant to be.

That was seven years ago. Over that time, Moose has seen hairstyles, jobs, and boyfriends come and go. I'd like to say he's a good gauge for who's a good guy or not, but he pretty much likes everyone, which does me absolutely no good whatsoever.

Most nights, after my shift at the station ends, I meet Natalie at the diner. Admission: I eat dinner every night after midnight. I know it's unhealthy, but the hours I keep don't allow me to eat at a normal dinnertime. Plus, I love the cast of characters who have come to be my friends. Call me a creature of habit, but there's something so comforting about a waitress who already knows my order. I like my short-order cook who winks and smiles at me when I come in; occasionally, the light hits his mouth so perfectly that his front left gold tooth sparkles like a diamond (and when it does, I know the next day is going to be stellar). I like sitting at the counter, always in the same seat, if possible. Natalie just tolerates it, which is fair enough—it's hard to shell out cash at a diner when you own your own restaurant. Eat It is Nat's culinary gem. Of course, there's a command in the name. The customer is not always right when Nat is in the kitchen, and she's not shy about letting them know. She's been written up in every local paper and some nationals. She's kind of famous for being a bit ornery, but people come to the restaurant expecting it. She has certain rules that customers have to adhere to.

1) No two people at the same table can order the same dish. This encourages the trying of new things and the finding of new favorites.
2) No substitutions. She doesn't care if you're allergic— in that case, order something else.
3) Natalie reserves the right to kick anyone out at any time. This could be because of disagreements stemming from rules one and two, or it could be because she doesn't like your hairstyle.
But it's not all bad . . .

4) Tablecloths are made of paper, and each table is
    equipped with colored pencils. At least once a night,
    Natalie will stroll around to examine tablecloth
    artwork, and every night at least one dinner is on the
    house due to exemplary doodling.

Natalie works only dinners, so her hours are pretty similar to mine. The restaurant usually dies down around eleven or eleven-thirty, and by the time she finishes cashing out the waiters and planning the specials for the following night, we are walking out the door at almost the same moment. The diner is right down the street from the station and not too far from Nat's apartment, so it's a convenient place to meet most nights after work. Mostly she listens to me regale her with tales of random callers, and I listen to her restaurant stories, which are always equally if not more entertaining.

Nat doesn't eat diner food—perish the thought—but she does drink coffee, and lots of it. How she'll drink coffee from midnight to two a.m. and then lie down and go to sleep is beyond me, but she claims to have ADD and says that coffee has the opposite effect on her.

U

Tonight Nat walks in with a determined look on her face, her blond hair still tied back in restaurant mode, her normally gorgeous brown eyes (I know, most people hate brown eyes. Or maybe it's just those of us who have them and wish we had something more exciting—but her blond hair/brown eyes combo is exceptionally pretty) oddly panicky—darting back and forth, and she looks around the restaurant as she makes her way toward me.

"It's bad," Natalie says, bracing me, as soon as she sits down.

I assume she's going to tell me something bad happened to her—something along the lines of a customer ruining her poached salmon by asking for salt—because what could have happened in my life that she would know before me?

"Just tell me," I say. I can handle it.

"So, Umbrella Guy?" she says, her face twisted to the side, like she's not sure how to get the next part out.

"What?" I say. "He heard me on the radio? He came into the restaurant? He thinks I'm an even bigger loser than he apparently already thought I was, hence the never calling me? He was with a girl? A prettier and skinnier girl? What did she look like? I hate her already."

"Berry, I'm so sorry, sweetie."

"She's a supermodel? *What?*"

"He's dead."

I blink a few times as it registers. *He's dead? How? Why? When?* (The "when" is key. The "when" is my ego wondering if he died on his way home and that's why he never called. But, no, it's five days later. That can't be how it happened.)

"They had a memorial service for him tonight," she says. "A bunch of musician-type people. They reserved the back room at the restaurant. It was packed. Celebs and everything. They had these great flowers—"

"Nat!" I interrupt. "*How did he die?* Did he die driving home from my apartment?" This would be worse than I even thought. Forget that bad "open an umbrella indoors" luck—I might have essentially killed him by sending him home! "Please tell me my decision to not be a slut didn't kill him."

"You didn't kill him. He died the next day. I got the whole story."

"Well, what? What happened? Oh my God, I can't believe he's dead."

"It was stupid. He was being stupid. He was shooting a video with some friends. Some band. They were drunk and racing go-karts, and apparently he stood up in his go-kart to celebrate his victory as he crossed the finish line. I guess he took off his helmet as he stood up in his seat, not realizing that he was putting all his weight on the accelerator, and . . . he crashed into the concession stand."

"That's . . . unbelievable."

"I know."

"Awful," I say, still trying to wrap my head around it.

"I know."

My breath catches, and I look at Natalie with dread.

"Oh, Jesus, here it comes," she says, falling back in her seat.

"It was the umbrella he opened indoors," I say. "I knew it. I knew it!"

"Next thing you'll tell me is you weren't wearing your lucky bandana because you had a bout of too much head sweat."

"I don't have head sweat."

"Everyone has head sweat at some point or another. I get it at the hairdresser when they highlight. I can't help it—all that pawing over my scalp, blech. And by the way, I notice you're not wearing your evil-warding bandana. So . . ."

"So what?" This is about to turn into an inquisition, but I'm trapped.

"So what is it? Lucky shirt? Belt you were wearing when you won five bucks in an instant lottery scratch-off game? Pants you wore to see the Dalai Lama at the Hollywood Bowl and got a group blessing? Or some hidden gem—like a lucky suppository?"

I look away. It's a sore subject, meaning she's right, but it irritates me to have it talked about, almost as though her mention of it is leaching away the power. I hold up my arm and rattle my wrist.

Nat nods, waits. She wants to hear it. She always wants to hear it.

"The bangles I was wearing when the cable company gave me free premium channels for a year to apologize for accidentally shutting off my service."

"I was going to mock you, but that really is lucky. My cable company usually says they're sorry for my inconvenience and to please stop calling. At least stop calling and breathing into the phone and hanging up. I guess everyone has caller ID these days."

She's trying to lighten my mood, and it's working. She motions for me to show her the wrist again, and traces the bangles.

"Still, this hardly qualifies as lucky clothing. I don't think you're holding true to your principles."

"I can accessorize. Who says accessories can't be lucky?"

"True," she says. "My road bike came with a racing-seat accessory, and sometimes that makes me feel like I'm getting very lucky."

"Stop it. You can't tell me you don't at least see the coincidence in this guy meeting me, opening the umbrella, and dying the next day. Not to mention the 'Everybody Dies' shirt!"

"You left out some critical details, like the fact that he was driving drunk, standing up in a go-kart with his foot on the accelerator. But, yes, I do see the coincidence. And it's just that: coincidence. Accident. Fate sliding by. Oops—guy doing dumb thing dies. Stop the presses, we've got one for the 'lighter side of the news' section."

Natalie, sensitive as usual. Meanwhile, I think I might cry. Not only because it's very sad to hear of his death but because deep down, I can't shake the notion that I had a hand in it, not only with the umbrella but with the post-umbrella chatter about him accepting all the unsolicited bad luck. Before I know it, tears are streaming down my cheeks.

"Oh, God, honey, don't cry," Nat says, waving the waitress over and getting a few more napkins for us. "This is why I was afraid to tell you. Berry, he was drunk and being stupid. It had nothing to do with you or the umbrella."

"Right," I say. Now, more than ever, I believe everything I've always believed.

"But hey—the good news is he probably would have called you."

"Hooray." *Yeah.* Not quite as satisfying as you'd think. Gallows humor doesn't really go with my self-pity. Or my Cobb salad.

The rest of our meal is a bit of a downer. There's no good way to come back from news like that, so I just eat fast while she drinks coffee and then we ask for the check.

"Uh-oh," she says, as she glances down at it.

"What now?" I ask, though I already know it's bad. It can't be good. I mean, how many people open a piece of mail and say, "Uh-oh," and then you ask, "What is it?" and they say, "I've just inherited eighty million dollars." Doesn't happen.

"Nat, what?" I persist.

"Well, it's nothing," she says, conveniently crumpling the little strip of paper in her right hand and reaching for her purse. "Probably. No, Berry. Really. It's stupid. I shouldn't have said anything."

By this time, I'm practically shaking with curiosity and dread. "Natalie, tell me. You know I need to know."

She sighs and turns her head slightly away, then very purposefully turns back and locks eyes with me.

"What do you make of this?" she says, smoothing the wrinkled bill on the counter between us with both hands.

"Um, well, I had . . ." I struggle with the restaurant's abbreviations. "I had the salad and the iced tea. . . ."

"No, no, no," she says, and then points to the bottom. "Look at the number."

And there it is, staring back at me like the very eyes of the devil.

A total so unsettling I feel a literal chill spiriting through me. $17.17.

Seventeen seventeen! The split seven. Worse than a triple four or a reverse nine descending. Not quite as bad as a quadruple duple (four twos) or a runzie—five zeroes in a row in the middle of a number. But pretty bad.

I know Nat doesn't believe in any of it, and she's just pointing it out because she knows how upset I am and she cares about me. But this $17.17 I simply cannot abide. Not now.

I call over Ashley, the waitress who tells me almost every time I come in about how the audition she had that day is gonna be the one and how she's going to finally "tell these assholes where they can go."

"I'm so sorry to bother, but I think there's maybe a mistake somewhere."

She takes up the bill with a barely suppressed sigh and ticks off the items.

"Ah, you didn't charge for the fruit," I say, relieved that I'd spotted the problem. No dread split seven after all!

"No, we don't charge for your side. You had the fruit in place of the muffin we normally serve with our big salads. That came with it."

"Right . . ." I say dubiously. Natalie and the waitress eye me expectantly for a moment. "I don't suppose . . . I wonder if you could charge for the fruit. Just, you know, the normal fruit charge."

Ashley assumes that expression of profoundest concern and sympathy that waitresses and waiters get when they're about to go back to the kitchen and tell everyone on the shift what a dumbass you are.

"I can't because of the way they have the system programmed. If

I don't actually request something from the kitchen, I can't charge for it."

I look up at her, pleading.

"So the only way I could charge you would be . . . if you actually ordered another fruit side."

"No," Natalie says. "You're not going to buy something you're not going to eat. I'm not going to watch you do that."

I stare at Natalie, and she stares back. Ashley stands before us awkwardly.

"I'll just give you two a minute to figure it out," she finally says, and escapes back into the kitchen.

"I'll eat the fruit later," I say.

"It's got to stop," Nat says.

"Natalie, did my potential next boyfriend not die the day after he opened an umbrella indoors?"

"It was a coincidence, Berry," she says, and sighs. "A total coincidence. And I wrestled with myself about telling you. Do I tell you to make you feel better about him not calling? Or do I not tell you because I know you'll make yourself even more crazy with this stuff. I opted for the ego boost. Don't punish me for that."

My cellphone interrupts us. I look at the caller ID and see my dad's number.

Now, if *your* father called you after midnight, you might automatically go into panic mode. Old men aren't supposed to be up making phone calls in the middle of the night. They're supposed to be half asleep in a big fluffy bed, watching Craig Ferguson make an ass out of himself. At this point in my life, I would pay for a little adrenaline rush when I see my dad's number come up on the caller ID. Unfortunately, these calls became part of near-daily life so long ago that I know just what he's after.

"Hey, Dad," I say, trying hard to keep the resignation out of my voice. "What are you doing up so late?"

"How's my lucky charm?" he says.

"Not feeling so lucky at the moment," I tell him.

"Me neither. So let's change it for both of us. I'm losing, baby. I'm losing big. Can you come by and just sit with me for a little bit? I know my luck will turn around."

"Dad, it's almost one a.m. I just got off work, and I'm tired."

"Just stop by, then, on your way home? Give me a hug for good luck?"

How could anyone—anyone who loves her father, anyway; anyone who once idolized her father—say no to that?

"See you in a few," I say, as I hang up and wave Ashley back over. "Could you please add a side of fruit to this tab and pack it to go? I'm going to bring it to my dad."

"Sure thing," she says, and I look back at Natalie, who rolls her eyes.

"Unnecessary."

"Which, the extra fruit or the fact that I'm going to now drive half an hour so I can give my father a lucky hug?"

"Both."

"Says you," I say, as I take my to-go fruit, kiss Nat on the cheek, and walk to my car. She might be right about my dad, but she is dead wrong about the fruit.

◡

To know and understand my relationship with my dad is, well, something I've strived to do myself for the majority of my life. I can't explain why I jump when he calls, why I want to please him so badly, why I need his approval. I guess at its most base level, it's your typical daddy issues. But that's a term you usually hear when someone has a strained relationship with her father, or when her relationship with her father and the issues that stem from it make her unable to have emotional connections. Unable to have successful romantic relationships. And I refuse to cop to that this early in my adult dating life. I'm no lost cause, so I don't need to put a label on my problem. I think.

I walk into my dad's apartment and am as immediately saddened by the décor as I always am whenever I visit. It's not so much the décor as the lack of it. It's the same "temporary" apartment he moved into when I was young and my mom and he split. Or at least he thought it was temporary, and so did I. Now, twenty-three years later . . . not so temporary. He has two TVs that are on almost all the time. They're both old and look like he picked them up at a pawn shop. Which he probably did. He has a couch facing the TVs, a long coffee table in front of it, and a sad and dying plant in the corner. That's it.

His bedroom consists of a tiny end table with chipped paint, a lamp that looks too small even for the tiny table, and a mattress on the ground. He takes "no frills" to new heights.

"There's my Care Bear!" he says, as he pulls me into a hug, forcing me to snap out of my standard once-over and wince.

"Hi, Daddy," I say, and hand him the white paper bag.

"What's this?"

"Fruit," I say. "It's good for you."

"Who's the parent here?" he asks.

Excellent question, I think, but I bite my tongue. "My bill had a split seven on it, so I needed to order something else," I explain. "That became your fruit."

"Say no more," my dad says, nodding solemnly. He's the one who taught me about the dangers of the split seven to begin with.

I yawn and look at his coffee table. He's stacked bunches of torn pieces of paper in curious piles, but I don't want to invade his privacy, so I just avert my eyes and smile.

"So what's going on, Pop? Why the need for a good-luck rub of the Buddha's belly?"

"Berry's belly," he corrects with a smile. "Well, honey . . . there was a Hold 'Em tourney at the Bicycle Club in Bell Gardens."

"Okay . . ."

"So I wanted in, but I was a little strapped. There were a bunch of donkeys at the table, you know, tourists, trust-fund types, easy pickings. I knew if I played tight, played smart, it was an easy score. Easy way to cash five hundred dollars. The buy-in was fifty dollars, but I didn't have it, and nobody will stake me anymore—"

"Slow down," I interrupt. "Maybe there's a reason nobody will stake you anymore."

You see, staking is when poker players lend one another buy-in money for a percentage of the player's potential winnings. Sometimes your "generosity" turns into a very tidy profit. Sometimes you end up with nothing. So you're not likely to continue staking a guy who's been on a fairly steady losing streak.

"So nobody would stake me, so I borrowed the buy-in straight up. I knew I'd win it and pay it back. Then I'd clear four hundred fifty dollars."

I remain silent. I've heard it too many times before. How Dad played every hand perfectly, but some donkey made a stupid call but caught the winning card. How if it wasn't for these housewives and retirees and college kids coming in and making a mockery of the game, he would be rolling in cash.

"So, Dad, you're out the fifty dollars. And you can't get by without it."

"Baby, I just needed to see your pretty face. My good-luck charm so that when I get in a game tomorrow, I can win it back and pay this guy off."

"Right. But you'll have to borrow more money to play tomorrow."

"Yes, but when I win it back, it won't matter."

And now you understand what I go through at least once a week. This is not a new dialogue. This conversation has played out so many times I could say it backward in three languages even though I don't know three languages or have the ability to speak backward. Point is—it isn't anything new.

It doesn't even have anything to do with the money. It doesn't matter if he wins or loses. For gamblers, it's all about what they call "action." It's the excitement as the cards are coming out. It's the rush before the dealer flips that card over. It's addicting. Another way to think about it is this: Gamblers love winning more than they hate losing. And then when they do win, they get so excited they want to win more. So they keep playing. And lose what they won.

I, on the other hand, hate losing more than I love winning.

"Dad, I'll give you the fifty dollars. You take the day off tomorrow."

My dad bristles, as always. "No, honey . . . I can't take your money."

But he'll also end up taking it, just as he does every single time. And I'm tired after having worked all night and then found out that the last guy I kissed is now dead. So I'd like some time to process this. And I tell my dad as much without the gory details.

"Dad, I'm tired. I need to go. I'm leaving you fifty dollars. Take the day off tomorrow and do something outside. Go for a walk. Take a book to the park and read. Or a magazine. Don't go to the casinos, don't stay here and play online poker. . . . Go out."

And so he doesn't have the opportunity to argue or keep me there any longer, I kiss him on the cheek and walk out without looking back.

U

I always feel a sense of relief when I'm home. I'm sure that's how it is for most people, but my place is also a veritable potpourri of lucky charms. Although there are no leprechauns anywhere here. I loathe them. They're fake and childish, and seem like they exist (or don't) to mock everything I believe in.

I also hate even numbers. Anything even-numbered is never a good thing. If I have multiple anything I have three or seven. I don't love five even though it's odd, because it seems so "evenly" between one and ten. I have three rabbit's feet, which are actually quite morbid when you think about it—we know they weren't lucky for the particular rabbits they came from—but my dad gave each of them to me on different momentous occasions when I was little, and in addition to being superstitious I am also sentimental. And probably many other words that start with *s* and have four syllables. (Don't go there: Psychotic is three syllables and starts with a *p*.)

Yes, I'm quirky. As much as I hate that word, it's true. But, I hope, quirky in a good way. Not like, say, Jeffrey Dahmer quirky. I'm not like every other person, but I choose to believe it makes me unique . . . perhaps even charming. Regardless, I'm me. And I know I'm not like anyone else, for better or worse. So I have the three rabbit's feet hanging by their little ball keychain–type thingies all in a row on my wall. I have an elephant with his trunk pointed toward my front door. The elephant is believed to be a good-luck animal in many countries, though there is a lot of debate about whether the lucky figures should have their trunks pointed up or down: Pointed down "dispenses" good luck, and pointed up "stores" it. I haven't had such great luck of late, so mine is pointed down. No need to store the luck I've had.

I also have a large brass horseshoe up on my front wall, a larger version of the rose-gold and pavé-diamond one that my dad gave me for my sixteenth birthday. I did stop wearing it briefly after Carrie wore hers on *Sex and the City;* the horseshoe necklace was my thing—kind of like my trademark, not to mention the sentimental value multiplied by what it stood for and the safety I felt in wearing it for added luck protection. Then one day there they were on the necks of impressionable young girls everywhere. So I took mine off. And promptly put it back on when I slipped and fell a day later just as I passed a cute guy at the post office. There was a slippery next-day mailer on the ground. Apparently. All I know is I went zooming past him right after we'd made eye contact and I'd smiled what I thought was a confident and welcoming smile. I took two more steps, and the tile floor came up and hit me in the chin. Back on went the necklace.

I also have a four-leaf clover in my wallet that's supposed to bring money, but anyone who works in radio and isn't Don Imus will tell you that if you're in this business, you do it for the love of the job, or the music, or even the thrill—but definitely not for the money. So I'm hoping the money will arrive some other way, like via Lotto, aka the tax on people who are bad at math, although as I've already noted, I don't play—so perhaps via some rich uncle I never knew I had who's been watching me from afar and admires my scrappiness. An uncle who never had kids of his own and got into a fight with my mom or dad before I was even born, and they stopped speaking so I never even knew I had an uncle. I even asked my parents once if I had any aunts or uncles that I didn't know about, living in Monaco, perhaps, and they looked at me like I was nuts. More nuts than usual. Anyway, why give up hope? I say.

Moose greets me at the door with his big brown eyes, and it's the perfect antidote to the one-two punch of the dreadful go-kart news coupled with witnessing my father's slightly less tragic but still death-by-a-thousand-cuts everyday existence. I take a look around my apartment and know that nothing "good-newsy" is going to happen between now and when I go to sleep. It's just one of those days. So to take myself out of the funk, I throw on one of my favorite cover songs, Annie Lennox singing Neil Young's "Don't Let It Bring You Down." Even though I've never quite understood it. Where are the castles, why are they burning, and why should a raging inferno be considered trivial? Still, I'm a sucker for a good cover song. Especially if I love the original and the artist does it justice. This one does just that, and it has a message that I need to hear.

Radio is a medium of entertainment which permits millions of people to listen to the same joke at the same time, and yet remain lonesome.

—T. S. ELIOT

Chapter Four

My definition of urgent must be different from that of Bill, my station manager. I nearly break a sweat getting to the office twenty minutes early because I got two emails marked with those little red exclamation points and an "urgent" voicemail from him, yet for the life of me I can't see the emergency.

"Are you ready?" Bill asks, when finally I walk into his office. He had been on a phone call, so our "urgent" meeting had been delayed ten minutes.

"I'm ready. . . ." I say, thinking, *This better be good. Raise, maybe?*

"Good," he says.

And that's . . . that?

I sit there, blinking at him, waiting for his achingly urgent news that I apparently needed to be ready for, but he just goes back to shuffling some paper around his desk and then looks at his computer. I take him in as he basically ignores me even though he's the one who called me in for this urgent meeting. He's about five-eight, I guess. Not tall by any means, but not short. In between. My being five-seven makes me taller than him in most shoes. He has a mostly shaved head combined with a ridiculous comb-over, but you can tell from the would-be hairline that it wasn't a first choice. His nose is a bit "puggish," which is cute on a dog but less so on a station manager who is ignoring you.

Finally he looks up. "You can go."

I sit there incredulous. *Is this a joke? Am I on* Candid Camera? *Did he not just ask me if I was ready for some urgent news and is he now excusing me before even delivering it?*

I let out an involuntary guffaw, which causes him to look back up at me.

"Did you have a question?" he asks.

"Well . . . yes," I say. "You wanted me here, I thought, for an urgent meeting? And then you asked me if I was ready . . . and then you didn't tell me anything."

"Because you said you were ready," he says.

"Perhaps there was some miscommunication, then. What were you asking me if I was ready for?"

"The contest," he says. "To announce the winner, hello?"

"Oh," I say, and try my best not to look at him like he's a complete idiot, while simultaneously wondering if I'm the idiot, all the while willing my head not to explode.

We've been running a contest with a few of our sister stations in different cities. One winner from each station will be flown to New York for the opening night of the Rolling Stones' latest "comeback" tour. Side note: How many times should we allow bands to do "farewell" tours and then "comeback" tours before we call bullshit on them? It's really gotten out of hand.

Anyway, the contest is called "Ten from Ten to Ten," and it's really not that complicated to win—you just have to have no life, not sleep, and never leave your radio. It's that simple. We've played eight Rolling Stones songs during the past twenty-one hours. I started us off last night at about ten p.m., and the station kept it going all day today. I'll play two more songs between when my shift starts at seven and ten p.m. tonight, bringing us to a total of ten Stones songs. You can imagine how I feel having three even numbers thrust into my life in a significant way like this, but it's offset by the fact that there are three "tens," so I'm choosing to believe the odd number balances it out.

Our winner will get front-row tickets and backstage passes, and will participate in an after-show "meet and greet" with the band, winners from other radio stations, and a handful of DJs. I get to fly out to New York and warm up the crowd before the show. While public speaking is something I do daily on the radio, it's something I never do in public. I wonder if I chose radio because I wanted to be heard more than seen. There will be cameras everywhere and an audience upward of twenty thousand people. To say I'm nervous about the appearance would be like saying that dropping a baby on its head isn't recommended. I'm terrified. But I will rise to the occasion, and just to be on the safe side, I'll ask Natalie for one of those Xanax pills she's always taking when she's stressed, or if she's anxious, or if the sun rose that day.

My theory: Bill picked me instead of our morning radio personalities because they're trying to reclaim the "youth" factor even though we play classic rock, which "youths" don't really tend to listen to—at least not the youth demographic our owners are after. I knew that Jed and Daryl, our on-air morning team, were pissed off from the looks I was getting when I'd pass them in the hallway. Anyone who thinks that we're one big happy family at the station should spend five minutes with us at shift change. If only I had a nickel for every time I picked up my headphones to find the volume cranked to maximum and a piece of tape over the mute button . . .

Almost nobody is friends with anyone else, inside or outside the station. Take that general animosity and then couple it with the fact that our building houses five other stations under the same media conglomerate and you have a human demolition derby of petty competition. Our morning drive team hates the rush-hour DJ, the rush-hour DJ hates the competing rush-hour DJ on KDAY, they all hate the "Dr. Love" DJ who's on KKRL because they're secretly jealous that he's younger, better-looking, and probably smarter than them. Every intern wants the assistant's job. Every assistant wants to be a board operator, and every board operator wants to be the star of the show. If you mix that all together, you've got one giant bowl of bitter batter.

I suppose it's no different from any other workplace. You'll always have climbers and backstabbers, but I guess because we have it times six, it just seems to make my everyday working environment that much more of an adventure in screeching feedback.

"I'm sorry," I finally say. "Yes, I'm ready. I thought there was perhaps something else. My bad." I hate the phrase "my bad," and I hate that I said it, but the situation is already awkward enough and I just need a transition to get me out of his office.

We've done contests before. I've picked winners before. I suppose on the off chance that every caller, one after the next, got the answers wrong there could possibly be a problem, but I doubt that's ever happened in the history of call-in radio contests. I'm not sure why he needed me there twenty minutes early just to ask me if I'm ready, but I need to let it go or it will ruin my day.

I pass Jed and Daryl, who are in the studio, taping an on-air segment for their cable show.

"Hey, Berry," Daryl shouts, and I pretend not to hear him, but Jed taps on the glass to get my attention.

"Hey, guys," I say. "How's it going?"

I don't want to be part of whatever they have going on. Usually it's some sort of offensive stunt they're pulling in an effort to grab the audience Howard Stern lost when he went to satellite radio, with the attendant "What size are those?" and "How many times have you taken it in the butt?" sprinkled here and there.

"Berry, come on in here. This is Jasmine, and that's Desiree."

Of course they are "Jasmine" and "Desiree." From the bad dye-jobs, the barely there clothing, and the copious amounts of lip gloss, I'd be disappointed if their names were anything but "Jasmine" and "Desiree." Their boobs look like if you got too close with a sharp object they'd burst, causing the gals to go whizzing around the room like deflating balloons.

"Hello," I say, and keep my head down. I don't want to give them anything that can be reworked into a sound bite.

"Berry's going to New York City to introduce a lucky winning fan to the Rolling Stones," Jed says. "Isn't that cool?"

"Awesome," one of the Barbie Twins says.

"Oh my God," the other chimes in. "I would totally do Mick Jagger, even though he's like a hundred years old."

"Well, I'll be sure to pass along the message," I say, and try to duck back out of the room.

"What would you be willing to do to be that lucky winner?" Daryl asks the girls.

"Anything," they say simultaneously. As if we didn't expect that.

"Would you make out with each other?" Daryl asks.

They look at each other and giggle, start running their fingers through each other's overly processed hair.

"They probably do that all the time," Jed interjects. "What about Berry here? Do you think she's hot?"

"That's okay," I interrupt. "You don't need to answer. I was just leaving."

"She's cute," one of them says. I don't see which one, because I'm trying to leave. I also hate the word "cute," so I'm glad I didn't see who said it. Not that I expected a "She's gorgeous" or "breathtaking" or "She's too beautiful! Don't look directly at her—it's like staring at the sun, you'll go blind." But "cute" just feels like such a consolation prize. Particularly for women who never describe other women as less than "cute." Men hear a woman describe another woman as "cute" and they hear "cyclops."

"Would you want to make out with her?" Jed asks.

"I would," Tweedle Dumb says. Then she adds, "Especially if I get to meet Mick Jagger."

"I'd do it just because," Tweedle Dumber says, and while my ego appreciates the vote of confidence, my soul feels like it's being sucked farther out of my body every second that I remain in Daryl and Jed's lair.

"I'd pay for her plane ticket myself if—" Jed starts, but I cut him off.

"Thanks, guys," I say, a bit too loudly. "And gals," I add to the strippers. "I'm flattered. So we're clear that for money or concert tickets these lovely ladies would make out with me. But what America really wants to know is whether there's enough money in the world to get one of them to make out with either of you. Now I really have to go prepare for my show, if you'll excuse me."

"Oh! Snap!" Daryl says. "Thanks for stopping by, Berry." He

sneers up at me from the mic. "Remember, folks, if you want all classic rock and a chick who really needs some bleep, tune in to Berry's nighttime show from seven p.m. to midnight. Maybe call in and see if she'll change her mind. . . ."

I can still hear him blathering as I walk down the hallway. There's only one Howard Stern. Just because there are two of these guys doesn't mean they're twice as potent. Just makes them twice as pathetic for biting someone else's style. One upside to my hostile work environment? Absolutely zero chance of stumbling into an awkward sexual relationship with a co-worker.

As soon as I start the second-to-last Stones song, the phones start ringing. *No, dummies. That's only nine.*

"KKCR," I say, as I answer the phone.

"Am I it? Did I win? Is this Berry?" says the caller.

"No, no, and yes," I say.

"But—"

"This is the ninth song. I'm sorry, but we have one more to go."

"And what are the odds of me getting through again when it's the tenth," he asks.

I'm stumped. I'm not sure how to answer him. I know the odds can't be that good, but then again, how many people are so committed that they've listened to the station for twenty-four hours straight?

"Well . . ." I start.

"It's okay," he says. "I know I won't get through."

He sounds so defeated.

"You never know," I say. "I hope you do."

"My mom is sick, and she really loves the Stones so much. I was hoping to win so I could take her. She has cancer."

"Oh, gosh," I say, genuinely feeling like crap. "I'm so sorry to hear that."

"How about a date to make it up to me?" he asks, changing the subject rather quickly.

"I don't date callers," I say. "It sets a bad precedent."

"Pretend I didn't call," he says. "I'll forfeit my chances of winning and not call back when you play the next song if you will have dinner with me."

Something's definitely off. "I'm very flattered," I answer, "but I really can't say yes. Plus, there's still a chance you can win and then take your mom to the concert."

Then I hear a giggle, which confirms it. Someone's messing with me. This is the trouble with radio. And phones. And people.

"Please!" he says now, in a loud, aggressive wail. Clearly mocking me. "Please!"

"I'm going to do what you asked and pretend you didn't call." I hang up and take a few breaths. I wish I could say this was the first or fifth of fiftieth time I've had a prank caller, but I couldn't even begin to count the number of prank calls I've had if my life depended on it.

The thing is, everyone wants their fifteen minutes of fame, even if they get there by being a complete jerk. What the majority of these people don't realize is that just because someone at the station answers their call, it does not mean that they will be heard live on the radio. We have screening processes for that exact reason. The screeners haven't failed me in a long time, and it takes me a second to recover—who lies about their mother having cancer? I wait until I've successfully started the next song and then get up to take a short walk to shake it off. I know we're going into a commercial break after the song, so I have at least six minutes to regroup, long enough for a little trip to the vending machines.

No highfalutin cafeteria for us here at the station. Nope, we've got two vending machines and a pseudo-Starbucks coffeemaker. I put my dollar in and opt for the seventy-five-cent bag of pretzels. Deciding that the bag is not large enough, I put another dollar in and buy another bag. Now I have two quarters, and it will cost only one more to get a third bag, and I'm pretty sure I have one in my pocket. . . . Yup, there it is, so I insert the three quarters into the machine and get my third bag. Of course, I'll feel required to eat them all, and I'm moments from being a walking ball of bad carbohydrates and refined flour and sodium, but it was really the only move that made sense. Fiscally, I mean. It was just one more quarter. And two bags would have been an even number, and we all know I don't like even things.

I spin around with enough pretzels to feed Haitian refugees for a decade and suddenly I'm face-to-face with none other than Ryan Riley, aka Dr. Love on KKRL. We've somehow never met, but I see him on billboards, and his show has gotten so popular recently that it's impossible not to know who he is. He's shorter than I would have imagined. He's still tall. Taller than me for sure. He's just not a billboard.

"Hungry?" he asks, motioning to the three bags of pretzels in my hands.

"Just how many pretzels can one consume before their innards turn to cement?" I reply. "I aim to find out."

And with that, I rush off to get in the elevator and back to my booth to play the final Stones song. I've already decided on "Tumbling Dice," a gambling song. Maybe my father will be the tenth caller?

Once I'm settled back into my chair, headphones on, half a bag of pretzels consumed, I already feel better. The most amusing part of telling a caller that they are the winner is the scream of elation when I let them know. And by "amusing," I mean "makes my ears bleed."

The board lights up, and I answer the first call.

"This is Berry, but you're the first caller. Try back!" I disconnect and do more or less the same thing for the next eight callers. Then I answer the winning call.

"Hello, caller number ten!" I say.

"Really?" says the woman on the line. "I won?"

"Well, you're the tenth caller," I answer. "Provided you get all ten songs right, yes, you will win."

"Oh my God!" she screeches.

"What's your name?"

"Katie Preston."

"Hi, Katie Preston. Are you a big Stones fan?"

"Huge. Like . . . huge! I haven't slept in thirty-two hours. I listened nonstop."

"Well, all right then, my sleep-deprived friend . . . Let 'er rip!"

"Okay, okay . . . um . . . 'Start Me Up' . . . 'Brown Sugar' . . . um . . . 'Angie' . . . 'Satisfaction' . . . 'Monkey Man' . . . 'Gimme Shelter' . . . I said 'Satisfaction,' right?"

"Yes," I say. "You're doing great. Four more . . ."

" 'You Can't Always Get What You Want.' "

"Ain't that the truth," I find myself saying out loud.

" 'Beast of Burden.' "

"Right, two more, almost there . . ." I say.

" 'Ruby Tuesday' and 'Tumbling Dice'!"

I pause for effect. You always have to pause for dramatic effect in moments like this. But not too long, because it's radio and you never want dead air.

"Congratulations, Katie," I say. "You're going to New York City to meet the Rolling Stones!"

There's more screeching, and then I place her on hold so she can give our station manager her contact information and they can work out all the details. It definitely feels good to make this girl's dream come true. I've gotten used to some of the perks and maybe even a little jaded—but it's moments like these when I'm reminded that not everybody gets to do this for a living. I take a second to breathe that in and remember that I am so fortunate to share in that moment of unadulterated joy with a fellow human being. So blessed. You could almost say . . . lucky.

But that would be jinxing it. So I tap the strip of wood trim that rims the booth at about waist level.

There are only two reasons to sit in the back row of an airplane: either you have diarrhea, or you're anxious to meet people who do.

—HENRY KISSINGER

Chapter Five

If you ask people to choose the "best rock-and-roll band of all time," you're frequently going to hear strong opinions from two camps: Team Beatles and Team Rolling Stones. I can see the arguments for both. The rivalry was never actually between the bands, as far as I know. They were clearly each their own thing. The Beatles wanted to "Hold Your Hand," and the Stones suggested you make a dead man . . . well . . . come.

With the Beatles, you have a group that strived to push new boundaries with production and songwriting. You'd hear extreme growth from them, in every way, on each record. They stopped touring at a very early stage in their career, which permitted them to be without creative limitation in their record making. No worries regarding how to reproduce something live, because they never played live.

In the case of the Rolling Stones, you have a band that basically limited themselves to rock and blues but remained exciting and after forty-five-plus years are still kicking ass. And they have written not one but lots of the greatest rock-and-roll songs of all time. Not bad. Not to mention they were once a kick-ass blues band. If you haven't heard *Exile on Main Street*—get it.

Personally, I'm Switzerland in that debate. I can see both sides. There will also always be a soft spot in my heart for the Kinks, who were Oasis years before Oasis. Their fights were real and born out of creativity. And who else had the balls to write an arena anthem based on the humiliation of making out with a dude?

You'll also hear arguments for the Clash, and I would absolutely be the first in line to rally for them, but a) longevity matters, and b) being declared "best band of all time" makes you part of the "establishment," which would just about kill the remaining living members of the Clash.

My mom, in any event, is Team Stones, which I'm reminded of over breakfast the morning before my flight to New York.

"Are you ready for your trip?" she asks. Ever the mother. She's far more concerned with the contents of my suitcase than I am.

"Define 'ready,' " I say.

"Why do you always wait until the last minute to pack?"

"Because I do. I don't know why. Because I like to have everything I need until I don't need it. Because I don't know until the last minute what I'm going to wear or bring."

"Aren't you excited?"

"Not really. It's a pretty standard trip—in and out."

"Says the girl seeing the band that her mom stayed up all night, outside in line in the pouring rain, to get concert tickets for before she was even born."

"I can't decide if that makes you or the Stones older, but it's kind of profound."

"It's me," she says. "I'm ancient."

"Yet unlike Keith Richards, you don't get full-body blood transfusions every few years to keep your corpse alive."

"Does he really do that?"

"Supposedly," I say, tentatively poking at that last, less-than-perfect strawberry on my plate. "Although he denies this in his book."

How would I know for sure? That's the rumor. But then there are so many rumors about the bands that make up our playlist, it's actually quite fascinating. Take Stevie Nicks. Supposedly Stevie's assistant had to blow coke up her ass because she'd completely destroyed her nasal passages from snorting. Is that true? I doubt it somehow. Something kept alive by bitter Christine McVie fans, maybe. But the rumor lives on.

Then there's the rumor that Mama Cass died choking on a ham sandwich. That one is absolutely not true. But people will swear it is. Rod Stewart supposedly got his stomach pumped after swallowing a gallon of semen. Let's pause there for a minute. Do you know how much a gallon is? Think of putting down a full gallon jug of milk. I mean, who comes up with this stuff?

"Have you seen your father?"

I wait a beat before I answer. She still loves him. I know she does. She'd never admit it, and maybe she can't even see past her disappointment to find the love, but I know it's there. "Yeah, I saw him a couple days ago."

"Did you give him money?" she asks. Straight to the point, as always.

"No."

"Are you lying?"

"Yes."

"Why, baby?" she asks, not angry but sad. "Why do you let him guilt you like that? He's supposed to be the parent."

"He does the best he can," I say.

"His best is pretty pathetic."

"I know, Mom. Just let it go. We know he's not the Prince Charming you signed up for, and he's not breaking any records for excellence in parenting. But he's still my dad. He's the only one I have. And you're not ancient."

"Tell that to my smooth neck skin if you run into it somewhere."

My mom is really beautiful. Far more beautiful than she thinks she is. I guess when your husband is more interested in playing with a deck of cards than playing with you, it does wonders for your self-esteem. But he's an addict in the truest sense, and she knows that, so I wish she wouldn't take it personally. Gauge your self-worth by the opinions of people whose opinions aren't worth a rat's rear end and pretty soon you're going to be living in a cave.

My mom is my rock. She's calm and cool; she's rational and level-headed; she's the complete opposite of me. She's not the type of person who walks through a casino in her lilac-and-butterflies nightgown. And then yells at her husband. Hysterically. For all to see. She's refined. She doesn't lose control like that. That night was the first time I ever saw her cry. And the last time. Sometimes I wish she would let go a little more, throw caution to the wind, drink regular milk instead of nonfat. But then she wouldn't be the person I count on, I guess. Or the person here at this restaurant who will not send back her runny eggs even though she asked for them to be well done.

"It's fine, honey," she says.

"It's not fine, Mom," I counter. "You ordered them well done. You should have what you asked for. And also not get salmonella."

"I'd rather not bother them," she says. "It's fine."

With her, everything's "fine." I once heard that "fine" is an acronym for "fucked up, insecure, neurotic, emotional." It's what people say they are when they're trying not to be what they really are—one or all of those descriptors. I love that she's considerate of other people—even the kitchen staff, whom she'll never meet—and that she doesn't want to put anyone out, but sometimes I think she puts everyone's happiness before her own. The only time she will ever raise her voice even a little is when she's concerned about me.

I give up on the eggs, because she's already dug in.

"I brought you this," she says as she pulls something out of her pocket.

"What is it?" I ask, because all I can see is that it's a small item wrapped in white tissue paper.

"Open it," she says. "It's nothing. Just a little something." My mom has always given me little keepsakes to carry with me, and I always do it. It's a nice way to take her with me wherever I go.

I unwrap the tissue and see that there's a pink quartz inside. A touchstone. It warms my heart immediately, which I imagine is precisely what it's supposed to do. And as someone who buys into things like superstitions, of course I'm inclined to believe that it will bring some of the good stuff my way.

"It's rose quartz," she explains. "For love."

"Thanks, Mama."

"I want you to do me a favor," she says, now more serious than before.

"Okay . . . ?" I say, one eyebrow cocked a teensy bit higher than the other.

"I want you to do two things, actually," she says as she inhales. "First, your father—"

"Mom," I interrupt.

"Just hear me out. You're enabling him. Plus, you spend so much time worrying about him and taking care of him that you don't do thing number two: Make yourself or perhaps some as-yet-unknown significant other your priority."

"Exactly," I say. "The as-yet-unknown factor being key. As in 'he doesn't exist.' "

"Oh, he exists, young lady," she says, sounding stern, almost as if she was about to break out my first and middle name the way parents do when you're in trouble. "He does exist. But your eyes aren't open to him. And neither is your heart. So I want you to keep that quartz with you—always, as a reminder to keep your heart open. Do we have a deal?"

"Yes, we have a deal. But I'm not sure a closed heart is my problem. You do know I work nights, right?"

"Don't try to deflect. We have a deal. Now, shake," my mom says, and I hold out my hand and shake hers, solidifying this new pact: Eyes open . . . heart open . . . but I'm keeping the night shift for now.

∪

Last-minute packing is only one of my travel rituals. Another is to wear my Saint Christopher medal—Saint Christopher being the Patron Saint of Travelers—not because of any fervent religious beliefs (I haven't been to church in God knows how long) but because it makes me feel good. A third is that I always need to sit in the back of the plane, as close to the last row as possible. If it's a cross-country flight, the flight attendants will often commandeer the last couple rows for their belongings and also for catnaps. (While we're on the topic—really? You get to take a catnap during a five-hour flight? That's a pretty short workday to be busting up with some shut-eye.) But not when Berry's on board.

Some people say that there is no safest seat on the plane. They are wrong—but not for the reasons you'd think. They've done research and the truth is that passengers who are seated near the tail of a plane are forty percent more likely to survive a crash than those in the first few rows up front. But they've also done a study proving that research is a crock like thirty-two percent of the time. No, my reason is simpler and sounder: The back of the plane is the counterintuitively lucky spot. Think of it: How many people jump for joy when they find out they've just been assigned a forward seat? Everyone, right? But we know that luck is a precious commodity. There's only so much to go around. And even if you do have a good-luck streak, some balancing bad luck is right around the corner. Just ask any honest gambler. If you can find one. So if all those people up front are competing for such a small supply of luck, odds are it's going to be exhausted by the time I come around. Not in the rear. Almost everyone there feels he or she got hosed. Ergo ipso facto, there's lots of luck left for the back of the plane. If I have to wait five extra minutes to deplane, I will gladly take it.

Of course, I'm not taking any chances. The last thing I always do is tap the body of the plane three times with my right hand as I'm boarding. People wonder why I set my bag down at that inauspicious moment, when we're all rushing to board and panicking over a shortage of space in the overheads. I don't let it bother me. No matter where you're sitting, it always helps to take every possible safety precaution.

This time, though, there is a small problem: My Saint Christopher medal seems to be missing.

This.

Is.

Not.

Good.

I feel my heart start to pound, perspiration starting to bead on my temples, on the nape of my neck, on my chest—you know, all the usual beady places. I try to calm down, to get a grip. I'm sure there's a small chance they would sell one at the airport, but that would probably be a very small chance, and it wouldn't be the same medal I've worn since I was a child. I spend seventeen minutes looking everywhere for it, cutting it closer and closer, breaking into a full-on sweat and swearing pretty steadily before I give up and leave for the airport.

The Traffic Gods are smiling upon me, and I miraculously arrive on time, cruise through the airport, do my ritual fuselage taps, and take my seat in the third-to-last row of the plane. The window seat to my left is empty, and the seat to my right across the aisle is also empty. All other seats are taken. I'm about to take a moment to hope whoever was supposed to sit next to me doesn't show when I see two more people walking down the aisle: an older businessman-type and a guy who looks roughly my age, give or take five years.

Businessman Bob takes the seat next to me and introduces himself without introducing himself. You know, that thing you do when you don't exchange names but you acknowledge that there's someone you're about to spend the next five hours a mere few inches from.

"Hi there," he says, as he props up the window shade to look out, practically blinding me in the process.

"Hi," I say as I squint, probably giving away the fact that I'm annoyed because I had just pulled that shade down two minutes before he arrived.

"You flying home or away?" he asks.

"Away," I say as I catch the eye of the my-age-ish guy across the aisle. He's listening to Old Man River make small talk with me, and I think he can tell I'm not into it. He smiles at me, and for some reason I feel compelled to reach into my pocket and pull out the rose quartz my mom gave me and hold it in my hand.

"Are these seats not the worst?" My-age-ish asks. Thank God, I think he's trying to save me from having to talk to my seatmate.

"The absolute worst," I agree emphatically, because, as a general rule, you don't want to let someone know just how neurotic you are within the first five minutes of meeting them.

"I missed the earlier flight, so I flew standby on this one. This was the only seat they had."

"My company booked my ticket," I embellish, "so I wasn't given a choice."

"Bummer," he says.

"Yeah," I say, and sigh. Then add, "But they do say the tail of the plane is the safest place to be. So we've got that going for us."

"Which is nice," he says, and smiles. That was a tired *Caddyshack* reference, but he not only got it, he was gracious enough to leave it unacknowledged. I swear I feel the rose quartz heating up in my hand.

"I'm Kyle," he says.

"I'm Berry," I say.

"Like the fruit?"

"One and the same."

"That's cute," he says, and I instantly deduct five points. We know how I feel about the word "cute."

"Are you traveling for work or . . ." I ask.

"Nah, just gonna see a buddy of mine for the weekend."

A little girl who looks to be about five years old walks past us with her mother. She stops and looks at me purposefully. "I go potty by myself," she says.

I stifle a laugh and sneak a look at Kyle. His eyes have gone big, but he's managing not to laugh. "That is wonderful," I say. "I go to the potty by myself, too."

"I go poop on the potty," she adds, and then marches off to the bathroom.

Kyle and I both start to laugh once she's out of earshot.

"I love how kids make grand declarations to complete strangers," I say.

"You mean you don't do that?" he asks.

"Are you asking if I poop on the potty or if I make grand declarations to strangers? Because I can assure you I do neither."

The next five hours and thirty-four minutes fly by, so to speak, faster than I could imagine. We're practically shouting across the aisle to speak to each other the whole time, annoying the other passengers, just guessing (from the nasty looks and raised middle fingers people are giving us two rows up), but not really caring because we're having too much fun talking, laughing, and cultivating a stable of inside jokes about everyone in our eye-line or anyone who passes us to use the restroom. People always talk about how much fun people-watching is, especially with a friend. Not true. The watching is only the first half. It's the people-critiquing that brings it all home.

There's the couple who try not once but three times to join the "mile-high" club by secreting away into the bathroom together. Each time they're foiled by either a flight attendant, an impatient parent and child knocking to see "if everything's okay," or just too many eyes on them at the crucial slipping-in moment. Slipping into the bathroom, I mean.

Then there's the couple who share a headset to watch the in-flight movie and then end up fighting over it, neither of them enjoying the movie, but really—what were you thinking sharing a headset?

There's the guy who stands in the back, pretending to want another soda while unsuccessfully trying to chat up the flight attendant—and failing to the point that he gets asked to "please return to your seat." That's gotta sting.

A whole cast of characters for us to mock, empathize with, or create backstories for, all of which are probably wildly more interesting than their actual existence.

"Cats or dogs?" I ask.

"I have a cat," he answers. This is of greater concern than one might think. No disrespect to cats, but . . . I'm a dog person. And dudes with cats have always struck me as somewhat effeminate. I just don't trust them completely. Of course, this could also be my secret fear that I will one day end up a cat lady. God forbid I start dating a "cat guy," and then we move in together . . . and then we break up and for some reason he leaves the cat behind . . . that's Cat Number One. It's all downhill from there.

Cat thing aside, by the time we land we've covered all kinds of territory. I feel like I've known Kyle my whole life. There's a certain ease to it—talking to him, laughing with him. I wasn't ready to part ways as strangers who would never see each other again. Thankfully, neither was he.

We stand together at the baggage claim for twenty minutes, waiting for our bags, continuing to talk about everything from airport Muzak to parents who keep their kids on a leash to how there's always that one ridiculous bag that comes down the carousel held together by an excessive amount of duct tape. What kind of person travels like that?

Then I see my bag tumbling down the slide.

"That's mine," I say. The excitement you feel when you see your bag is something I think we can all relate to, not just because you're being reunited with your belongings but really because the odds of your bag getting lost are so good that it's almost a miracle if it doesn't.

"Which one?" he asks.

"The gray one. Swiss Army."

He grabs it like a perfect gentleman.

Then we stand, looking at each other for the quintessential awkward moment. I have my bag. I don't want to say goodbye. But I have nothing else to wait for. There's no real reason for me to stay . . . but I don't want to leave. Finally I speak up, looking away from him, back at the carousel, because I feel like I might be turning a bright shade of tomato.

"How many bags do you have?" I ask.

He looks down and away now, and if I'm not mistaken he's turning a bit tomato himself.

"I don't have any bags," he admits. "I was just keeping you company."

What's that I feel? My heart skipping a beat, perhaps? Is that not the most charming thing ever?

"I'm kind of embarrassed," he says. "I didn't know how this was gonna pan out. I thought maybe your bag might get lost and I could pretend mine was, too."

"That's really cute," I say, breaking my own rule.

"Cute, like George Clooney? Or cute like a pathetic puppy trying to jump up on a couch, but his legs are too tiny so he misses every time?"

"Are you suggesting that you want to jump on me?"

"Depends which way you answer," he says, and we hold each other's gaze.

I look away first. I'm never great with extended eye contact. There's always a bit of a creepy factor, even if it is someone you like. When is enough? When does it become a staring contest?

"Well, your legs aren't tiny," I say, trying to subtly tell him I meant "cute like Clooney" but somehow managing to make it clumsy.

"I'd ask if you want to share a ride into the city, but I don't want to seem too forward," he says. "But can I get your phone number? Or your email? So we can stay in touch?"

"Absolutely," I say, wishing we were actually sharing the ride but not wanting to come across as desperate, so I leave it alone. I dig through my things to find a pen and write down both my cell number and my email, and together we walk to the taxi stand and then make our ways into separate cabs.

I'm not five minutes into my journey when my cellphone rings. "Hello?"

"Is it too soon to call?" he says.

I laugh. He took the initiative. He stood at the baggage claim with me for no other reason than to keep me company. He asked for my number, and he called within the hour. Practically within the minute. I decide that it's okay if I invite him to the concert. I mean, why not? Who wouldn't want to go to a Rolling Stones show? Even if he didn't like me. But I hope he likes me.

"Not at all."

"This is Kyle."

"I know," I say.

"What are you wearing?" he asks.

"Something lacy," I answer.

"Man, I wish we didn't take separate cabs. I knew you were gonna change into something lacy the minute you took off."

"You know me so well," I say. "Hey, what are you doing tomorrow night?" I say, not giving him a chance to respond in case he has plans but he will tell me he doesn't once he hears what I'm offering. "I'm going to see the Rolling Stones . . . for work. It's part of my job, so I'll have to do a little bit of work stuff, but mostly I'll be able to hang out and enjoy it. And if you want to come . . ."

"Awesome," Kyle says. "I'd love to."

"Okay, then," I say.

"Okay."

We end up talking for almost three hours. Through the cab ride, through my checking in to the hotel and unpacking, through him showing up at his friend's house. Pretty ridiculous.

"Is your jaw tired?" I ask him.

"Depends why you're asking," he says. I get where he's going, but I'm not ready to wander down that path. Yet.

"I'm asking because we've now talked for six hours in person and three hours over the phone. I feel like I'm in junior high."

"I'm not gonna hang up till you hang up first."

"Exactly!"

"Okay, I can take a hint," he says.

"No, no," I say, but it probably is time to hang up.

"No, you're right. Plus, I don't want you to get sick of me."

"Too soon for that," I say.

U

When I spot Kyle outside Madison Square Garden, he lights up— his face, not a cigarette; I don't do smokers, and thankfully, he isn't one—and we wave hello and embrace in an awkward first-time hug.

Once we navigate our way through the Garden to our seats, Kyle sits to my left. I must say that after staring at the left side of his face for six hours yesterday, the right side is equally riveting.

On my right is Katie Contest Winner, and she couldn't be more excited to be here. She's in her late thirties; what you'd call "pleasantly plump," I'd say; and is practically bouncing in her seat with glee. It's nice to see our winner be so appreciative. The camera crew that's shooting coverage for the local radio station and our website shows up to interview Katie, and as I toss her questions about how she stayed up drinking Mountain Dew for twenty-four hours in order to win the contest, I try to sneak a glance at Kyle, to let him know I know he's still there—just so he doesn't feel left out—but he's nowhere to be seen.

We wrap the interview, and there's still no sign of Kyle. It's getting dangerously close to the time I have to introduce the band, so I tell Katie I think he's gone to the concession stand and ask her to keep an eye out for him as I make my way down toward the stage.

Even with my credentials, it's hard to get backstage. There's a wall of burly security guys in yellow jackets that say "Event Staff" in big block letters on the backs. Finally someone from another radio station recognizes me and tells one of the guys in the yellow jackets to let me through.

Everyone's rushing around, pushing people out of the way, tripping over cables. It's pure chaos. Rock and roll has no calm before the storm. I look for Sam, the Stones' tour manager, who I'm supposed to report to, and when I finally spot what I think is him, he guides me to the side of stage left and then leans down so we're face-to-face. A little too close for my liking, actually.

"Are you ready?" he asks me.

"No," I say. "But I'm gonna do it anyway."

"It'll be over before you know it. And if you pass out from nerves, we have paramedics here."

"Comforting, thanks."

I walk up the steps, and the spotlight follows me. *Wow, that's a lot of people out there.* I speed up a bit as I make my way over to the mic and hope it doesn't blast feedback when I speak into it. The crowd gets quiet as I approach the mic stand, and I'm aware of my every movement. Each step, each breath, hyper-realized. I take my place, and I look out into the crowd. *Oh my God, that really is a shit-load of people,* I think. And my next thought is, *I wonder if I know any of them, like, say, Jason Goldstein, whom I had a giant crush on throughout high school even though he gave me dirty looks every single time he saw me. How do you like me now, Jason?* And then I look at the crowd again and think, *I might very well faint.*

I try taking deep breaths. In. Out. I do a quick mental check-in. Tell myself reassuring things. *You're fine. This will be over in a heart-beat. Don't think about the quadrillion people who are looking at you right now. Don't pee in your pants. What? Where'd that come from?* Suddenly I'm panicking, thinking I'm going to pee in my pants or faint or pee in my pants and then faint and be unconscious with wet pee pants.

Breathe.

In.

Out.

I grab ahold of the mic, as much to steady myself as to appear like I know what I'm doing.

"Hello, New York City," I say, and the quiet disappears again as thousands of people cheer. One sentence down. "I'm Berry Lambert from KKCR, and I'm so excited for the opportunity to be here tonight and bring this legendary rock royalty to the stage."

The audience cheers, and surprisingly I'm feeling a little more steady and fairly certain that I won't be urinating or passing out. Yay me. I've done my bit by mentioning the station and now I should probably get off the stage as quickly as I possibly can, so I pose a question I know will garner some cheers and get me the hell out of Dodge.

"I wanna know one thing, people: Are you guys ready to see the Rolling Stones?" Louder cheering. "Then let's start it up!"

The lights go down, and I hear Keith Richards's first three strums of the iconic power chords in "Start Me Up." I practically run off the stage as the silk curtain that's hiding the band falls to the ground, revealing the Rolling Stones.

Midway through the first song, Kyle appears at my side again. No drink, no hot dog.

"Hey, Houdini," I say.

"Sorry about that!" he says. "I got a phone call and I couldn't hear, so I had to go where it wasn't so loud."

"Everything okay?"

"Yeah. Just my buddy wanting to let me know he left the keys for me in case he's not home before I get back there. And telling me how jealous he is that he lives here and couldn't get tickets but I snagged them on my plane trip."

At least that's what it sounds like he says. I only get every third word or so, because he's shouting over the music.

"I missed your intro!" he yells. "I'm sorry!"

"No worries," I say. "I introduce the Rolling Stones at Madison Square Garden every day. You'll catch it another time." I wink and smile to let him know I'm completely teasing, and we settle into the concert.

Throughout the show we sneak glances at each other, perfectly timed with innuendo-laden lyrics. When during "Beast of Burden" we lock eyes as Mick sings, "All I want is for you to make love to me," there's no turning back. He leans in to kiss me, and it's almost downright cheesy when you think about it. Or even if you don't think about it. Imagine the eye-rolling that would ensue if we ever told our future teenage kids that our first kiss was at a Rolling Stones concert, perfectly timed with sexy lyrics. Still, I manage to get lost in the kiss and the promise that it holds.

Unlike the song, there will be no "making love" tonight. I just met this guy with the chiseled jawline and perfect eyebrows and sexy arms twenty-four hours ago, and I wouldn't want him to think I was a total slut. No, I am clear on this much: There will be no sex. Absolutely. Positively. None. This is the part where if it were a movie, you'd cut to Kyle and me midway through a clumsy, steamy sex scene. But this is not a movie.

It's on our way to the Club at the Garden, where we're holding the meet and greet for contest winners, when Kyle disappears again. We get to the entrance and pass a sign that reads, "By entering these premises you agree to be filmed on camera." I pull out my credentials and am about to walk us in when Kyle points behind us.

"You know we passed a bathroom a few steps back. I'm gonna hit that, so why don't I catch up with you two in there?"

"There's a bathroom in the club," I say.

"I need a remote location," he says.

I take this in, and it dawns on me that maybe Kyle's having stomach issues. Maybe his friend didn't even call before when he disappeared for so long. Maybe he has crippling diarrhea, the poor thing. Which, actually, might explain how he ended up near the bathroom on the plane?

"Okay," I say, trying to play it off like I have no idea what he's talking about. I point to Kyle and get the security guard's attention. "He's with me, KKCR. Can you please let him in when he comes back?"

The security guard grunts a yes, so I tell Kyle to text me if he has any problems getting in.

Twenty minutes later, Katie is on cloud nine, but even she realizes that Kyle's been gone a long time. I walk over to the entrance and find the security guard.

"That guy didn't come back, did he?" I ask.

"Nope," he says.

"You remember what he looked like, right?"

"Yup," he says, and looks away. A man of few words.

After forty-five minutes I start to worry about him. I don't want to barge into the bathroom, but if he's in pain or something I'd feel terrible—him being stuck in there alone. I tell Katie I'm going to go check on him when we hit the hour mark, because really—who spends an hour in the bathroom when something's not seriously wrong?

I exit the club and walk to the men's bathroom. I'm not sure what to do, so I stand outside the bathroom for an additional five minutes as about twelve people come and go. Finally I stop someone on his way in.

"Hi. Could you do me a favor and just ask if there's a Kyle in there, and if there is, tell him that Berry is outside if he needs anything?"

The guy looks at me like I'm nuts. "Sure, I guess," he says, and he walks in.

A few moments later he walks out. "Nobody answered to Kyle."

"Did you speak loudly?" I ask.

"Lady, I gotta get home," he says as he brushes past me. That's fine. We all have places to be, I'm sure, but clearly this is a sensitive situation. I think. And thanks for making me feel like the crazy lady stalking the men's bathroom.

I watch and wait, and when I'm pretty sure nobody else is in there, I tiptoe into the bathroom.

"Hello?" I say, tentatively. And get no response. Then I try again, louder, making it clear that if anyone is in the bathroom I am looking for an answer. "Hello!"

Nothing. I walk past each stall, peeking under for dangling legs, feeling creepier with every step—even more so when a man walks in.

"I'm sorry," he says, as he puts his hands up and backs away, almost as if I have a gun. "I thought this was the men's room."

"No," I say. "It is."

And rather than give any more explanation, I quickly walk past him and out of the bathroom. Once I'm in the main MSG corridor again, I pull out my cellphone to see if he's tried to call. Nothing. So I text him: Where are you?

And then I wait.

And wait.

And wait.

Then I text him again: Kyle, are you okay? Are you sick? I tried to find you in the bathroom. Nobody was in there. Are you in a different bathroom?

Send.

He writes back: So sorry. Friend texted me to say someone found the keys and broke into the apartment! Was kind of my fault so left to help him out. Tomorrow?

The rest, as they say, is history. Except this is my life, so it's not good history, like the end of apartheid or women's suffrage. This is A-bomb history, Jonestown history.

Much like Jim Jones offering up the Flavor Aid, I wake up to a text from Kyle, asking if he can take me to breakfast at Norma's in the Parker Meridien hotel.

The menu is obscene. Not just because of their beyond gluttonous menu items, which they have aplenty (Caramelized Chocolate Banana Waffle Napoleon, anyone?), but because they have a "Zillion-Dollar Lobster Frittata" that costs a hundred dollars, and in case that's not enough, you also have the option to "supersize" the caviar portion for the totally reasonable price of a thousand dollars. Are. They. Kidding. Me. I'd like to meet the person who spends a grand on a plate of eggs. And then smack them.

"So what happened with your friend's place?" I ask. "Was he home? Did they catch the burglars? Did anything get stolen?"

"It was awful," Kyle answers. "A neighbor noticed something was up, and he called my buddy and my buddy called me to see if I was moving stuff out of his apartment, and I told him no and he said to get to his place as fast as I could and that he was calling the police."

"Oh my God. Weren't you scared? I mean, what if the burglars were there when you got there? Were they?"

"No . . . Well, yes, but the police got there first, so they already had them handcuffed."

"That is unbelievable," I say. And somewhere in the back of my mind, a tiny voice is suggesting to me, *That really is unbelievable.* But I dismiss it and move on.

"I know, right?" He shakes his head and looks away. I've noticed he hasn't made a lot of eye contact with me, and I'm wondering if he's decided he doesn't like me as much two days later or if the subject of the break-in is just making him uncomfortable.

I decide to change the subject. "Anyway," I say, in that oh-so-awkward way when you actually have nothing to say but you're trying to signal a change of subject. I settle on, "This place is great."

"It's awesome," he says. "I try to come here whenever I'm in New York. I love to bring people who haven't been here before."

"Virgins," I say.

"I hope not," he says with a wink, and now he's making eye contact again. Conversation becomes easy, and from Norma's we walk to the MoMA. I'm typically not even a museum person but read about the Tim Burton exhibit a couple years ago and was so bummed to have missed it.

Kyle pays for our entrance. "After you, m'lady."

We spend the rest of the day wandering aimlessly throughout the museum, making up stories behind the paintings, much like we did with the passengers on our flight. By four o'clock we're back in the comfortable groove that made me think I could really like this guy.

Somewhere along Fifth Avenue, Kyle abruptly stops walking and lets go of my hand. We'd skipped lunch because we were still stuffed from breakfast, but our stomachs are both starting to grumble so we're discussing what we'd like for dinner when he just oh so casually reclaims his hand.

"We don't have to do Indian," I say, trying to make light of the situation.

"Sorry," he says. "Be right back."

Kyle ducks around the corner, and I stand alone on Fifth Avenue, wondering if he's having stomach issues again and if the mere mention of Indian food sent him over the edge, searching for a bathroom.

Six minutes pass, and I'm still standing next to a NY1 reporter who's doing a man-on-the-street piece about the resurgence of high-top sneakers. The door is open to the NY1 news van, and the tape operator sitting in the van amid all of the electronics smiles at me.

"I'm waiting for my friend," I self-consciously tell him. "Too bad he disappeared. Maybe he'd have something to say on the matter." He nods and goes back to what he's doing.

Twelve minutes later my annoyance level has skyrocketed. I pull out my phone and text him:

Kyle—are you okay?

I wait. I stand there getting more and more angry as he doesn't respond.

I send another text:

Hello????

Finally I hear the sound of a text message coming in. He wrote back:

Berry, I'm sorry. I'm married. I know that I probably should have told you. But I saw that news van & freaked. I just can't risk being on camera and having m (part one of two)

It stops there. There's a hundred-sixty-character limit, so I wait patiently for part two. Married? In our marathon conversation he never thought to bring up that teensy little detail? Or perhaps not kiss me during the concert? Or spend today with me like he was becoming my new boyfriend?

Ding. Part two: y wife see us. If you're upset, I understand. If you want me to come by your hotel later tonight, I'd like that. If not, no hard feelings. —Kyle

And that's it. "No hard feelings"? You have no hard feelings? How about my feelings? They, in fact, are extremely hard feelings. Solid. Rigor mortis feelings.

U

I retrace everything Kyle said when I'm back in my hotel room. No ring. No discussion of a significant other. But to be fair, no direct questions were asked about a significant other. He disappeared the first time the camera crew showed up, but why would I think anything of it? The second time . . . Sure, perhaps I could have given it some thought . . . if I was a completely suspicious psychopath. Is that what I need to be? In order to protect myself, do I have to be offensively defensive?

I just want to get the hell out of New York and go back home to my comfort zone. Erase that kiss. Erase today. Erase all things Kyle. Erase, erase, erase.

I pull out my iPod and put KKCR's live podcast on to make me feel a little more at home. Black Sabbath's "Immaculate Deception" is blaring.

"Sweeter than the dream, the reality of you, immaculate, deception."

Perfect.

No doubt exists that all women are crazy; it's only a question
of degree.

—W. C. FIELDS

Chapter Six

I have a blown-up picture of Jimi Hendrix's headstone hanging on
my wall at home. It's a black-and-white photo that I took when I actually went to Renton, outside Seattle, to visit the grave site. It has
the lyrics to "Angel" scrawled in Jimi's recognizable handwriting—
recognizable to anyone who's a Jimi Hendrix fan—and then somehow transferred onto marble. To me it's a beautiful reminder of talent and recklessness and how sadly they often go hand in hand. A
reminder to share your gift, whatever it is, while simultaneously not
being an idiot.

The grave itself is pretty monumental—which is only a recent
development, because apparently when Jimi died from an acciden-

tal overdose in London, his family barely had the funds to bring his body back to the States. For more than twenty-five years Jimi's grave was nothing to speak of, but after a drawn-out legal battle, Jimi's father finally regained the rights to Jimi's musical legacy, and the first thing he did with the money was build a beautiful memorial for Jimi—a resting place fit for a legend.

When I walk back into my apartment after the trip I'd like to forget, I find myself staring at the photograph, looking at Jimi's handwriting, taunted to rejoin the land of the living by the lyrics "Today is the day for you to rise."

Okay, Jimi. I'll rise. I will overcome. I will put this weekend behind me and move forward. That said, I'm swearing off men for a while. Because, seriously? Two complimentary shit cocktails in a row? Some might call that a "one-two punch." I, however, know exactly what it was.

So what do I have to look forward to in the next guy I date? Guy Number Three in the screw-it-I-might-as-well-join-the-convent series? I can only imagine. And I don't want to imagine. I've had one die and one be married—thus technically dead to me, and possibly also dead inside. What fresh hell could be next? Psychopath? Social disease? Drummer in a band? One, two, uh, one, two, three . . . Count me out.

But before I can take heed of Jimi's words and rise anywhere, I need to wash off the thin layer of travel grime that I'm certain is coating my entire body. Between the radiation from airport scanners and the general airplane filth, even thinking about the many unseemly violations of my person makes me a bit nauseated. So I jump into the shower to do a thorough post-travel scrub.

Then I do the most stupid thing a girl can do after she gets rejected by a boy: I step on my scale. And, yes, I know technically he was willing to come to my hotel—how gracious—but the fact that it would be completely meaningless and that he had some poor unsuspecting wife at home still makes it feel like a rejection. I wasn't worthy of being seen in public with, from one of the biggest stages in the world to a common city street. I was worthy of a morally bankrupt booty call. Blech.

You know how you step up and the number bobs around, up and down, finding center, and when it lands, you think, "God, no. It's broken. It's gone nuts. When did this cheap thing break down?"

Well, after the third or fourth time resetting it and stepping back up, hoping for a miracle, I literally gasp when I read the number before me. I'm six pounds heavier than I was the last time I weighed myself. Six. It's not that I'm saying I'm fat. I'm not one of those girls who's skinny and complains about how fat she is all the time, making you want to force-feed her frosting so she really knows what fat is. I don't even weigh myself regularly. Once every week or two. And as far as my weight goes, I'd say I'm normal. Healthy. I'm in fairly decent shape. And I fluctuate like everyone else. But by two or three pounds up or down. Not six. And, yes, if we're going to be honest, I've been hitting the crumb cakes more often than the gym of late. But this is appalling. It's more than five. Closer to ten than to one. Six. Of course it's an evil even number.

Nat calls me as I'm toweling off to tell me that she's just spilled salt in the kitchen.

"Which shoulder am I supposed to throw the salt over?" she asks. She's probably just humoring me, but screw it, I need humor.

"The left," I say.

"Okay," she says.

"With your right," I add.

"Wait—what? Left or right?"

"Throw the salt over your left shoulder with your right hand."

"Oh," she says. "I'll have to do it again."

Now, for a moment, I almost forget the misery, as I ponder this advanced concept from the superstition rulebook: If you spill salt, then incorrectly administer the antidote by using the wrong hand to toss more over the wrong shoulder, should you do the shoulder toss twice? That makes me think about the maximum amount of bad luck you could bank before a painting scaffold fell on your head, and that makes me think about general wallopings, and that of course leads me back to New York and my affair to forget.

"You will not believe the whirlwind romance I just experienced over the weekend."

"Spill!" she squeals. "Is he tall? Funny? Mortgage holder? Fully vested? Does he have a brother?"

"Yes, yes, a bunch of I-don't-knows, and for his mother's sake I sure as hell hope not, because one son of his kind would be enough to make you want to shoot yourself," I say. Then I add needlessly, "He's history."

"Oh, God," she says. "Please tell me he's not dead."

"Cute," I say. "Dead to me. But sadly, still alive."

"I think we have different definitions of 'whirlwind romance,'" she says.

She has a point. Plus, if we're going to be honest about the term "whirlwind romance," isn't it really used only in cases of celebrity? And doesn't it usually just mean "They got engaged/married too soon, but they're too important and/or we're too polite to say it"? And at minimum, I have to acknowledge you can't really have a "whirlwind romance" with one kiss and no sex. So perhaps I'm exaggerating a tad.

"No, it started out great," I say. And then proceed to tell her how quickly it devolved into complete crap. I tell her all of this in between her shouting at the line cook for "more this," "less that," and "Rodrigo, are you trying to kill that piece of meat a second time? It's already dead!"

"I should let you go," I say.

"No, you shouldn't. I mean, yes, you should, but come to the restaurant."

"I can't," I say. "I've gained six pounds."

"My pastry chef is gonna be pissed he had no part in that," she says. "So you can't even fit out your door now? Get your fat ass over here."

I sit in silence for a minute, listening to the sounds of her crazy kitchen, knowing that it would be nice to get my mind off Vile Kyle. I look around, and my apartment is empty. I don't even have Moose, because the doggie day care closes at seven and my flight didn't get me home in time to pick him up.

"Fine," I say. "I'll be there in thirty."

When I walk into Eat It, I'm impressed, as usual, by the fact that Nat really has her own restaurant. And it's a hit. I know the restaurant business is impossible to begin with, and she didn't have some trust fund to fall back on or keep sinking into the place if it failed. Yet she took the chance and did it.

The place is full of Los Angeles hipsters, and on any given night you can often find a celebrity tucked away in one of the corners. I do a cursory scan as I make my way into the kitchen because I don't want her to say, "Did you see so-and-so?" when I get there, and then have to sneak a totally obvious peek. I don't see anyone.

The kitchen always amazes me. So many people, each doing their part to bring together this well-oiled machine of complete chaos. I would probably have an anxiety attack if I was responsible for not overcooking someone's line-caught wild salmon, yet I just stood on a stage and introduced the Rolling Stones to thousands of people. I guess we all have our comfort zone.

"I thought I felt an earthquake," Nat says as I walk in. "But it's just my obese friend."

I roll my eyes and give her a hug.

"You'd be the same if six pounds crept up on you out of nowhere," I say.

"I gain six pounds after a good meal."

"Whatever."

"Did you see Leo?" she says.

"DiCaprio?" I turn my head back reflexively, distracted from my unpleasantness by the prospect. "No."

"Good," Nat says. "He's not here. I was just checking if the extra poundage was causing hallucinations."

"Well, I can tell you it's about to start causing some pain and suffering," I say as she fends me off with a spatula.

Nat shakes her head and moves on. "I started painting my apartment," she says. "And now I regret it, because I'm being photographed at home for a 'Hot Chefs of L.A.' article in *Los Angeles* magazine. They didn't want to have ten pictures of ten people all in similar-looking kitchens, so we're being pictured 'elsewhere.' Stupid. Especially when you consider that if I was truly hot, they'd have asked me to pose in a bikini, casually grilling up wieners at the beach. So annoying."

"How about, 'amazing'?" I challenge. "You're being profiled in a magazine. One that people actually read, no less!"

"I know, I know," she says, dipping a wooden spoon into a sauce and tasting it, then twisting her face sideways like it needs something. "But I passed out after doing the one wall. I don't know what I was thinking deciding to paint my own apartment."

"What color?" I ask. "And you need to paint the entry wall first."

"Red," she says. "It's bold."

I'm absolutely certain that red is a bad color for her. I know this because it's also bad for me; in numerology you have good colors and bad colors based on your Life Path number, which is determined by the date and month of your birth. Nat's birthday is the eighth of November. I was born on the seventh of the same month, so of course we get along. Our bad colors are red and black. Nightmare, right? I mean, fine, I don't need to wear red . . . but black? It's only the most stylish, slimming color there is. So to answer the question you must be asking yourself: Yes, I wear black. But never all black, and always with a good-luck color to balance it out, and only because it's black, which really can't be avoided. I do not wear red. And I would never paint the walls of my apartment either color—that would just be asking for trouble.

I pull out my iPhone and Google it to confirm I'm right about the color catastrophe. Sure enough. I look up at Nat, panicked.

"You can't paint your walls red," I say. "It's a bad-luck color for you."

She gives me her usual "That's your burden, Berry" look. "It's gonna be okay. Relax."

"Nat, no. Seriously. You need to paint over it. You've only done one wall."

"No," she says, abruptly annoyed.

"Then can you make it an accent wall?" I suggest. "My friend Brady used to have one wall painted blue, and the rest of the walls in his apartment were white. It was an accent wall. It was cool. Not overbearing."

"You mean bold," she corrects.

"I mean unlucky," I reply, looking back down at my phone. "How about yellow? Yellow is bold. And cheerful."

"And jaundiced. Are you high?"

We go back and forth for a while, me trying to convince her that a pale yellow would be soothing and pleasant and a bright yellow would be bold just like red, so really yellow is the way to go. She says yellow is the color of piss and "La Cage." I'd have gone with "the sun," but Nat's a little more acerbic.

I know that this interview and photo shoot are going to mean big things for Nat, and I don't want her to screw it up. I also know that in my bathroom I have two full canisters of white paint from when I repainted my own walls.

"I just remembered something," I say, and tell her I have to go.

"You didn't even eat!" she says.

"What part of six pounds did you not hear?" I call behind me as I'm leaving. "I just came by to see your warm self."

"You said 'warm.' You should have said 'hot,' " she shouts. "Bite me!"

"Not eating," I shout back.

Here's the thing: It's not breaking and entering if you have a key. Um, I think. And Nat and I each have keys to each other's apartments in case of emergency. She may not realize this, or necessarily agree, but this is totally an emergency.

♀

M-E-S-S-Y! Jesus, is Nat's place messy. I hate clutter. Leaving dirty dishes in your sink is not only an invitation to ants and roaches—it's just disgusting. It's amazing that this girl runs an immaculate kitchen, yet her own kitchen is a total pigsty. Once I've washed and towel-dried everything, I feel I deserve a mini-break, so I sit down in front of her TV and I'm three-quarters of the way through *The Bachelor* when I realize I'm totally getting sucked into this crappy fake reality show and whatever person gets chosen will never end up in a real marriage because that only happened once and I'm still not convinced that Trista and Ryan aren't getting paid boatloads of cash by ABC to stay together so they can keep the dream alive. Disgusted with myself for getting (once again) lured into that trap (I may or may not have seen every previous season of *The Bachelor*), I head back to Nat's foyer and get down to business.

I roll up my sleeves and embark upon the cover-up. There is no way she will have that interview tomorrow with one red wall. She's one of ten Hot Chefs in L.A. An inexplicable aversion to clean dishes and a tendency to wear pigtails ten years too late aside, Nat has her life together—not partially painted walls in unlucky colors. This is what best friends do.

I've brought a drop cloth and a bunch of newspaper to put on the floor, which I lay out as I prepare to undo the Red. She'll thank me later. Nobody would want an entire apartment full of red like this. It's abrasive.

U

And that's what I find myself telling the police two hours later when they are banging on the door because Nat came home after work, heard movement in her apartment, and tearfully called to report a burglary in progress.

"Please turn around, ma'am, and put your hands behind your head," the first officer says.

"Ma'am?" I say. "Really? How old do I look? Can I put the paintbrush down first?"

"Hands behind your head, ma'am. Drop the paintbrush."

Again with the ma'am. I'm six pounds fatter, and now I'm a ma'am. This day keeps getting better and better. I drop the paintbrush on the floor—thank God I put the newspaper down—turn around, and put my hands behind my head. A second officer pats me down.

"My name is Berry. Natalie Engle, the person who lives here, is my best friend. You can ask her."

"The woman who lives here is the person who called the police," Officer Ma'am says. "You have the right to remain silent . . ."

They just don't get that I'm her best friend and there's no need to read me my rights. I try to tell them as much. "Well," I say. "You can tell her it's me and— Oh! Ouch!"

They're actually putting handcuffs on me. This is new.

"Please step out of the apartment, ma'am." It's Officer Ma'am who says this, and Officer McFeely guides me out into the hallway and then keeps me facing the wall.

"Do you have ID?" McFeely asks.

"Yes," I say. "In my bag, in there on the floor."

Officer Ma'am goes to collect my bag and get my ID while McFeely stays with me. Once Ma'am has my wallet, he takes off in the elevator.

"Where is he going with my ID?" I ask.

McFeely ignores me.

"I was just painting my friend's apartment. Is house-painting a crime?"

"No, but breaking and entering is," he says.

"*Berry!*" shouts Natalie, when she exits the elevator with Officer Ma'am. "Yes, I know her."

"Thank you," I say.

"What the hell, Berry? Why didn't you tell me you were heading over?"

Natalie is not amused. "I came home and heard noises in my apartment. I thought I was being robbed! Or about to be raped."

"Neither," I say. "See? Lucky you!"

"What were you doing?" she asks.

"I was painting," I say. "And I finished. And *you're welcome*. You have all white walls again now, and your place will not look crazy when the interviewers come tomorrow."

Natalie shakes her head and crosses her arms in front of her chest. "No, I'm looking at the only crazy around here," she says.

"Ladies, we're going to need to run checks on you both, so if you could accompany us back downstairs," McFeely says.

"Checks for what?" Natalie says.

"Warrants . . . missing persons . . . wanted persons," he says. "We're required by law."

"So help me God, Berry, if I have some parking ticket warrant and I get arrested now because of you I will kill you."

"I'll have to make sure they put us in different cells, then."

The two officers guide us downstairs and put us where they can maintain a visual while they sit in the car and run us through their system. The handcuffs are still on me, and they're uncomfortable, to say the least. I have no idea how people willingly use these things during sex, but please continue to count me out.

Despite the fact that I feel a little bit like we're in an episode of *I Love Lucy*, Natalie is fuming.

"I'm sorry," I say, quietly. "I really was just trying to help you. I guess I had some extra energy after my disastrous weekend and I tried to channel it into preventing you from tempting the Bad Luck Gods, since they've been causing such havoc with me lately. At least where men are involved."

She doesn't say anything.

"I'm sorry," I say again. "It was stupid."

"It's okay," she finally says. "I know you meant well."

"I did. And now the place is ready for your close-up. I even tidied up for you."

"You didn't have to do that," she says. "The tidying. We know you didn't have to do the painting."

"I just wanted you to have a good interview."

"Thank you," she says. "You are a lunatic. But I know you meant well."

"Okay, ladies," Officer Ma'am says. "You're both clear." McFeely uncuffs me and walks back to the car.

"Sorry for the confusion," I say. Neither cop responds. "And feel free to never call me ma'am again," I add under my breath.

I imagine I hear McFeely say "whack jobs" under his breath, but I know that's impossible because he's here to serve and protect, not denigrate.

Natalie and I walk back upstairs so I can get my bag, and I apologize about seventeen more times. Finally, when I'm sure she's not angry, I leave. But I call her on the way home just to make sure.

I wanted to buy a candleholder, but the store didn't have one.
So I got a cake.

—MITCH HEDBERG

Chapter Seven

If there's one more thing you should know about me, it's this: I tell it like it is. Always. Sometimes, that makes things uncomfortable. Sometimes, it's made me unpopular. But for the most part it's what's made me *me*.

So when I'm walking into work on a warm Tuesday evening and there are a dozen or so guys camped out in front of our building to watch contestants sign up for Daryl and Jed's "Best Chest in the West" contest and one of them shouts, "Show us your tits!" my re-action is slightly less classy than perhaps I'd have wanted. "If I wanted to show my tits I'd work in TV, not radio," I say, which gets a laugh from some and encouragement from others. All of which I ignore. When your nickname at puberty was "The Young and the Breastless," you tend to be sensitive about these sorts of things. Granted, I grew into myself eventually. Or, rather, they grew out of myself, but when you come from humble beginnings such as those, you don't soon forget.

I walk past the long line of girls who are signing up and take note of their buckled boots, multiple tattoos and piercings. I'd say the girls range in age from about eighteen to thirty-five, with the exception of one woman standing in line who, I'm certain, is confused about where she is. She looks to be at least eighty-five years old—possibly older—and there's no way she's in line to show her boobs. I see more scalp on her head than hair, and her husband or companion is in a wheelchair for chrissakes. No, she is definitely not here to sign up for the contest.

My wanting to save her the trouble of waiting unnecessarily in the long line and possibly being embarrassed by the mere suggestion of her entering a wet T-shirt contest compels me to walk over to her.

"Hi, excuse me," I say, but she doesn't answer. Hearing-impaired, perhaps. I speak up again, this time tapping her gently on the shoulder, feeling her fragile bones so thinly covered by translucent skin. "Hello?"

Startled, she turns to see who touched her. "Yes?"

"Hi," I say. "Can I help you find . . . something?"

"Er . . . I don't think so," she says, sneering—yes, sneering—as she looks me up and down.

"I work here at the station," I say. "My name is Berry, and, well, it's just this line is for a contest that they're having on our morning show tomorrow. Daryl and Jed."

She just stares at me uncomfortably.

So I go on. "This line you're standing in is for a . . . silly contest."

"Get to your point, missy," she says, baring teeth, sounding not so much like the sweet grandmother who knits you a quilt or bakes you cookies but like the one you'll have nightmares about tonight. And by "you" I mean "me."

They say no good deed goes unpunished, but I've already started this, so I keep going.

"Ma'am," I say, conjuring my least favorite word for the occasion. "This line is for a wet T-shirt contest."

"I know what the line's for, you nosy *broad*. Why don't you mind your own damn business?"

At this point, Grandpa comes wheeling over in his chair and slides to a sideways stop right beside me, almost as if he's on ice skates.

"You got a problem?" he asks, chin jutted forward and up.

"No, sir," I say. "I was just trying to be helpful."

He gestures to his wife. "There some kinda age cutoff on this contest?"

"Well, no . . . I don't think so, no . . ." I say, stumbling for the right words, and my balance. *Are they serious?*

"You don't think Mama has nice boobs? I'll bet she has better boobs than anyone else in this line." He looks me up and down. "Definitely better than yours."

"Hey—I'm sure you're right," I say, backing away slowly. "I'm really sorry. I was just trying to be helpful."

"Ageist!" he says. And then says it again, louder, "*Ageist!* You hate the elderly!" He gets more and more agitated and starts to point at me. "She hates the elderly!"

"Sir," I say, now walking toward him, trying to calm him. Christ, I don't want him to have a heart attack or something. "I don't hate the elderly. I love the elderly. Love. I hope to be an elderly . . . person . . . someday."

"Mama," he says, as he turns to his wife. "Show her what you got."

I raise my hands up before me. "That's not necessary. Really."

But Mama doesn't listen to me. She raises up her shirt, exposing her breasts, and I quickly look away.

"Look at Mama," he insists.

"Sir, I don't want to look at your wife's breasts. Ma'am, please pull your shirt down, there's no need for this—"

Now I sound like Officer Ma'am. I'm ma'am-ing her. Which makes me feel even worse, because I know how crappy it feels to be ma'am-ed.

"Look at 'em!" Wheelchair Willie says, more forcefully.

How has this happened? How did a gesture to help a sweet old lady become an assault on my eyes? Is this not a sexual assault, if we're really going to get technical about it? This woman is flashing me. Okay, so maybe it's not assault. It's certainly indecent. How do I make it stop? By looking?

"Fine," I say, putting my hands on my hips to brace myself.

Her breasts hang well below her belly button. The skin is stretched and almost pulling, and the majority of them seem hollow, until you get to the bottom, where the rest of them are.

"Wow," I say. "I've never seen a pair like that before."

"Told you," Grandpa says.

She shakes them at me, and her husband lights up like a Christmas tree.

"That's it, Mama," he says. "Shake it!"

The other girls in line start egging her on and cheering. It's becoming a bit of a situation, and I don't want to be held responsible for any part of it.

"Okay," I say, in a higher pitch than usual, trying to signify that "show and tell" is over. "Thank you for sharing them with me. I have to go to work now, but I wish you the best of luck in the contest."

I take off so fast that if my life were a cartoon you'd see my legs in hyper-speed as I try to get the hell away from them and into the elevator.

And as I watch the floors light up as I pass, I wonder, in the grand scheme of my life, why was it written somewhere that I would need to experience that?

My office is full of years of promo kitsch that I've collected. Some is from my tenure, and some has been passed down from friends or co-workers. You get to know people at record labels when you work in radio, and they are forever sending you "stuff" to promote their artists. Less so in the past couple years, as it seems we are in the late Cretaceous period of the record label, but I definitely have an odd collection, including some things that could even be considered museum-worthy, or at the very least Hard Rock Cafe–worthy.

Things as small as a signature Def Leppard guitar pick, to a train whistle from the House of Cash and signed by Johnny Cash himself, to a guitar played by Stone Gossard during Pearl Jam's unplugged session, to the actual angel wings from R.E.M.'s "Losing My Religion" video.

But my prize possession is a Coolio head. It belonged to Tommy Boy records—apparently, in Coolio's heyday they had a life-size animatronic Coolio in their lobby. As Coolio's career disintegrated, so did animatronic Coolio, until eventually all that was left was the head, sitting atop one of the exec's desks, the mangled, broken-down body shoved in a closet. The head is complete with dreadlocks and eyes that moved back and forth—when animated. It was incredibly lifelike, and once I saw it I couldn't let it go. I needed it to be part of my collection. I basically harassed the entire staff of Tommy Boy for months until I finally broke them. Now the head is mine. At certain times of the day Coolio looks almost as placid and wise as a Buddha. Most other times of the day he just frightens me.

Safe and sound in the eclectic mess that is my office, I scan the gossip sites to see if there's anything breaking that I'll need to cover or make fun of. It's sad that I even look at this stuff, but it's what our zeitgeist is these days so it can't be avoided. There's nothing terribly exciting, so I decide to walk into our pathetic kitchen to see if anyone's left something out for the scavengers to nibble on. Every now and then, there will be some event in-house or some label that sends over doughnuts and you can score something yummy. But usually you're stuck with the downstairs vending machine.

When I turn the corner into our kitchen, I see a rear end I'm not sure I recognize from our floor poking out of our refrigerator. I take a few quiet steps to the side and see that it's Ryan, aka Dr. Love from KKRL. He does not work on this floor. KKRL is on the fifth floor. Is he actually sneaking onto our floor to see what kind of food we have? And I thought I was sick of the vending machines downstairs. Ballsy.

I watch him cut a tiny sliver off someone's cheesecake and take a bite. Then I clear my throat to get his attention. He turns around, caught red-handed.

"Are you eating my cake?" I ask.

At first he doesn't speak. I raise my eyebrows at him to say, "Well?"

"What cake?" he says, with a mouthful of food, accidentally spitting some out.

"At least chew and swallow it before you go on with this ruse."

He swallows and giggles like a kid who got caught with his hand in the cookie jar. Another family's cookie jar.

"I'm sorry," he says. "We never have anything good on our floor."

"So you just thought you'd help yourself to my cake," I say.

"Well . . . I didn't know it was yours."

"Would that have made a difference?"

"Probably," he says. "I've seen how many pretzels you eat at a time."

Really? He's going there? The cake isn't even mine, but now I'm gonna pour it on thick.

"It's good cake, right?" I ask.

"Mmm-hmm," he says, somewhat guiltily.

"It's from my favorite bakery. In San Francisco. Where it was flown in for me by my mom, who was just visiting and wanted to bring me a special treat: my favorite cheesecake."

"I'm sorry," he says.

"Oh, no, it gets better," I go on. "I'm on a diet. And that cake? Was my one treat for the entire week."

"Um . . ." he says. "Then I was doing you a favor?"

"Are you calling me fat?"

"As a gender, we have no response to that. Except 'No. Oh, no, not at all. Not you. God, no. Of course not.' "

"You've been trained well."

"Yes, well . . . that's why they pay me the not-so-big bucks to pretend I'm a relationship expert."

"How did you get that title, might I ask?"

"I have no idea," he says, looking sideways to make sure nobody is listening. "I suggested 'King of the Meerkats.' Didn't play with the bosses, though. So relationship expert it is. Though I'm unmeasurably unqualified. Please don't tell anyone."

"Your secret is safe with me," I say.

"And your diet is safe with me," he says. "Because I will apparently eat all of your food. I'm really sorry about that. Seriously."

He seems genuine at this point, and I can't take it any longer. Yes, I like to mess with people, but I can never keep it up. I always end up having to tell the truth.

"It wasn't my cake," I say as I breeze past him and open the fridge, slicing off a piece for myself and shoving it into my mouth. "I was just messing with you."

And with that I walk out of the kitchen and back toward my office.

U

The Red Line rings just as I settle into the studio and start one of my all-time favorite songs, "Can't Find My Way Home" by Blind Faith. If you could equate songs to comfort food, this is my mac 'n' cheese. But the Red Line is ruining the moment. There's always a feeling of panic when you see your red line light up. It could mean that there's an emergency; it could mean that when you thought your mic was muted, it wasn't and you said something on-air that wasn't meant to be heard; or it could mean that you said something that was meant to be heard but your boss didn't appreciate it at all and you may be fired momentarily.

I watch it ring in a state of panic before I answer. Finally, I do.

"This is Berry," I say, tentatively.

"It is so on," says the voice on the other end of the call.

"Huh?" I say, confused.

"It's Ryan," he says, clarifying.

"Oh!" I say, relieved that I didn't inadvertently let a cussword fly.

"You got me good in that kitchen," he says. "I felt terrible."

"Good," I say. "Because someone is going to be upset that their cheesecake was molested."

"You did it, too!" he says.

"I'm not saying I didn't."

"Well, you should know that you've started something here."

"Have I?"

"And two can play at that game," he warns.

"Bring it," I taunt.

"Oh, you have no idea," he says. "Listen to my show tomorrow."

"Why?" I ask.

"This is Ryan Riley . . . signing off. But remember . . . all you need is love."

Click.

God created the flirt as soon as he made the fool.

—VICTOR HUGO

Chapter Eight

"Here's the thing about Prince Charming: He doesn't exist. The truth is, 'Happily Ever After' is ruined in the space between 'Some-day, my prince will come' and 'Damn it, my prince came too soon.' You make your own happily ever after simply by choosing to be happy. Nobody's gonna be perfect, folks. Pick someone who doesn't drive you completely crazy and love them."

That would be Ryan on the radio. I'm listening to his show, as ordered. I'm a little pissed he can get away with a "came too soon" joke when I get warnings from the FCC simply for the occasional reference to Nickelback being the perfect arena rock band for the

Shithead Generation. I'm still not sure what I'm listening for, but I have to admit he can be amusing.

"That means they're allowed to drive you crazy part of the time. Because you'll drive them crazy, too—trust me. I try to go by the eighty-twenty rule. If your partner makes you want to scratch your own eyes out (or theirs) only twenty percent of the time? You're golden."

Interesting. I guess those are pretty good odds. From my past dating experience—Dead and Married excepted—I think they're actually pretty optimistic. The phonetic similarity between Dead and Buried and Dead and Married is actually quite interesting. Something to ponder if you have too much free time or are sitting in your car, listening to the radio, waiting for your parakeet's next missive.

"Okay, listeners. In the spirit of proving that 'Yes, anyone can find love,' I'm having a special contest tonight . . . and the winner gets a date with KKCR's classic-rock DJ, Berry Lambert."

Oh.

No.

He.

Didn't.

"Look her up if you don't know what she looks like. She's pretty cute."

And he called me "cute."

"Now, Berry loves cake. She's very protective of her cake. She'll bring cake in to work and leave it in the fridge and then guard it with her life, checking on it throughout the day to make sure nobody's stolen it."

Am I really hearing this? Have I nodded off into a narcoleptic lapse of consciousness while traversing the hallways? I pray not, because Lord knows what Daryl and Jed would do if they happened upon me. I'm never surprised by how low those two will go. Did they even watch that video human resources told us was required viewing?

"So I think a fair way to earn her love is to sing an emotional rendition of 'MacArthur Park.' "

Donna Summer's version of the tune is suddenly booming through my speakers: "Someone left the cake out in the rain. . . ."

"Callers, now's your chance to sing for her love and win a date with Berry Lambert. Compliments of the station, you will get dinner for two and . . ."

I don't even stay to hear what the "and" is. I race to his floor and charge in and out of offices until I see his studio and *bang* on the glass window. He looks up and smiles, giving me a thumbs-up.

I violently and repeatedly thrust my two thumbs down, which just makes him laugh. As soon as he takes a commercial break, he removes his headphones and steps out into the hall to join me.

"Are you kidding me?" I shriek.

"Well . . . kind of," he says. "I'd call it more of a 'getting you back' than a 'kidding' since, well, I did promise a date."

"I didn't agree to that. What makes you think I need a date? Or want a date? How do you know I'm not married?"

"I asked."

"Asked who?"

"You're single," he says.

"I don't even know you. You're a cake-stealing, fake-contest-making menace. And I'm not going on your date."

"Yeah, you will," he says, confidently.

"Uh—no, I won't."

"Sure you will," he says. "Because you're a good sport."

"This has nothing to do with being a good sport," I practically shout.

"I gotta go back in," he says, grinning like a schoolboy fresh from a prank in progress. And as he walks away, my cellphone rings. It's Bill. My boss.

"Hello?"

"Berry!" he screams, and I'm certain that not only has that idiot Ryan just procured me an unwanted date, he's also gotten me fired. "I love it! I just heard. Why didn't you tell me you were doing this, and why didn't you do it on KKCR?"

"Wait—what?" I ask. He's happy about this?

"We're gonna promote the hell out of it."

"Okay, there's nothing to promote. Ryan was kidding. And it was done without my knowledge or consent."

"Do you have any idea what the phone lines did when he announced that date with you?"

"Uh . . ." I stumble. "No?"

"They went nuts! Guys . . . girls . . . everybody wants a date with Berry Lambert!"

"Berry Lambert never agreed to this, Bill," I say sternly.

"Berry Lambert wants to keep her job, right?"

"Berry Lambert doesn't think you can possibly be serious. And Berry Lambert is extremely upset that you have caused Berry Lambert to resort to referring to herself in the third person."

"Berry, it's all in good fun. What's one night of your life? I'm talking to Wendell, the station manager at KKRL, and we're both going in on the money for the date. We're thinking a helicopter ride around the city after dinner. He's calling me back in five."

"I'm not getting into a helicopter, Bill!"

"It'll be great!" he says, ignoring me. "Call you later. I love this, Berry. Good stuff! Way to think outside the box!"

He hangs up. "Good stuff," I mimic, and then notice an intern standing about three feet to my left.

"Yes, occasionally I talk to myself," I say.

"Hey," she says. "We all need a pep talk every now and then."

I smile politely and walk to the elevator. I can't believe Ryan is doing this.

A helicopter? No. Bad enough that I'm now being forced on a date with some random stranger, but I will draw the line at the helicopter. How about my safety? Is that not something I have a right to? Fine, my time . . . can be sold. A dinner? To keep my job . . . whatever—I can deal. Helicopter? Hell, no. I call my dad to see if there's anything legitimately unlucky about helicopters. If there are any related superstitions, he'll know.

"Luck be a lady, tonight," my dad sings into the phone when he answers, channeling a not-too-bad Frank Sinatra. If he had a very bad cold. And was tone-deaf.

"Hi, Daddy," I say.

"What's wrong, pumpkin?" He can hear it in my voice.

"Are helicopters safe?" I ask. "And do you have a cold?"

"Sure they are," he says. Adding, "Except when they're not. They're like anything. Cars. Airplanes. Roller coasters. Why do you ask? Are you planning to ride in one?"

"Trying to avoid it, but, yes, there is a possibility that I will have to. I have a little situation brewing at work."

"As long as you don't step onto the helicopter with your left foot when boarding, you'll be fine."

"Are you sure?"

"Well," he says. "That, and if there isn't some engine malfunction or something gets stuck in the propeller."

"You are not helping!" I shout.

"Aaaa . . . choo!" He sneezes. "Berry, it's fine. It sounds exciting! Can I come?"

"Yes, Dad. That's what the contest winner will want. A date with me and my dad."

"Sounds like a new reality show," he says. "I like it!"

"While I have no doubt that somewhere, someone would pitch and probably sell that . . . I'm still going with 'no.' "

My call-waiting clicks, and I look to see it's Nat.

"Daddy, I gotta call you back."

"That's it?" he asks. "That's all I'm good for? Helicopter-safety inquiries?"

"No, I can hear that you're sick, so I'm gonna come by, but I gotta call you back," I say, and click over to take Nat's call. "Hey."

"Oh my Christ, you're auctioning yourself off for charity and there isn't even a charity?"

"Thanks for making me feel even worse," I say.

"It's what I'm here for," she says.

"You have no idea. This jerk DJ—"

"I know who Ryan Riley is, Berry," she cuts me off. "He's hot."

"He's a jackass," I say. "And he made that contest up to get me back for pretending cake was my cake when it wasn't."

"Can you say that in English?" she says. " 'Pretending cake was my cake when it wasn't'? What does that even mean?"

"There was a piece of cake in the refrigerator—on our floor, mind you, not his—and he was stealing it, and I pretended that it was mine to make him feel bad, but I was kidding."

"This is fascinating," she says.

"So he did this to get back at me. Which is like taking it five thousand steps too far. I didn't make a public mockery out of the fact that he can't get a date. Mainly because I'm sure he can get a date."

"Okay, a) he's flirting with you," she says. "And b) you could get a date if you wanted one. But let's focus on *a*."

"You think he's flirting?" I say incredulously. "That's how you flirt? You pimp the person out to the first person who can sound like Richard Harris howling his way through one of history's most overblown pop songs? No."

"I'm thinking they'll go for the Donna Summer disco cover version. She hits that 'again' note much better. But we'll agree to disagree on this one."

"We'll agree to nothing," I say. "That's not flirting. It's tormenting."

"It's totally flirting," Natalie says. "It's like boys who dunk girls' pigtails in inkwells when they're kids."

"Really, Nat?" I say. "Inkwells? Were there inkwells when you were a kid?"

"You're the one who went right past Donna Summer to Richard Harris."

"Did you walk uphill in the snow both ways carrying your inkwell to school every day? You never tripped and stabbed yourself on your quill, did you? That's gotta smart."

"Wow," she says. "You are really not happy."

"Ya think?"

"Okay, there's no even having fun with you right now, so I'm just gonna go."

"Yeah, not feeling super-fun right now," I agree. "Call you later."

I hang up, feeling like all I'm good for is "dish" about something I'd rather forget. A blind date. Involving a helicopter, which is simply terrifying, with a person who listens to Dr. Love on a regular basis—a male person, no less. It's so incredibly ridiculous that I can't even believe it's happening. And being forced on me with potential job loss as a repercussion for not partaking. How do you sit in the far back of a helicopter? There is no back! It's all front. And all of this practically in front of an audience. Have I died and gone to hell? No and yes.

Employees make the best dates. You don't have to pick them up, and they're always tax-deductible.

—ANDY WARHOL

Chapter Nine

Sudafed is a bastard. A tiny red pill of evil. And I tell my dad as much when I go to his apartment to bring him chicken noodle soup and find him, jacked up on pseudoephedrine, frantically writing out his will.

"Dad," I say. "I promise you're going to be fine. Calm down." Other than the occasional cold or flu, my dad is in perfect health. Well, physically.

"I feel like my head is going to explode and my heart is going to jump out of my chest and start punching me in the face."

"Sudafed is the devil," I say. "I've had more bad reactions to

Sudafed than to the burritos at Los Tacos, and that's saying something."

This gets a smile, and I feel relieved that he's calming down. I'm pretty sure the only actual ingredients in that stuff are speed and venom and sadness.

"Thanks for the soup, baby," he says.

"It's what I'm here for."

"No, I'm supposed to take care of you."

"Nah," I say. "Not once I'm over eighteen."

"That's going to be a great birthday, you know." He winks. "You're still a baby to me. You'll always be my baby."

"Eat your soup and let me clean up a bit here."

"My girl . . ." he says. "Why am I so lucky? Wait—I already know the answer. Because I have you: my lucky charm."

My dad does as he's told and sits at the small card table that doubles as his dining room. This is no way to live out your impending golden years. It's his choice, I guess, but it's not the man I knew when I was little. I look around and feel tremendous sadness. There are slips from racetrack bets, tallies of owed money scribbled on random pieces of paper, empty take-out food containers. . . . It doesn't exactly scream "good living." I start by organizing his betting receipts. I don't even know what is or isn't okay to throw out—although I'd like to throw it all away and pretend it never happened. I make three small piles of paper and wipe the table down with Windex until I can see my reflection. Once I've peered into my nostrils—not a bad look for me, I tell myself, immediately resolving to feel more self-confident around short men—I move to the kitchen.

Since Dad doesn't actually cook, the kitchen's not really in a bad state, although there appears to be what I think may have at one time been a banana but is now a black fossilized entity. I open his refrigerator, and he has an onion that has somehow grown into a plant, a carton of expired milk, and some moldy bread. I hold my breath and grab all three items to toss. For a moment I think I want to go shopping so he has food, but then I wonder if he'd just let it wither and die in here like everything else.

"Dad," I say. "If I went shopping and bought you some healthy food, would you eat it?"

"Don't go shopping for me, baby. You do too much."

"If you'll actually eat it, I want to." I hold up the banana. "But if this is going to happen, then . . ."

"I call that the 'Banana Experiment,' " he says.

"Yes," I say. "You also had an onion experiment in your refrigerator."

"I know!" he says, coming to life like a kid. "It kept growing. The little onion that could!"

"I think it can't, I think it can't. I think it can't stay here another second."

"Judge not lest ye be judged."

He has a point. I continue to tidy up the place while I listen to my dad slurp his soup. I've always known that everything comes full circle. Our parents take care of us when we're children, and then ultimately we take care of them—but that usually happens later, when they regress back into a childlike state. Or when they physically can't take care of themselves. This situation isn't that. I'm reminded of my mom warning me to let him go a little. But he has a bad cold. He needed soup.

U

"Good evening, boys and girls. First things first—you should know that Ryan Riley is kind of an ass," I say into my mic the moment I turn it on. "And that little contest he created out of nowhere was sort of a practical joke gone wrong. So to clarify, I will go on this date because . . . well, my boss is making me, but you need to all know that this was an incredibly immature act perpetrated by the same person you guys call for love advice."

My red light flashes. Great.

I start "More Than a Feeling" by Boston and pick up the phone.

"There's a problem," Bill says.

"What's the problem?"

"Your contest winner is fifteen years old."

"Of course he is," I say. Because in my alternate universe the winner would be tall, dark, and handsome, with a kick-ass sense of humor, solid morals, and a great job, and he'd fall in love with me at first sight. So, yes, it only makes sense that my date would be a fifteen-year-old boy. Assuming it is a boy. Knowing my luck, this will just get more and more complicated.

Bill tries—and, as usual, fails—to sound reassuring. "We're figuring out what to do."

"Gee, I don't know, how about you cancel it?" I practically screech at him. "I mean, it was foisted on me, anyway. It was a joke. But now the joke's on him. Can I discuss this on-air?"

I can hear Bill thinking about it. Weighing the all-in-good-fun potential rivalry in his head.

"Sure," he says. "Have fun with it."

"Always," I say, and hang up the phone.

When the song ends, I put my headphones back on and get comfortable.

"So get this, friends. The winner of the KKRL contest is all of fifteen years old, and therefore is unable to attend our date. Awwww. I'm so disappointed. Let's see if we can get Ryan on the phone."

I look up the direct line for Ryan's show and dial up the KKRL station.

"Ryan Riley," he says.

"Hi, Ryan," I say. "This is Berry Lambert, and you're live right now on KKCR."

"Well, hello, Berry Lambert."

"Hello," I say. "I was so disappointed to hear that my date turned out to be a teenager, but then it all made sense, because, well . . . what grown man would be taking dating advice from—no offense—you?"

"Oh," he says, and laughs. "No offense taken."

"Good, good," I say.

"The truth is everyone else who was willing to date you has already been tried as an adult."

I laugh audibly. He got me there. "Nice one, Ryan. Touché."

"We have a caller who wants to chime in," says Frank, Ryan's producer. They connect him.

"Hey," says the male caller. "Why don't you two go on the date? You're obviously into each other. Anyone can hear that."

"You couldn't be further from the truth," I say. "We barely even know each other."

"I'm hearing a lot of sexual tension," says the caller.

"What's your name, caller?" Ryan asks.

"It's Craig," he says.

"Well, Craaaig," Ryan says mockingly, adding an extra syllable to the guy's name. "That's a neat idea, but I don't know if I can do that. There's a difference between sexual tension and taking pity on the sexually frustrated."

No. He. Didn't. My entire body breaks out in a cold sweat. *Low blow, Ryan Riley. Below the belt, even. Ahem.* "Excuse me?" I chime in. "Who says I'm sexually frustrated?"

"Word on the street is the pizza boy refuses to go to your door without backup."

"Funny," I say.

"No tip will make up for that kind of terror," says Ryan.

"Wow," I say. "You hear that, caller? Is that what you call 'sexual tension'?"

"Yes," the caller answers. "You two have it bad for each other."

"I'm charming," Ryan says. "I sound like that with everyone."

"You're not as charming as you think you are," I say.

"Nobody is as charming as I think I am," Ryan says.

"No argument here."

"*If* we do this," Ryan says, "and you pay for dinner, don't think it entitles you to . . . anything. I'm not that kind of guy."

I can't tell if he's just playing this up for my benefit or if he's really this cocky. Oddly enough, I'm not sure it matters.

"So wait," I say. "A contest that you concocted in your tiny, tiny brain, a contest that was supposedly courtesy of the station, is now a dinner that I am somehow paying for?"

"Keep up with that attitude and I'm ordering the lobster."

I laugh again and find I'm genuinely smiling. "You're delusional."

"You mean adorably quirky?"

"You should get a dictionary," I say. " 'Delusional' means detached from reality, which is what you are if you think I am taking you to dinner."

"You are going to wear something nice, right? This is dinner, not poetry night at the Perpetually Single Café."

"You're hilarious."

"And I think you should wear a skirt. Your legs are not just for walking you to the grocery store to buy TV dinners for one."

This time he actually cackles, and Frank begins stomping his feet in the background. I take advantage.

"Dr. Love, huh? 'Dr. Love.' Wow. How did you get this job, anyway? Callers, what you've just listened to is exactly what *not* to do when wooing a person—take note."

"Wooing?" Ryan says. "Wooing? Did people use that term the last time you had a date?"

"Oh, I'm sorry," I say. "What I meant was when you are desperately gushing over a lovely female co-worker."

"Technically you're not a co-worker," he says. "You are sort of on a rival station. The old people's station."

"Good point," I say. "And speaking of that, I'm going to get back to my show and let you get back to giving extraordinarily misguided advice to poor unsuspecting souls. Remember, folks, those who can't do . . . "

"Nice to hear from you, Berry!" he says. "Call back anytime!"

I slam the phone down dramatically. But I can't stop grinning.

Bill runs into my office moments after I go off-air, and I'm sure that I'm about to get in trouble for going too far.

"KKRL is not a rival station," he says. "Both of us are owned by ClearWaves."

"I know," I say. "Sorry. He just got me so riled up."

"No kidding. But you both riled up a bunch of listeners. Great cross-promotion. Plus, we got seventy-five emails and counting from people saying they want you to go on a date."

"That's ridiculous," I say.

"You were already gonna go on a date with the winner."

"He's not the winner!" I say.

"He is now."

"Is there not some law against this? Something that says you can't pimp your DJs out for ratings?"

"Berry," he says as he pushes his greasy strand of hair out of his left eye and back over his barren scalp. "What's the harm?"

"There's just general harm," I say, really making no sense at all. Then I stretch the facts a tad for effect, adding, "There's harm in you treating me like a prostitute."

But the truth is that under normal circumstances there would be no harm. The truth is he's actually really cute and smart and funny, and maybe in some other circumstance I would really like to go on a date with him. Ryan, that is, not Bill. But not these circumstances. First of all, he's going out with me only because my date turned out to be in high school, and second, if I make one mild-to-extreme faux pas, his entire listenership will hear about it, in detail and embellished, I'm sure. No, thanks. And third, this technically makes Ryan Guy Number Three. Which I don't necessarily want him to be. This cannot mean good things.

"Berry," he says. "I really don't understand your reluctance. This is someone you know. A colleague, if you will."

"See, Bill," I say, at my wit's end. "That's just it. The phrase you just uttered, 'if you will,' hasn't come up at all—not once in this whole situation. Nobody has actually asked me if I will go on this date. It was assumed that I would go when it was some random caller, and again it's assumed that I'll go if it's with Ryan. You even semi-threatened my job rather than just saying 'Berry, will you go out on this date?' "

"Berry," he cuts me off. I know where he's going, and technically it's my fault; now, if he asks nicely, I pretty much have to say yes. "Will you go out on this date?"

"No."

"Berry . . ." he says.

"Fine."

"Thank you."

Bill walks out, looking satisfied, and I shake my head, wondering what I've gotten myself into.

○

Nat is practically jumping out of her skin with excitement when I meet her at the diner.

"Oh my God, you should have heard yourselves," Nat says.

"Were we embarrassing? Was I a total idiot?"

"No, you were hilarious!"

"Really?" I ask, surprised because I don't even remember exactly what we said, it all happened so fast.

"High-larious," she reiterates. "Seriously. And you guys have amazing chemistry. Kind of like Joe and Mika, except you're both single so it's not icky. I felt like I was listening to two people fall in love. In the 'Hate-at-First-Sight' version."

"Yeah, that wasn't falling in love."

"It was definitely falling in serious like," Nat says.

"No," I say. "He's too full of himself."

"He is not," she says.

"Oh, you suddenly know him?"

"He was just messing with you. You started it."

"He started it by being on my floor and eating the cake!"

"He was on the floor? Eating cake? Not gonna lie, Ber. Kinda hot. Very *9 1/2 Weeks*."

"No, not on the floor. On the floor I work on and not hot. I mean . . . I guess technically he is pretty good-looking, and I suppose what would qualify as 'hot' if you were—"

"You totally like him," she interrupts.

"What are we, thirteen? I do not."

"Dude, I heard it in your voice," she insists. "I know you."

"You heard nothing. You know nothing."

"Yeah, okay," she says.

"So did I tell you the worst part?"

"The worst part about this terrible situation where the good-looking, smart, and funny guy wants to take you out on a date? No, by all means, tell me. Because I'm on three online dating sites, and the only guys who're even remotely interesting are in jail. And can't spell."

"You're lying," I say.

"I'm not!" she says. "His headline said 'Will Be Released from Prison Soon. Need a Date.' So I thought he had our kind of sense of humor. 'Ha ha, how clever,' and we wrote back and forth for a bit before I realized that he was actually an inmate and wasn't kidding. Nor was he trying to be cute when he used 'California Penile Code' in his subject line. I prefer it when men talk dirty to me on purpose."

"Oh . . ."

"Yeah," she says. "So from where I'm sitting, your 'unfortunate' date seems pretty exceptional, so all I can imagine being the 'worst part' is—what?—he's taking you horseback riding at sunset?"

"Well, now I feel like an asshole for complaining."

"What?" she goes on. "He's flying you to Paris for dinner?"

"Actually you're not too far off. We have to go in a helicopter around the city."

"Oh my God, it's like an episode of *The Bachelor,* except he's not creepy, you're the only girl, and I'm now starting to sort of hate you like I hate every other girl on that show."

"I don't want to go on a helicopter, and it's not like a real date! It's a fake date, made doubly fake because my first fake date still wears Underoos. Anyway, the date is really annoying in its forcedness and publicness—"

"And awesomeness?" she interrupts. "I'm sorry, I'm just not seeing the downside here."

"You don't understand, and I don't expect you to, but let's just make it about the helicopter. Helicopters are scary."

"I disagree," she says. "I think you're going to have an amazing time, and I'm going to be completely jealous."

"Then we'll agree to disagree."

"Agreed," she says. "Or disagreed. Whatever."

Come fly with me.

—FRANK SINATRA

Chapter Ten

There are few things more exciting or more traumatic than getting ready for a first date. What do you wear? Does your apartment need to be clean in case you bring the guy home? Do you tempt bad fortune by cleaning in the hopes you'll bring the guy home? Will the gods of fate find that presumptuous? Do you shave? Do you tempt bad fortune in the hopes that you'll want him to discover you've shaved? Will the gods of fate find *that* presumptuous? These are all things that need to be considered. Clothes? Always stressful. I try on five different outfits and model them for Moose, who finally gets up and leaves the room, strongly suggesting the blue dress is a no.

Apartment cleaning? Sure, you always want your apartment clean, but the stress of having to do it in a mad rush at the last minute makes you get sweaty and need to take a whole other shower before getting dressed. Which leads us to the shaving thing. A lot of people say don't shave. That way you will force yourself to behave and come across as less of a slut. But then Murphy's Law will guarantee that you end up naked with the guy and he'll think you're a filthy Sasquatch.

Not that this is a real date.

Because it's not.

When Ryan and I are seated at our table at Pace, the conversation flows naturally. So naturally, in fact, that the waiter comes to our table three times before we've even looked at the menu.

"What made you get into our not-so-glamorous business?" he asks me as he wrestles with a piece of bread that doesn't seem to want to separate from the rest of the loaf in the bread basket.

"Music," I say, and shrug. "There's just never been anything I've had a more visceral reaction to. Memories, experiences . . . Pretty much everything in my life has a soundtrack that I can call up. I always just knew I wanted to work in music in some capacity, and I have no musical talent whatsoever, so . . . radio."

"No musical talent?" he balks. "I find that hard to believe. In fact, didn't I see you do a rendition of 'Sweet Child o' Mine' at that charity karaoke event two summers ago?"

I'm completely taken aback. He knew who I was two summers ago? I pretend I'm not excited to glean this little tidbit.

"You have quite a memory," I say. "That's my go-to karaoke song. I don't remember you singing that night."

"That's because I didn't."

"Why not?" I ask.

"Because unlike you, I actually mean it when I say I have no musical talent. I had a blue plastic recorder when I was in grade school, and that was the beginning, middle, and end of my music career."

"So what got you into radio?" I ask.

"My dad," he says. "He worked as a sound engineer, and one day he came home from work and said, 'Son, whatever you do . . . don't go into radio.' So of course I went into radio."

"Are you close with your dad?"

"We lost him," he says.

"Oh, I'm sorry."

"No, I mean we don't know where he is," he says.

"Oh," I say. "Did he go out for the proverbial pack of cigarettes and not come back?"

"Worse," he says. "Ice cream. I'd just had my tonsils out, and when we got back from the hospital, he promised me all the ice cream I could eat. He never came home. To this day, I cry when I see the number forty-eight."

"Why the number forty-eight?"

"Baskin-Robbins," he explains. "Forty-eight flavors."

"It's thirty-one flavors."

"Fuck." He bangs his hand on the table. "I've been crying at the wrong number this whole time?"

I can't help but smile. "None of this is true, is it?" I ask.

"I did get my tonsils out."

"Was your dad a sound engineer?"

"Yes," Ryan says. "And he did tell me not to go into it. And I was gonna listen. I got my degree in psychology and was going to be a therapist of some kind, but then my college radio show took off on a lark and . . . here we are."

Our food arrives, and I cut off a piece of my cedar-plank-grilled salmon and put it on his plate. He feeds a piece of his chicken directly to me. I'm trying not to like him, but he's making it increasingly difficult.

"You have great teeth," he says.

"Teeth?"

"Yeah," he says. "They're perfect. I'm sure everyone compliments you on your hair or your eyes—and don't get me wrong, I'm a fan of those, too—but those are some nice-looking chompers you have."

The solicitous way he says "chompers" makes me burst out laughing, and I accidentally spit out a shard of salmon.

"I'm still learning to eat," I say, completely embarrassed.

"I have that effect on women. They spit at me constantly."

"I believe it," I say, and wink, still mortified.

"But I like it," he says. "Sometimes when I'm lonely I'll go to the zoo and see if I can get a llama to spit at me."

"You're a weirdo," I say. "Stop trying to make me feel better."

"We should go to the zoo on our next date and see if we can get a large animal to spit at us. Make it a theme."

Our next date? Did he mean to say that? Is he thinking this is really a date? A real date?

"Are you calling me a large animal?" I ask, but then quickly add, "Don't answer that. I withdraw the question. But can we pick a different theme for the next date?"

"If you insist," he says.

For the most part, Ryan is completely unlike who he is on the radio. He's sweet and charismatic, he's interesting and interested—he's not just waiting for me to finish talking so he can speak, he really listens. I find myself totally engaged yet sometimes totally distracted and missing what he said completely because I'm thinking, *Oh my God, I might actually like this guy.*

Which would be bad. Because he's Guy Number Three, and Guy Number Three, we know, is gonna be bad news. Already I'm regretting having told the restaurant that it was Ryan's fortieth birthday. I know the fake birthday is an old gag, but I was going for the "old gag" in its most literal sense—saying he's ten years older than he actually is.

When the waiters bring the cake over and start singing a fancy jazz version of "Feliz Cumpleaños," he doesn't miss a beat.

"C'mon, guys," he says, all charm. "Look at me. Do I look like I could be forty years old? It's *her* fortieth birthday." And all eyes go back to me. He's a wily one, this Ryan Riley. "And you don't know this woman and cake. If you don't bring her a bigger piece, someone might seriously get hurt."

We're still laughing as we exit the restaurant and walk to the valet. Ryan offers to drive us to the heliport, and I don't refuse.

"I'm actually excited," he says. "I've never been in a helicopter."

"Me neither," I tell him. "And to be honest, I'm a little scared."

"Really?" he says, and places his hand on my knee and squeezes. His hand lingers on my knee, and I don't want him to move it. "Don't be nervous. It's totally safe. We're gonna be just fine."

Somehow, when he says it I believe it. Plus, what are the odds of our parent company losing two DJs in one night?

U

I'm pretty sure Pilot Dan is unstable. I'm not talking about piloting skills. I'm talking life skills, coping skills, confidence-inspiring skills. Never mind that his green-and-another-shade-of-green striped shirt immediately convinces me that if he's not full-on blind, he's at least color-blind. I'm generally not a paranoid person, but Dan's got a mild facial tic and keeps asking Ryan for relationship advice. In truth, he's more shouting than asking, because "so loud it's deafening" doesn't even begin to describe the situation. The incessant whir of the propeller sounds like a machine gun with a stuck trigger—not that I want it to stop propelling mid-flight; I'm terrified enough as it is. We're wearing headphones to block out some of the noise and enable us to communicate with each other.

"Hey, Doc?" Dan says to Ryan.

"I'm not actually a doctor," Ryan says. "I just play one on the radio." Then he turns to me. "What are the odds I would ever be able to say that in a real-life situation?"

I shake my head and clutch my seat.

"I've heard your show, and you know stuff," our pilot goes on. "What are the sure signs that your wife is cheating?" he asks.

"What?" Ryan shouts.

"How do you know your wife is cheating on you?" Dan shouts, and from here until we get used to the racket of the blades, we settle on a volume about fifty decibels above bloodcurdling scream.

"Well," Ryan says, "I'm not sure there are any one hundred percent sure signs—"

"Sure signs," the pilot says.

"Right, yes, sure signs," Ryan continues, "but often sudden changes in appearance can be a tip-off. Like if she usually goes around in sweats but suddenly starts caring more about how she looks . . . going out looking more put together . . . That can be a sign."

"Uh-huh," Pilot Dan says, nodding.

"Starting a new exercise regime. Also, if she's secretive about her phone," Ryan adds. "People who have nothing to hide will leave their communication devices lying around the house. But people who are composing secret text messages or emails will carry their phone everywhere."

"Even to the bathroom!" Dan says.

"Well," I chime in, "she could just be expecting a call . . . or a text."

I can see he's agitated, and I don't want the already scary and possibly color-blind pilot who is flying the already scary helicopter to be agitated. I suddenly remember a recent news story about how the army just abandoned plans for a new attack helicopter because after twelve billion dollars in development costs, it still kept crashing. Twelve billion and they can't get it to stay in the air? I'm resolved: No agitation for the pilot.

"She's not always expecting a call," Dan says.

"Nobody's always expecting a call," Ryan agrees.

"Exactly!" Dan says. "But she's clutching that phone at all times. Especially when she goes to the bathroom."

"I take my phone with me to the bathroom," I say. I don't really, but I don't want Creepy Pilot getting agitated.

"Not every time," Ryan says. "I'm positive that every time you go to the bathroom you do not—"

"No agitation for the pilot!" I shout, my panicked thoughts manifesting themselves into sentences spoken loudly.

Ryan looks at me, and I give him a pleading look.

"You know," Ryan says, "these are just theories. Sometimes a new outfit is just a new outfit."

And it's at that moment that Dan makes a sudden turn and takes off in the opposite direction, slamming me up against Ryan as though I'm pressing my face against a plate-glass window. Smoosh.

I know L.A. well enough, and we're flying low enough to know that this isn't the lame "Tour of L.A." route that Bill had booked.

I want to say something to Ryan, but I feel like I could be being paranoid so I just sit. And panic. And look out the window at the residential area we seem to be touring. And . . . circling?

"Are we going in a circle?" I ask Dan.

"That's what a tour is . . . one big circle . . ." he answers, but his already beady eyes have become shifty. I should have realized he was insane by the way he smiled at us when we boarded. I was too busy touching the fuselage with my right hand to really take into account that no one smiles that big at strangers unless they're about to crack.

"Seems like a smallish circle," I press.

Dan says nothing, but I see tiny beads of sweat forming on his brow and upper lip. I catch Ryan's eye and raise my eyebrows to say, "Are you not noticing that we are going in a tiny circle?"

Finally Ryan speaks up. "Bro, she's right. What's up?"

Dan doesn't answer, but I notice his nostrils flare.

"Dan?" Ryan says. "Everything okay?"

Dan points down at . . . something . . . and the helicopter drops a good twenty feet.

"Whoa!" Ryan and I simultaneously say.

"That's my house," Dan says.

The look that Ryan and I exchange is a knowing one. We're in a bad situation.

"Which one?" Ryan asks, feigning interest so as not to upset our not-so-dutiful pilot.

"The one down there . . . right . . . hang on . . ."

He does another loop and moves in closer.

"The one right there," he says. "The roof is white. It's a white roof. Do you know what a white roof is?"

"A roof . . . that's white?" I offer.

"Yes," he says. "It's white, and it reduces the cost of electricity by lessening your need to use air-conditioning. White reflects heat instead of absorbing it."

"That's interesting," I say. "Eco-friendly."

So he's earth-conscious in addition to being a psycho stalking his wife. From the friendly skies, no less. *How nice.*

"I have a pair of binoculars on the floor," he says.

"Neat," I say, and look at Ryan, who shakes his head.

"Could one of you get them for me and hand them over?"

"I get that you're going through something, man," Ryan says. "But maybe this isn't the best time to be . . . you know . . . checking up on your wife."

"It's absolutely the best time," he says. "She thinks I'm at work."

"Yeah, because you are." Ryan sounds a bit stern when he says this, and I'm glad. "We're paying customers here. And we're both radio DJs with a large audience, if you get my drift."

"The binoculars," Dan says. Then adds, "Please." As if that makes the situation any more palatable.

Ryan reluctantly reaches down and hands the man his binoculars.

"I'm so sorry," Ryan mouths to me, and the previous thirty minutes or so of fighting the noise has made me an excellent lip reader.

"It's not your fault," I say, trying to remain somewhat upbeat.

"It's totally my fault," he says. And I feel like we're Stillwater, the band in *Almost Famous,* when they think the plane's going down so they're panicking and saying whatever needs to be said.

"Hey," I say. "If we get out alive, this will make a good story."

That much is true for sure. Bill and Wendell have already prearranged for me to be in the studio with Ryan tomorrow to discuss our "date," so this is definitely fodder for that.

"I can't see anything," Dan says, and he loops around again.

"Maybe it's for the best we move along, then," Ryan says. "And really, we're California natives, so we don't mind cutting the tour short."

"Sure, no problem," Dan says, but he's just yessing Ryan and doesn't change his flight pattern at all.

"So you wanna bail on this little recon mission and head back to the heliport?" Ryan asks.

"In a few," Dan says, and makes another loop.

Ryan and I look at each other. I don't think he's going to suicide-bomb into his house, because first, he hasn't actually been able to even see anything, and second, he knows damn well that it would be a waste of a perfectly good white, heat-reflecting roof. A roof he's proud of. I keep telling myself this over and over as we go in circles over and over.

I change my mind about Ryan's culpability. "Assuming we make it to the station tomorrow, you are so not going to hear the end of this," I say to Ryan.

"I'd expect nothing less of you," Ryan says with a smile. A smile that even in this ridiculous and terrifying situation manages to make me feel a little bit better. Until we swerve.

"I think I see something!" Pilot Psycho shouts.

"I'm sure it's really hard to see from up here," I say.

"Seriously, man," Ryan chimes in.

"No, I saw . . . something," he insists. "Movement."

"Well, your wife is alive, right?" I ask, thinking, *Oh God oh God oh God I hope she's still alive.* "She's allowed to move around your home." *Oh God oh God oh God she's chained up in the cellar.*

Dan squints his eyes and does that tic thing he does when he's plotting or thinking or existing. He jerks his head slightly to the right. Really quickly.

"You're right," he says, and I think reason is finding its way into his less-than-reasonable brain. "We should get closer."

My stomach drops as the whirlybird does the same. I grab onto Ryan's arm, and he places his hand over mine.

"That's not what I was saying," I tell him.

"Buddy," Ryan says, "chances are really strong that even if there is anything going on with your wife—and I'm not saying there is—she wouldn't do anything under your roof."

"He's right," I say, picking up his rationale, hoping we can convince him using the tag-team approach. "I can speak from a woman's perspective. You don't cheat in your own home."

"That would be an outward act of aggression," Ryan adds. "Not starter-cheating."

"Starter-cheating?" I parrot, concerned that this is even a thing. *Is this a thing?* Ryan just bulges his eyes out at me, and I get his point: Now is not the time.

"Your wife doesn't hate you, does she?" I ask.

"Not that I know of."

"Oh, you'd know," I say. "It takes a very angry woman to behave like that." Of course, I'm thinking, if she happens to notice a helicopter hovering overhead every single night, she's bound to be getting at least a little bit perturbed.

"It's true. She's not cheating in your home," Ryan says.

"How do you know?" Dan asks.

"I know," Ryan says.

"But how?" he presses.

Ryan looks at me, then back at our pilot. "Because I have ways of knowing. It's what I do. I'm a psychologist. And if you turn around and land this chopper right now, I will tell you everything you want to know. Just because she's not cheating in your house tonight doesn't mean she isn't cheating. Take us back right now and I'll give you five surefire ways to find out."

Dan turns the machine around so fast, I practically get whiplash.

Ryan winks at me as we head back to base. My heart rate starts getting back to normal, but it's not at my resting tempo until we are on the ground and out of the helicopter.

Ryan offers his hand and helps me climb down safely before turning back to Dan.

"You're lucky there was a lady on that plane," he says, putting his arm around me and turning us to walk away.

"But wait—" Pilot Unstable shouts. "What about the five things?"

Ryan doesn't even stop walking, he just swivels his head around enough to say, "Number one, get close enough to smell her. Preferably not from the cockpit of a hovering helicopter. But smell her. And if that stink on her isn't her or you, figure out who or what it is. Number two, if you do something incredibly stupid—and be imaginative on this—and she doesn't get really pissed off, it's usually not just a highly evolved capacity for forgiveness. It can be, but it's usually not. She's unwittingly giving you one back, throwing you a bone, trying to restore the cosmic balance. Number three is simple. If she says she's doing something somewhere or with someone, call there, or call that person. This will at least exhaust her alibis over time, or piss them off enough to push her to find someone else to cover until she finally runs out of people. Number four, ask yourself, *Am I a big enough dick that I deserve to be cheated on?* Number five, if the answer to number four is no, try asking again. You're probably not being honest with yourself."

While I don't consider it exactly profound, and I'm sure he was making almost all of it up on the fly, I'm impressed. Especially because I'm almost positive we're back on the freeway and halfway home before Dan gets it. Casualty of a life spent not being able to hear a damn thing anyone is saying.

Well, remember what you said, because in a day or two, I'll
have a witty and blistering retort! You'll be devastated then.
—CALVIN, OF CALVIN AND HOBBES

Chapter Eleven

Since the contest took place on KKRL and Bill and Wendell have
already completed what I can only imagine were some very juvenile
negotiation rituals, Ryan and I are broadcasting the follow-up to
our date during my show. Once we were safely on the ground and
away from that maniac, I barely even said a single word to Ryan. I
was literally shaking during the whole ride home, and when he
dropped me off I coughed up a "thank you" for at least the dinner
part of the evening and headed into my building without looking
back. I can't wait to skewer him for endangering my life with not
just a helicopter but an unstable pilot.

U

Ryan walks in with his usual swagger, and I want to roll my eyes at him but my body doesn't cooperate. Instead, I end up grinning like a moron the second I see him. *Stop it, mouth!*

"Hello there, pretty lady," he says.

Pretty lady? That's new. A bit cheesy, but good cheesy. He hasn't ever flattered me before. Except on the radio when he told people I was cute and they could Google me—which, for the record, never stops sounding dirty to me, but I suppose that's because I'm actually a twelve-year-old boy. Apparently. Ah, he also said I had nice "chompers." That one isn't quite as dirty-sounding, but I'm not sure it counts as flattery.

"Hello," I say back, flashing my chompers.

"Has your heart rate returned to a normal resting tempo yet?" he asks.

It had. Until he walked in. "Yes," I say.

"Good," he says with a wink as he pulls his headphones out of his messenger bag and puts them on.

Maybe I'm not alone in my superstitions. Lots of DJs have their special headphones, and they will never use any others. Even if they're old, broken, and put back together with duct tape and bobby pins, people are loyal to their headphones—and yes, some of the old-timers do still call them "cans," which always makes me giggle. I've heard of crazy stories—people stealing headphones of rival DJs, people taking their headphones with them out of town, even if they aren't doing radio, just so they aren't out of their sight— I mean crazy stories.

"Are those your lucky headphones?" I ask.

"Only because I wear them," he replies, cool as a cucumber.

"Maybe you should have worn them on our date, then," I say.

"Mrrrowr!" he growls.

"No," I blurt. "That didn't mean you would have 'gotten lucky' with me. I meant maybe then we wouldn't have had Psycho McFlyer as our pilot."

"Turn on the mic!" Bill's voice echoes, like the Wizard of Oz's. "This is gold!"

I look at Ryan and smile, now able to roll my eyes.

"Let's do this," he says.

"And we're live," I say into the mic. "Good evening, my friends. Welcome to Classic Rock With a Little Talk. I'm Berry Lambert, your barely-still-alive-after-a-disaster-date host, and with me is special guest KKRL's Ryan Riley—also known as the Man I Will Never Go Out With Again."

"I beg to differ," Ryan chimes in.

"Don't beg, Ryan. It's just embarrassing."

We lock eyes, and my heart speeds up a little. *Damn it, heart, relax, would ya?*

"So," Ryan says. "Who gets to start? Because I thought it was a pretty good date, all in all."

"You would," I say. "The station paid for it, and you got to live out a videogame."

"Okay, first of all, I paid."

"They'll reimburse you."

"Second of all . . . maybe that helicopter ride was a bit atypical, but there were no upside-downs and no guns, so that hardly qualifies as a videogame."

"Upside-downs?" I tease.

"We went in circles," he says. "We didn't do tricks."

"I know what you meant, you just sounded like a six-year-old boy. And the 'trick' was staying alive."

"Our pilot was going through some stuff," Ryan says.

"Our pilot was insane," I clarify. "Clinically. Criminally. And, folks, if you think I'm making this up, think again. He thought his wife was cheating on him, and we were basically stalking his house from a helicopter. At one point he thought he saw 'movement,' and I thought we were going to dive-bomb through the roof. It's a white, heat-reflecting roof, just in case his wife or her enormous stable of boyfriends are listening. Also, he was wearing a shirt that was hands down the most hideous shirt I've seen since *Magnum P.I.* was on the air. Boy, I don't usually wish bad things on people, but I hope his wife is sleeping with the entire USC offensive line. And speaking of 'offensive' lines, Ryan, nice planning. Would five minutes of due diligence on the flight crew have been so hard?"

"I got us out alive, did I not?"

"Am I supposed to thank you?"

"It would be the polite thing to do. . . ."

"I tend to define 'polite' as 'not endangering the life of your date.' "

"That doesn't sound like a thank-you," he says.

"Thank you, Ryan," I say. "Thank you for the cardiac arrhythmia I'll probably have for the rest of my life."

"See, folks? I made her heart skip a beat."

"You damn near caused it to stop beating altogether. All thanks to a truly memorable date that I hope to never repeat again."

"But you'd go out with me again."

"Says who?" I ask.

"If there was no psychotic aviator involved? You had fun. You had fun at dinner, and even in the helicopter you had fun."

"I did not have fun in the helicopter."

"But you did at dinner," he says. "You can admit it."

"It was . . . moderately tolerable. The food was good."

"So good that you spit it in my eye while laughing at my brilliant banter. Such a crock!" Ryan says.

"You certainly are sure of yourself," I say.

"I only call it like I see it."

"Perhaps you need glasses," I say.

The phone lines are ringing off the hook, and Bill is frantically motioning through the glass for us to take a few calls. I pick up line one.

"This is Berry. You're live on KKCR. . . ."

"Hi, Berry! Hi, Ryan!" the caller says. "Sounds like you guys had quite the date. But, Berry, if Ryan asked you out on a real date . . . no publicity stunt, no debriefing, would you go?"

I'm completely flustered by the question. Before it was just shtick, but now this is sounding real. My real life is personal and none of her business, and Ryan is, of course, leaning in now, waiting for my answer.

"What would you do, Berry?" Ryan asks.

The caller perks up again. "What would Berry do if Ryan asked her out on a real date?"

Really? What would Berry do?

After what feels like an eternity but is probably only about twenty seconds, I finally speak.

"Well, caller," I say, "that's extremely hypothetical. Plus, it's hardly a real date if we're plotting it on the radio. And, Ryan, I'm sure you don't normally ask women what they'd say *if* you asked them out, so we'll just pretend you're not losing your touch and just got caught up in the moment."

He leans back in his chair and kicks his feet up on the table, placing his hands behind his head.

"I was just having fun watching you squirm," he says. "The truth is I already know what your answer would be.

"Let me give all you fellas out there a little tip," he goes on. "You never ask the question if you don't already know the answer is yes. That goes triple when proposing. If you don't know the answer is yes, you don't ask. Why put yourself through it? Why put the girl through it? We've all seen the YouTube video of that poor guy asking his lady to marry him on the Diamond Vision screen at a filled sports stadium, and what happens—she runs off crying. That's not just a no. That's a humiliating virtual kick in the crotch. You. Don't. Do. It. You only ask . . . when you know the answer is yes. End of story."

"So what would my answer be?" I say.

"You'd say yes," he answers.

"There goes that sure-of-yourself thing. Too bad it's based entirely on delusion."

"I stand firm on my answer," he says.

"You mean my answer," I say. "We'll just have to cross that bridge if we get to it."

"Berry?" he says, and my heart starts beating faster. Is he really about to do this? Publicly? The brat in me wants to say no, just to prove him wrong, but then again—we know that he's Guy Number Three, and since I already know it won't work out with him, I should say yes just to get him out of the way and make room for Mr. Right. Plus, truth be told, if I did say no after that speech of his, Dr. Love might find himself instantly unemployed and unemployable.

"Yes, Ryan?"

"Would you like to go out on a date with me?"

Was.

Not.

Expecting.

That.

Even with all the windup, I still somehow didn't think he was really going to do it. "Are you asking me out?" I challenge. "Because that almost sounded like you asking if I'd *like* to go . . . *if* you asked me out."

"I would like to take you out on a real date," Ryan says. His tone is absolutely earnest and a little unsure. I think I even detect a little quiver in his voice. Surprising. "Will you go out with me?"

"Sure, Ryan," I say. "I'll go out with you. Even if only to see what you do when left to your own devices."

"I don't usually incorporate devices until later in the relationship. You know, to spice things up."

"Yeah, that's not what I meant."

"Right," he says with a smile.

"Well," he says. "I for one am looking forward to our date."

And I . . . am looking forward to not having to discuss it on the radio.

Like a river flows surely to the sea
Darling, so it goes
Some things are meant to be.

—ELVIS PRESLEY

Chapter Twelve

I'm struck by the irony of just escaping serious injury in a helicopter mishap only to experience a massive cardiac arrest when the cute guy you're desperately trying not to fall for asks you out—live, on the radio, of all places. My mom used to say (constantly), "When you least expect it, expect it," which is probably the closest thing I have to a mantra, even though it basically leaves you expecting the worst nearly one hundred percent of the time. Rule number one in the superstition handbook: Bad luck never sleeps. Okay, I'm not one hundred percent sure which rule that is, but it's definitely in the top ten.

So after I inhale two Diet Cokes in my office, I gather my things

to meet Nat—very uncharacteristically—for a jog. This we've decided is going to be our new routine. Rather than meeting at the
diner every night and packing on the pounds, we're going to take
up exercising three nights a week and potentially take off a few.

"You so like him," she says between heaves of out-of-shape
breath.

"False."

"It's me, Ber. You can be honest here."

"I can't like him," I say. "He's the third asshole."

"That's gonna be hell when you become incontinent."

"This is serious."

"I know it is. Third asshole. Come to think of it, I may have read
a novel with that title."

"My autobiography."

"Then you can write your own ending," she says, and then gags.
"Wow, that was cheezalicious. Forgive me for saying that."

"No can do."

"But really. Maybe you should give this guy a chance?"

"No," I say, standing firm.

"Then go out with him once more and then dump him. Get it
over with, and then Asshole Number Three will be out of the way."

"That's the plan."

"Yeah," she says. "Just keep in mind what they say about best-
laid plans."

"I forget," I reply. "Was it something about friends not just
being cheesy but also turning into walking clichés?"

"Yes, I think it was," she says, and makes a face at me. But I've
made my point.

"So," I say, trying to change the subject. "What else?"

"I think Victor is stealing food."

"Victor?"

"The line cook. You know him, Berry, he's the one who always makes you chicken paillard. He's always been really good—he's one of my best. But I'm pretty sure he's a thief. Which sucks."

"What's he stealing?" I ask.

"Does it matter? Stealing is stealing."

"No, I get it," I say. "But . . . there's a difference between grabbing a handful of grapes at the supermarket when you're not buying grapes and loading your pockets up with cans of Wolfgang Puck soup."

"That's pretty specific, Ber."

"I've never stolen soup," I clarify. "But . . . I've been known to swipe a grape or three."

"I get it. You know they're unwashed, right? Given any thought to where those grapes have been?"

For as much of a slob as she is in her apartment, there's a difference between being messy and being dirty, and Nat is a total germophobe. She could single-handedly keep the antibacterial-hand-sanitizer companies in business. I stand by my theory that the main ingredient in hand sanitizer is paranoia.

"Okay, Nat," I say, and sigh. "You've just successfully detoured me from my life of fruit crime. Now spill."

"What?"

"What do you mean 'what'? I'm dying to know what he's stealing."

"You really need a hobby," she says. "He's stealing staples."

"Staples? Staples are cheap. You can get staples for less than a dollar at Office Depot. Or, for that matter, Staples."

"Not staples staples. Food staples. Pretty much everything. Eggs, milk, pasta, tomatoes, cheese, flour—"

"Flour?"

"Eggs, milk, pasta, tomatoes, and cheese are fine, but you draw the line at flour?"

"No," I say. "None of it is fine, but you said 'staples' first of all. Those other things qualify. But flour . . . I mean, it's bulky. . . . It's not a staple per se, unless you're a baker. I don't know, it just seems odd."

"Yes," she says. "Odd, and just as much of a theft as the other items."

"Have you confronted him?"

"No," she says.

"That's unlike you."

"I know. Because I have even worse things to deal with right now."

"Like?" I prod. "And why don't I know about them?"

"Just happened," she says, and then looks sideways both ways, indicating that this one is big. "It's bad."

"Take a breath and spit it out."

Nat slows to a stop and exhales. She looks at the ground as if the words she's trying to find are somewhere down there. Finally, she looks back up at me. "You know my dad," she says. "E.T."

I nod and smile. Nat's father's name is Donald. "E.T." stands for "Enemy of Technology." He's incapable of figuring out the simplest computer issues and constantly bothers Nat to come help him out.

"Yes, I'm familiar. But we do this because we love our parents. You know, we're probably the last generation that will ever even have this opportunity, because I think kids these days are hardwired at birth to be tech-savvy."

I notice Nat shifting from foot to foot as I get off topic. "Sorry," I say. "Go on."

Nat takes a deep breath. "Last night I was over there because his email had supposedly 'disappeared.' How he manages to find new and inventive things to screw up on his computer is beyond me."

"It's kind of an art."

"Yeah." She rolls her eyes. "Art."

"Maybe he just wants to see you," I suggest. "Did you ever think it's just an excuse to get you to come over?"

"No. Because I see my parents plenty. Can I finish?"

"Finish . . ."

"So last night I go over there to help him find his email, which as you can imagine wasn't 'lost,' but he'd done some cockamamy thing that made it appear that way. So I restore his settings and then decide to check match.com to see if there's anyone interesting who hasn't already been on the site for the past seven years, and when I go to type the URL into his drop-down menu bar, a bunch of his 'recently visited sites' expose themselves."

"Uh-oh . . ." I say.

"And I do mean expose."

"Double uh-oh . . ." I say.

"Beyond double uh-oh."

"How bad?"

"Not just regular porn. Asian girl porn. Asian teen-girl porn."

I twist my face while trying to think of something I can say either to defend how this porn could have accidentally found its way to his computer ("I thought your dad couldn't find a website on purpose if his life depended on it!") or to perhaps initiate a fast subject change, like, "Look! George Clooney just walked by! With his arm around Matthew McConaughey!"

She goes on. "I mean . . . not just one site . . . dozens."

So much for my brilliant defense. Your Honor, we'd like to discuss a plea.

"That's . . . awful."

"No shit!" she says. "Do I tell my mom? Do I bring it up to my dad?"

"Never talk to a man about his porn habits," I say. "That's a sure way to get rid of him."

"It's my dad," she reminds me. "Much as I may like to right now, I can't 'get rid of him.' "

"Still applies," I say. "I just don't think you wanna go there."

"Asian cheerleaders," she says, with a look on her face like she just realized the milk she guzzled was sour. "Pom-poms and innocence lost."

"What can come of it?" I ask, immediately regretting my choice of words, so I keep going. "You bring it up to him and he's embarrassed and you're condemning and God forbid you tell your mom and she hates him for the rest of their marriage—"

"Oh, she's hated him since 1985."

"Still. It's a different kind of hate."

"I'm horrified," she says. "I can't even look at him."

"I'm sorry," I say. "That is profoundly awkward. I feel for you."

"It's revolting."

"Dads are handfuls," I say.

"Yours gambles and thinks the sun rises and sets around you. Mine is a pedophile! Slight difference. I can't even say 'handful' and 'dad' in the same sentence anymore without conjuring up mental images that will drive me right into therapy."

"You already see a therapist twice a week."

"And now I need a third day. This is not just horrifying. It's expensive."

"Okay," I say, trying to find a bright side. "But he's not acting on it, right? He's just . . . looking . . . ?"

"Why are you defending him?"

"I'm not. I just . . . He's still gonna be your dad, so I'm trying to soften the blow." Why does every turn of phrase I utter somehow sound perverted in this context?

Nat sinks her head into her hands. "Can we talk about you again?"

"Yes," I say as my cellphone rings and I look at the caller ID but don't recognize the number.

"Hello?"

"So I was serious about wanting to go on a date," he says. It's Ryan.

I nudge Natalie and point to the phone, mouthing "Ryan" as I practically bounce out of my skin.

"Well . . ." I say. "You know where to find me." *What does that even mean? Why did I say that? He just found me. Idiot.*

"Well . . . that's what I'm doing now," he says. "I'm finding you."

"Okay, then," I say. "Hello."

"Hi," he says. "What are you doing tomorrow?"

"Tomorrow?" I repeat back, looking to Nat for help with my answer. She nods. "I'm, well . . . I'm on the radio from seven to midnight."

"And I'm on the radio from four to seven," he says. "So what about lunch?"

"I eat lunch."

"As do I. Would you like to do that together?"

"Sure," I say. "That sounds . . . fun."

"I promise we'll stay on the ground."

"Otherwise you'll be six feet under it," I reply warmly.

Ryan tells me to "wear something nice" and says he'll pick me up at twelve-thirty.

"You soooooo like him," Natalie says the second I hang up. "I could see it in your face. And your voice changed into your 'I like you' voice."

"I don't have an 'I like you' voice."

"Oh, you totally have an 'I like you' voice."

We stand in silence for a minute before I can no longer take it and am sure that I will explode from excitement.

"I have a date tomorrow," I say. "A real one."

U

Ryan arrives at twelve-twenty-nine, wearing a great-looking suit. He's so handsome that he almost looks like he belongs on a red carpet somewhere. He hands me three lilac orchids wrapped in plastic as soon as I open the door. Three. A perfectly odd number.

"For the lady," he says.

"Thank you," I say, blushing. "Come in while I put these in something."

Ryan follows me inside my apartment and takes a cursory glance around. I get self-conscious immediately, wondering what he's looking at, what he's thinking, why I still have that stupid bright green stuffed frog I won at the arcade two summers ago—what am I, fourteen years old? But my memory quickly relives the sequence of that night: I'd won the balloon-water-gun game, besting a thirteen-year-old—who no doubt spent about fifteen hours a day parked in front of a PlayStation—after eating not one, not two, but three cones of cotton candy (the third hadn't gone down nearly as easily as the first and second, but two was an even-numbered no-go, and one wasn't cutting it); after riding the Witch's Wheel not once (or twice, which would have been unthinkable) but three times; after wasting three nickels on the wishing well (low percentage, admittedly); after watching the odometer roll through a triple seven; after brushing my hair for three minutes with my lucky Vidal Sassoon brush. That little hopper was luckier than a squirrel in a nuthouse, as my dad says. It was my reward for doing everything right that day and a reminder to be vigilant about superstitions. So it wasn't going anywhere.

"That's a pretty dress," he says, taking in the seventh outfit I tried on—a slightly nicer-than-average sundress with medium-heeled ankle boots. Moose loves the boots, perhaps a touch too much, which is why they reside on the top shelf of my closet.

"Thank you," I say. "You look pretty sharp as well. Am I dressed okay for our destination?"

"You're perfect," he says, and I find myself wishing he was talking about me and not just my outfit.

I notice him looking over my shoulder at the horseshoe on my wall.

"It's a horseshoe," I say, and then wonder why I said it. Duh. He can clearly see it's a horseshoe.

"Is there a story behind it?" he asks. "Do you ride horses?"

"I have ridden horses," I say. "But not since . . . I don't even know when. That's not why I have the horseshoe. I mean . . . horses are great and all, but that's not . . . I'm not a horse aficionado or anything." *Can someone stop my mouth from moving? Jesus!*

"Okay," he says, with an easy smile. "I'm officially clear on what it doesn't represent, then."

"It's important that the . . . you know, the curvy part, that the shoe be mounted upright, you see? Like so."

And I trace the shape in the air, illustrating. "It's to ward off bad luck," I blurt.

"I see. And how's that working out for you?"

Fine, until I stopped being able to form an intelligent sentence. "It's working out very well," I say, and then once I've placed the orchids in a shallow jade vase, I walk back toward the door. "Shall we?"

Ryan opens the car door for me and then walks around to let himself in. I wonder whether he'll have a radio station on or a CD that will provide a glimpse into his inner soul, but when he starts the car . . . nothing.

"So where are we going?" I ask.

"It's a surprise," he says, and then quickly changes the subject. "Did you know that Big Brad Stevens does traffic on KRST in a fake voice under a pseudonym?"

Brad Stevens is our sports guy. He's the most mild-mannered psychopath you'll ever meet. I always exchange pleasantries with him in the hall when I pass him because I want to remain on his good side, and he has always been entirely pleasant, but I've heard stories about him flipping out, making interns cry. And there's a rumor that he once got into a fight with Bill and tried to choke him. Which would explain a lot, including the giant dent next to Bill's Adam's apple.

"No way," I say. "How can he get away with it?"

"He just does. A lot of people do it. He has a mortgage to pay and, well . . . KKCR—"

I interrupt him at that point. "Oh, you don't have to tell me how pathetic the pay is at KKCR."

"I mean . . . don't blow his cover."

"Are you kidding? You think I want to be on that guy's bad side? He's like Jekyll and Hyde, and with plenty to Hyde. And apparently he's two different radio hosts as well. Fitting."

"Now if he ever gets on your bad side, you'll have something to hold against him," he says with a wink. I have visions of my black-mail note in uneven newsprint cut and pasted together in different fonts:

I KNOW THAT's YOU DOiNG THE TRAFFiC REPORTS.
NOw LEAVE $10,000 In UNMARKED BILLS
uNDER THE TrEE OR ELSE....

After about a twenty-minute drive—everywhere in L.A. pretty much takes twenty minutes to get to—we turn onto La Tijera and I start getting nervous. This is the way to the airport. If he thinks I'm getting on any type of aircraft with him, ever again, he's nuts. I keep my mouth shut, though, and after a few short blocks we pull into a driveway, and wouldn't you know it . . . Ryan has managed to outdo himself.

And by "outdo himself" I mean make a quasi-mockery of our date while further convincing me that he and I just might see the world through the same bizarre, twisted tinted lenses. Hilarious.

"Welcome to Chuck E. Cheese's," the hostess says as she looks around, behind and beyond us, to locate the children we should have with us if we're at all self-conscious or self-respecting, which, as it turns out, neither of us is.

But then Ryan says something that catches me completely off guard.

"I heard you'd never been to Chuck E. Cheese's before."

"That's true," I reply. "But where did you hear that?"

"On the radio," he answers. "Someone requested Jonathan Coulton, and you said that you assumed all Jonathan Coulton fans spent a lot of time at places like Medieval Times—which is uncool, by the way; he's great, and 'Skullcrusher Mountain' is a hilarious and beautiful song—and then you went on to say that you'd never been there or to any theme restaurant. Not even Chuck E. Cheese's when you were little. And I thought, *How sad.*"

That was nearly six months ago. I remember saying that on the radio, but that was way before Ryan and I met cute over cheesecake. He's been keeping tabs on me from afar! (I hope not from a helicopter. Come to think: *Did he and Pilot Dan already know each other? Did I bring my pepper spray?*)

I refocus. "Gee, Ryan, you have a pretty good memory for inconsequential stuff."

"I'd hardly call Chuck deprivation inconsequential," he balks. "Everyone should go to Chuck E. Cheese's at least once."

"Yeah, it wasn't exactly on my bucket list. And I don't recall it showing up on the one hundred, one thousand, or even one million things to see before you die. But thanks for taking such an active role in making sure my life is complete." I'm giving him a hard time, but inside my transition to total mush is nearing completion.

"I complete you, I know. It's what I'm here for."

Once we're seated and the "rules and regulations" have been laid down by Lloyd, our pimple-faced waiter, who seems as enthused about his job as he would be if you offered him some more acne, we peruse the menu, settling on the Barbecue Chicken Pizza, the Garden Fresh Salad Bar, and Cinnamon Sticks for dessert, which I can only hope will be like churros.

I'm a sucker for the old-school games—Galaga, Centipede, Ms. Pac-Man—and it turns out so is Ryan. So when we've finally eaten ourselves firmly to the point of gluttony, we march over to the arcade and let the games begin.

It should be noted that I'm totally comfortable eating like a pig in front of him, which is normally not the case when I'm crushing on a guy. That's not to say that I like Ryan any less. There's just an ease that allows me to shove pizza into my mouth like, if I don't eat fast enough, a basket of puppies will be killed.

It should also be noted that we play videogames for two hours, laughing our overstuffed guts off, and when it's time to call it a day, neither of us wants to. We sit in his car for about twenty-five minutes, after which time it's really getting obvious that either I need to just get out of the car or he needs to kiss me, 'cause otherwise he's gonna be really late for his shift.

I reach for the door handle just as he reaches for me.

"Wait," he says, and I turn back to face him.

"Waiting . . ." I say, with nervous anticipation.

And he leans in, stopping just before our lips meet. He looks me in the eyes, and we're just centimeters from each other but I can see by the tiny crinkles forming next to his eyes that he's smiling. I close my eyes and feel things I have never felt until now. Like these are the lips that were created to kiss mine. This is a kiss that I would never get bored of. This is that thing you read about but think doesn't really exist. But it turns out it does.

Double uh-oh.

Jerry, don't you see? This world here, this is George's
sanctuary. If Susan comes into contact with this world, his
worlds collide. You know what happens then? Ka-shha-shha-
shha-pkooo [exploding sound].

—KRAMER, ON *SEINFELD*

Chapter Thirteen

So, yes, the next six weeks are pure bliss. My show ends later than
his, but our days are open to spend time together. I constantly re-
mind myself that he's Guy Number Three and I shouldn't get my
hopes up—I even push him a little at times, testing him, giving
him reason to be a jerk or show his true colors or introduce me to
his wife and family—but each passing day seems to prove me
wrong. A rare case where I'm happy to be proven wrong.

We spend our first weekend away together at a bed-and-
breakfast in Laguna, and my heart melts when I find out he's made
special arrangements for Moose to come with us. Ryan is consider-

ate and charming—and his biting sense of humor and severe case of the smarts give him balance. His obvious good looks, when you add everything else up, are just a bonus. Looking at *la package totale,* it's virtually impossible not to fall for him.

Everyone at both stations knows we're a couple, and while at first we tried to hide it, we ultimately decided there was no point. Even interest from callers has quieted to a dull roar since we've stopped divulging the date dirt. And we don't work at the same station, so if by some stroke of bad luck things go south—which, who am I kidding, they always inevitably do—he can stay on his floor, I'll stay on mine, and we'll just pretend this never happened.

As if.

I'm a pretty private person by nature. While, yes, I scan all of the gossip blogs every morning so I can have fodder for my show and be in the know so I'm not blindsided by caller questions, the truth is I find them all to be completely vile. Each crotch shot more disgusting than the next. I can't imagine what it's like for these celebrities to be under a microscope 24/7, and you can argue that "this is the life they chose" so they deserve it, but I disagree. These people chose to play a sport or act in films or on TV or on the stage; they didn't go into those careers because they were desperately seeking an invasion of their privacy. The same does not hold true for reality stars of any kind. Those people get what they deserve, and I have no sympathy for the Kates and Kardashians of the world. And, yes, on occasion I'll give out a few random tidbits about my life on the air here and there, but only if it's wildly interesting or, alternatively, a sign that I'm completely unraveling. It's never the focus of a show, not that anything in my life is interesting enough to hold people's attention any longer than someone fixing a flat tire on the freeway shoulder.

So you can imagine my surprise when Bill calls me into his office on a Monday morning to tell me that they want Ryan—Unprivate "Dr. Love" Ryan, mind you—and me to co-host a new morning show. The privatization of our relationship has resulted in a drop in listenership, or that's how they perceive it, and they want to reclaim some of that traffic.

"Berry, did you hear what I said?" Bill nudges.

But I stand there, staring at his gross poster of Lita Ford in a bathing suit, holding a guitar, while I ponder what I've just heard. The poster in and of itself isn't gross. Lita's gorgeous, and we should all be so lucky to have a body like that. What's gross is that it's the only poster in his office. The only thing on his walls. There are no family photos on his desk, no finger-painted masterpieces framed on the bookshelf. Lita Ford is the focal point of this creepy man's office.

"Berry! Hello!"

Finally I tear my eyes away from Lita and answer. "Yes, hello."

"This is great news," he says, trying to convince me.

"I don't know, Bill," I say, and start backing out of his office without even realizing I'm doing it.

"Where are you going?" he asks.

"Me? Nowhere."

"Berry, this is what we need. It's what the station needs. The show will be on KKCR. You can still keep your nighttime slot, Ryan can keep his evening, and you'll have this show in the mornings."

"And when do we have our own life?"

"You don't get to have a life right now, Berry."

Even Bill realizes that the way he just said that sounded awful, so he starts backpedaling as he pushes his comb-over farther back on his head, one lone sprout now sticking up uncomfortably. "You'll be like Regis and Kelly without Regis. Kelly and Hot Guy."

"They're on TV," I counter.

"You'll be on billboards," he says. "Bus stops. We're gonna do the full-court press."

"I'll talk about it with Ryan," I say. "It's not just up to me."

"He'll do it."

"You don't know that for sure."

"I'll bet you he says yes with minimal discussion," Bill says, quite sure of himself.

"Can I go now?" I say. "I need to prep for my show."

"You're acting like this isn't great news," Bill says. "This is a big deal, Berry."

"I get it," I say. "I appreciate the offer. I don't mean to come off as ungrateful."

"Think about it, Berry."

"I will."

♉

I weigh the pros and cons as I walk to my office. It seems like a no-brainer, right? A big morning radio show? Morning is "prime time" in radio. It's a big deal. *Pro.* Having my private life made public on a daily basis? *Con.* I didn't even get into the money thing, but it would double my pay at the very least, I'd assume. *Pro.* Navigating a brand-new relationship, live on the radio? *Con.* Having to work all day and then work all night? *Con.*

Before I even get back to my office, my cellphone rings. I know it's Ryan before I even answer. Not just because he has his own per-sonalized ring on my cellphone, which has changed four times since we've started dating. The first song was "Wish You Were Here" by Pink Floyd. No matter how much time we spent together, I always missed him when we were apart, so it seemed fitting. But it got old. Plus, one day when we were having our first mini-argument—neither of us felt like choosing where we were going to eat for dinner, and we got into a stupid disagreement over who picked where we ate more often (pretty sure it was me, but Ryan would disagree)—I decided that I did not in fact wish he were here. And that I was starving and going to kill him if he didn't just pick a restaurant. I changed his song to "Hungry Like the Wolf" by Duran Duran. Then I felt guilty, and once my hypoglycemia faded and the hungry beast turned back into normal girl, I changed it to "Happy Together" by The Turtles. I mean, why would his ringtone be "Hungry Like the Wolf"? It made no sense. Unless he was obese, and then it would just be insulting. Then "Happy Together" just seemed too . . . happy, so after much internal deliberation, I settled on "No One Like You" by the Scorpions.

And that's what's blaring as I walk through the hall and try to hold off on answering until I get to my office so we can at least have some privacy. I pick up my pace and rush into my office, kicking the door shut behind me.

"I can't imagine what you're calling about," I say, when I pick up.

"This is amazing," he says. "Are you freaking out?"

"Kind of," I say, but I don't let on that my freak-out is not necessarily of the "Oh my God, I'm so happy" variety.

"You're on the fence," he says.

Through laughter that's only half forced, I reply, "You know me so well already."

"It's a no-brainer," he says.

"For you," I counter.

"For us," he says. Then adds, "For anyone."

"Anyone who is used to just . . . talking on the radio. That's your deal, not mine. I only talk if there's something interesting going on or it's been a while since I've introed a song. I don't just blabber."

"But you can," he says. "You have. You did it with me for the contest, and you were great."

"I don't know, Ryan."

"Berry, this is huge."

"I know it is."

"It's prime time," he adds.

"I know, I know. . . ."

"I know you can do it. I know it's weird for you to talk for a whole show. It's not what you're used to. . . . But it's fun. I think once you got used to it, you'd love it."

"I know you want it . . . which, honestly, Ryan, is the only reason I'm even considering it."

"But you are. . . ." he says. "You are considering it?"

"Yes," I say. "I'm considering it."

"That's all I ask."

"Anything else?" I ask. "Because I need to prep for my show."

"You're beautiful?" he says playfully.

"Am I more beautiful because I'm considering doing this show?"

"Infinitely."

"So I'll be less beautiful if I don't agree to it?"

"Beyond. You'll be hideous. Children will run screaming when they see you."

"Uh-huh."

"You'll be just as beautiful," he quickly corrects. But then he adds, "But seriously . . . you'll be thirty-five percent prettier if you do it."

"Goodbye, Ryan."

"Goodbye, Berry."

And as I walk to the studio, I count my steps, looking for some sign that this will work out. Twenty-four. A decidedly neutral number. But still an even number . . . which I take as a bad sign.

○

I'm almost at the diner, where Nat is waiting for me, when my cell-phone rings. I know it's my father without looking because just last week I changed his ringtone to "The Gambler" by Kenny Rogers. It wasn't a very nice thing to do, now that I think about it, but he'd needed two hundred dollars to pay back someone named Fred, and I was feeling very put-upon at the time.

"Berry," he says, sounding panicked. "It's Dad."

"You okay?"

"I'm down. I'm losing big. I need my lucky girl."

"Where are you?"

"Carson."

"Dad," I say, and sigh. "Really? You really want me to drive there?"

"I know it'll turn around when you get here. You're my lucky charm."

I can hear the desperation in his voice, but I just got off my shift, and I tell him exactly that.

"I know," he says. "I was listening. I always listen. I have my one-ear RadioShack headphone in whenever you're on so I don't miss it."

Guilt.

Guilt.

Guilt.

"I was about to meet Natalie at the diner," I say. "She's there waiting for me now."

"Bring her," he says. "I'd love to see her."

"Yeah, I'm not so sure she'd love to drive an hour and a half to a casino right now."

"Never know until you ask."

"I'm pretty sure, Dad."

"I was winning for a while. . . ." he says, and then trails off.

I stand at the diner entrance and see Natalie at the counter. She turns around and waves to me. I roll my eyes, and she nods knowingly. When I hang up the phone I walk in and shrug.

"I can't say no to him."

"I wish we were talking about Ryan," she says. "And I wish you were recapping some sordid sexcapade. . . . But from the roll of your eyes and that fact that you're Berry Lambert . . . I'm pretty certain we're talking about your dad."

"Bingo," I say.

"If only that were his vice," she replies.

"I gotta go meet him at the casino. You're invited. . . ."

"Yeah, tempting as that sounds . . . the cigarette smoke and the desperation and all that velour . . ." She shudders. "I'll pass."

"Lucky," I say.

"No, that's you," she corrects.

"Well, I need to talk to you," I say. "I needed our debriefing tonight. Something happened. It's big."

"Can you tell me quickly?"

"Yes, but I know what you're going to say, and I need you to consider all of the different factors before you just try to bully me into doing it."

"Cryptic," she says.

"I'll call you from the car. We'll discuss."

"No, you can't just leave me hanging like this."

"It'll be one minute!"

"Berry, you tell me right now." Natalie is one whine away from stomping her foot.

"They want me to do a morning show. With Ryan. Talk radio. Talking the whole time. No music. Just me and Ryan. Just talk."

"Just say yes!" she exclaims.

"I said no bullying until we discuss!"

"Berry, that is an incredible opportunity," she says. "You can't say no to that."

"I'll call you from the car."

"You're doing this."

"I'll call you in forty-seven seconds."

"You're so doing this."

"Aargh!" I growl as I walk to my car and put my headset on.

Before I've even turned the key in the ignition, Natalie is calling me. I start the car and answer the call.

"This is amazing," she goes on. "I can't let you even consider not doing this."

"Okay, Nat?" I try to rationalize. "That isn't who I am. I'm not a talk-radio person. I like my privacy. Plus, I don't know how those people even do it. How do you talk for two or three hours nonstop like that—I can't imagine."

"It will go by so fast," she says.

"You don't know that. It could be long and painful."

"No way," she says. "The rush, the people calling in, the chemistry between you and Ryan?"

"Yeah," I say. "That's the other thing. Ryan and I are still new. We're still getting to know each other. You expect us to do that live on the radio for everyone in the world to hear?"

"Yes!"

"What if we have a fight? And we have to go be all happy and coupley on the radio the next day?"

"You cross that bridge when you get to it," she says. "Maybe you have people call in and decide who was wrong and who was right! That could be fun."

"Have we met?" I say. "This is me. I don't like my business being aired to the public. And this would be that in the most literal sense."

"This would be amazing. I am so freakin' excited for you that I'm about to get mad at you for not squealing and being excited about this."

"What if we break up?" I say.

"You guys are crazy about each other," she says.

"We haven't even said the L word," I counter.

"I miss that show!" she interrupts.

"The other L word. The real L word. The four-letter, oh fuck, what-did-he-just-say word."

"Oh, that L word."

"Don't you think you should say 'I love you' before you jump into a commitment like this?"

"I love you," Natalie says.

"Very funny," I reply. "Seriously. It's too soon."

"You'd never feel like it was the right time to do this, Ber. I know you. Even if you'd said your I-love-yous and you guys were married with kids. You'd have a million other excuses."

"This show is a little bit like a marriage, though," I say. "It is. We're not ready."

"You're doing this," she says. "I can't believe you have to go meet your dad right now. I need to smack some sense into you. You were right there. I missed my chance."

"I need someone to see this rationally with me."

"I am seeing this rationally. I am the rational one in this friendship. That's why you need to listen to me. You're doing this."

My call-waiting chimes, and I look to see that it's Ryan.

"Ryan's calling," I say.

"Answer it and tell him you'll do this."

"We're not ready to be married!" I shout.

"Stop being dramatic," Natalie says.

"I'll call you tomorrow."

"Call me tonight. After you say yes!"

I click over to Ryan.

"Is this my beautiful co-host?" he says. "The girl who was stunningly beautiful when she woke up this morning but is somehow thirty-five percent more beautiful now?"

"You drive a hard bargain," I say.

"Is that a yes?"

"I don't even get to sleep on it?"

"I was hoping you'd sleep on me," he says. "Come over. We can celebrate properly."

"I'm going eighty on the 405 Freeway South."

"Wrong direction," he says.

"My dad . . . needs me."

Confession: I haven't really given Ryan the whole rundown on my dad. In the beginning, I suppose it was because I didn't expect Ryan to be around that long. Now I guess the whole situation is just more embarrassing than I'd like to admit. They've never even met. Not that I've met Ryan's parents, but I'm so close to my dad that usually by this point in a relationship he's somehow met whomever I'm dating. If I were being honest with myself, I guess because I like Ryan that much more I'm that much more afraid of what he'll think.

"Is everything okay?" Ryan asks, concerned.

"Yeah," I say, and sigh. "It's kind of a long story."

"Do you need me to meet you?"

"No, no," I say. "It's not a real crisis. He's . . . at a casino."

I guess now's as good a time as any for Ryan to find out the crazy superstitious apple doesn't fall far from a crazier, compulsive-gambling tree.

"Oh . . ."

"This isn't really a phone conversation, but I guess there's never a great time to tell someone your father is consumed by gambling in all forms and he considers you his lucky charm so whenever he gets in a bind you have to come to the rescue and either bring him good luck or cover his debts." *There. I said it.*

"Wow," Ryan says. "That must be exhausting for you."

"It can be," I say. "But I'm also pretty used to it."

"I'm sorry," Ryan says. "The offer's still good if you want me to meet you there."

"That's sweet of you, but I'd rather you meet my dad in a better situation. He'll be all wild-eyed and shouting things like, 'Come on, seven! Come to Papa!' And then I would just proceed to die a slow, mortified death. . . ."

"You don't have to be embarrassed in front of me, Ber."

"I know," I say. *Crap.*

"We should be together tonight. To celebrate."

"I didn't say yes yet."

"But you will," he says. "And I want to be able to grab you and kiss you when you do."

"Then we'll just have to put the decision off until tomorrow."

"You're killing me!"

"You're too used to girls saying yes to you, anyway," I tease. "It'll do you some good."

"Breakfast tomorrow?" Ryan asks. "I mean . . . pretty soon we'll be spending every morning together. . . . Why not get used to it?"

"So cocky," I say.

"Pick you up at eight-thirty?"

"Nine."

"Morning radio starts early. There'll be no more sleeping in. You might want to get used to it."

"Or," I say, "I might want to enjoy it while I still can."

U

My dad is smoking when I find him at the blackjack table. He hasn't smoked in fifteen years. I thought. He also doesn't usually go in for blackjack; he considers it a rookie game.

"Dad," I say as I pull the cigarette out of his mouth. "What is this?"

"Well, it ain't a breadstick," he says. "Hi, cookie. Thanks for coming. I knew I could count on you."

"When did you start smoking again?"

He stands up and gestures to me. "This is my lucky baby," he says to anyone within earshot who's paying attention. "My lucky charm."

Is he drunk?

"Now we're all gonna start winning!" he shouts, and then stumbles back to the table.

"Dad, what's going on?" I ask gently. "You're smoking and . . . drinking?"

My father has never been a drunk. I always consoled myself with the fact that while he may be a gambling addict, he didn't have a taste for booze. I rationalized that this somehow kept him on the "classier" side of addiction.

I sit down next to him at the table and hope that for some reason I do bring him luck. Luck enough to help him win some so we can get out of here.

He's up for about an hour, and for a minute I think there's something to his crazy belief that I'm his lucky clover. My dad's "friend" Jonesy keeps leaning in a little too close to speak to me, and when I feel his hand on my thigh I take the opportunity to step outside for some fresh air. I'm gone only ten minutes, but when I return to the table my dad's somehow both lost another three hundred dollars and gotten into a fight with the dealer.

I, of course, end up paying off his tab, we leave his car in the lot, and I drive him home, him waking up only every so often to reminisce about how he was up for that one golden hour. And how if we'd stayed just a little longer he'd have won it back.

Decide that you want it more than you are afraid of it.

—BILL COSBY

Chapter Fourteen

Days of the week may not be odd or even per se, but in my estimation they are. Monday is odd, Tuesday is even—while odd sounding it is the second day of the week, which is an even number—therefore Wednesday is odd, but I feel the same way about Wednesday as I do the number five. It's so "in the middle" it feels borderline, but it's not. And Thursday feels odd . . . but it's not. And so on. Sunday and Monday are both odd in my estimation. So, much like I don't like even numbers, I also don't like even days. They tend to be the least lucky. But today is Wednesday, and that makes it a toss-up.

I know, I'm bizarre. Even I can see that.

Ryan calls. "You ready for breakfast?" he asks.

"Almost," I say. "I'm washing the balcony." Holding the phone to my ear, I lean into a rag sliding across the railing, almost doing a header off the ledge onto my neighbor's patio below.

"Washing—what? Why?"

"A dragonfly landed on the hibachi." I splash the sponge into the bucket, washing dirty, soapy water over the edge and onto the decking, where it drips down.

"Hey!" my neighbor shouts. I realize I should have checked more carefully before launching into my routine, but desperate times call for desperate measures.

"I thought dragonflies were supposed to be good luck."

"Not on the hibachi."

Nothing. Then maybe a long sigh on the other end of the line.

"It's not something I'm prepared to talk about at this moment," I say, like a scandal-plagued politician. Not the image a person wants to send.

"Look," I say, "the patio needed cleaning, anyway. It was just an inspiration. I'm not being OCD about it. It's more like . . . like a religious exercise. A cleansing."

"Hallelujah, Berry is losing it," he says.

That stings a little. Not enough to make me stop cleaning, and not enough to make me call him on it. Something about that smacks of bad luck, like sawing three-quarters of the way through a tree and then having a picnic lunch under it. It's better to leave that sort of thing alone. In the Book of Berry.

〇

While I may not be a morning person, I am absolutely a breakfast person. I love breakfast with all of my being. I love breakfast so profoundly that if love of breakfast could be measured, I could quite possibly win some sort of Guinness World Record.

So when Ryan suggests the Griddle, he quickly puts us on the road to recovery. I couldn't be happier. The Griddle is one of those places that serve way too much food but it's so delicious you'll practically kill yourself trying to finish it.

We make small talk in the car, and I can tell Ryan is itching to ask me if I've made a decision, and I have, but I'm enjoying watching him fidget and awkwardly try not to just come right out and ask me.

"How'd you sleep?" he asks.

"Like a baby," I say. "And by that I mean I got up every few hours and cried for my mommy."

"As long as you didn't wet the bed."

"No," I say. "I stopped doing that in college."

Driving.

Driving.

Looking out the window.

Ryan taps his hands on the steering wheel.

I smile at him and look away.

"You're really milking this one, aren't you?" he finally says, when he can't take it any longer.

"What do you mean?"

Ryan widens his eyes and bats his eyelashes as he mimics me, "What do you mean?"

I can't help but laugh. We pull up to the Griddle and park in the lot behind it. He takes my hand as we walk up the ramp to enter through the back. I give his hand a squeeze, and he whips me around to face him.

"Whatever you choose," he says, "you're still the prettiest girl I know."

I can tell I'm blushing, and I hate when I blush, so I rush forward to give him a big kiss, because I love kissing him, of course, but also so he can't see me blush.

We sit and peruse the menu and decide on two equally ridiculous pancake orders. Ryan wants the coconut-chocolate pancakes topped with whipped cream, but the dish is called Mounds of Pleasure, and he refuses to order it by name. He points to the menu, amusing me and our waiter. "You want the . . . ?" our waiter asks, as he winks at me, helping me egg him on.

"No, the one above it," Ryan says.

"Which one, Ryan?" I tease. "The pumpkin?"

"That one," Ryan says, pointing again to Mounds of Pleasure.

"Sorry, guy," the waiter says, grinning widely. "I didn't put in my contacts this morning. Which one are you pointing at?"

Ryan looks back and forth between the two of us. "Fuck you both," he says.

"That's not on the menu," our waiter replies.

"I'm not sayin' it." Ryan shakes his head.

"I can't wait to tell everyone about this on the radio," I say. "I am gonna tease the shit outta you."

"Does that mean yes?" Ryan says, sitting up at attention. "Is that a yes?"

"That's a yes," I confirm, with a huge grin that I can't contain as much as I'd like to.

Ryan jumps up and grabs me. He yanks me out of my seat and twirls me around.

"She said yes!" he says, and a few people at nearby tables start to clap.

"Did I just witness something momentous?" Clever Waiter asks.

"Not the kind of momentous you're probably thinking," I try to clarify, but news seems to spread like wildfire, and now everyone in the restaurant thinks we've just gotten engaged. There's clapping and cheering and well-wishing, and it almost seems cruel to disappoint these people by shouting, "It's not what it looks like!" and holding up my ring finger. "See? No ring!"

"Congratulations, you two," our waiter says, though he's probably thinking, *If this guy proposed to her at a pancake joint, I give this marriage six months at best.*

"Thank you," Ryan answers.

As far as this restaurant is concerned, we're engaged. A couple of Japanese tourists sheepishly walk to our table and ask if they can take our photo.

Ryan, of course, says yes, and hams it up for the camera.

"This is bad luck," I say. "Or at the very least, bad karma."

"Smile for the camera?" Ryan says, pretending he misheard me. "You bet." And he puts his arm around me and smiles big. I'm pretty sure I'm rolling my eyes in the picture, but luckily I'll never know.

"Now, where were we, sir," our waiter asks. "Oh, yes. You were ordering the . . ."

"Say it, Ryan," I tease.

"Who names something that on a menu? Do they not want people to order it?"

"Look at the rest of the names!" I say. "They're all a bit . . . quirky."

"I would have no problem ordering any other item on this menu."

"Yet you draw the line at Mounds of Pleasure."

"It's important that we stand up for what really matters. Racial equality. Equal pay for equal work . . . five-dollar footlongs, sneaking our own candy into the movies, choosing white rice over brown rice even if it's bad for you, the right to brutally make fun of guys who are into magic . . . and breakfast dishes that don't sound like they should be served at Ta-Ta's House of Hoo-Has."

I turn to our waiter. "He will have the Mounds of Pleasure."

"He's no fun," the waiter says.

"He's plenty of fun!" Ryan counters.

"He is," I say, backing him up. "And I will have the 'Tis the Season and a very large cup of coffee."

"'Tis the season?" Ryan asks.

"Pumpkin-pie pancakes," our waiter says. "They're really good. Both are great celebratory dishes." With that, he walks off.

"You really should have gotten me a ring," I tease.

"Seriously," he says. "Without the spectacle and the fake engagement of it all . . . I am really, really psyched that we're gonna do this. It's gonna be great."

"Why do I feel like those are going to be famous last words?"

"They're too boring to be famous last words."

"They're foreboding. They're exactly what famous last words are made of. Some casually tossed-out declaration that will turn around and manifest the exact opposite."

"So this is a superstition," he says. "Just to be clear. This is one of your nine million gazillion superstitions."

"No," I correct. "It's Murphy's Law."

"Fuck Murphy," Ryan says. "And fuck his law. Here's Ryan's Law: We are gonna be great. Our show is gonna be so much fun. You'll see. Trust."

Funny he should say "trust." That's the one thing I seem to be having trouble with lately. And I was never that person. I was never the guilty-until-proven-innocent type. But I want to trust this. I want to trust him. So I tell him I will.

"Oh, believe me. I'm trusting. I just hope you realize that the only reason I'm—"

"I know," he cuts me off. "You don't even have to say it. I know this isn't your thing. I know you're doing it for me. And I hope you know I appreciate it. Because I do."

"You'll make it up to me."

"I'm sure you'll find creative ways to task me," he says, flashing a sly smile.

Before I can get creative with my retort, our waiter returns with our ridiculously gluttonous pancakes. Ryan holds up his fork to clink. I knock my fork against his, and we dig in.

∪

When we ask for our check, we are informed that not only is breakfast on the house, the Griddle wishes us a long and happy life together.

"No," I practically shout. "That's so sweet, but we can't accept that."

"How generous of you," Ryan tells the waiter, ignoring my protest.

"Ryan," I say, eyes wide, trying to send him a telepathic message. A message that says: It would be really bad luck to accept an engagement gift for a fake engagement. "We really can't accept that generous offer."

"It would be rude not to, Berry," he says pointedly. "They're trying to celebrate our momentous occasion."

We stare at each other for a long beat. It becomes a bit of a contest. Neither of us looks away. Neither of us blinks. *This is how it's gonna go down?* I don't care if my eyes dry up and fall out of their sockets. I'm not losing this one.

Or so I think. Our waiter shakes Ryan's hand and moves on to a table where the customers aren't at a telepathic stalemate.

"That's so wrong," I say.

"I'll leave him a good tip," Ryan says as he tosses a twenty onto the table. "Look—we are celebrating. We did have a momentous occasion. We just made a big decision. Together. So what if it's a different decision than he thinks? It is a big deal, and it is worthy of celebrating."

"Whatever you say."

"You disagree?"

"It just wasn't what he thought," I say.

"Nothing ever is," Ryan says, and there's a hint of something sharp behind it that if I thought too hard about would probably send me into a downward spiral, so instead I stop being such a pessimist and shake it off.

"Fine," I say. "Whatever. I'm over it."

"Good," Ryan says. "What should we do next?"

"Go to Seven-Eleven and steal a candy bar?"

"You said you were over it!" Ryan laughs. "We did nothing wrong. We were and are celebrating."

"Okay, okay," I say.

"But I will say this." He cocks his head sideways and studies me for a moment. "For all your superstitions and what-have-yous—"

"My what-have-yous?" I interrupt. "What exactly are my what-have-yous?"

"I'm trying to say something nice here. May I finish?"

"Go ahead," I say.

"I was going to say, you're a really good person. An honest person. With good, strong morals. It's sweet. Very endearing."

"Thank you."

"You're welcome."

"Does that make me less exciting?" I ask. "Should I be out tripping old ladies and running Ponzi schemes on unwitting investors? Would that be hotter?"

"That's where the what-have-yous come in. You could never be classified as boring. Are you kidding? It could be an odd day during an even hour and we could step on a crack and your uncle in Tallahassee would lose an eye."

"Very funny."

"I think you're incredible," he says, suddenly much more serious. "And I'm really excited to do this show with you. And I didn't think it was possible, but you might even be eleven percent prettier than you were five minutes ago."

On stage, I make love to twenty-five thousand people, then I
go home alone.

—JANIS JOPLIN

Chapter Fifteen

Working with the person you're falling in love with is not something I recommend. Not that Ryan or I have actually said the L
word. We still haven't. He's called me a loser, lunatic, and lesbian in
jest a few times—although there may have been an implicit wish
behind that third one—but he hasn't dropped the other L word.
Not even close. But he does do this thing where sometimes he'll be
looking at me in a way that seems to mean . . . something. And I'll
get self-conscious and ask, "What?" And he'll say, "Didn't I tell
you?" But he never tells me what he didn't tell me. He just leaves it
at that, with that devilish smile that makes me melt. And even if I

can resist his kryptonite enough to press and say, "No, you didn't tell me," it never goes beyond that. And I never push.

Logistically, *Morning Mayhem with Riley and Lambert* is no sweat. We get into a routine that involves spending the night at each other's apartment, taking turns every other night. We drive to the station in separate cars because his second show is earlier than mine and I can leave for a bit before my seven-to-twelve shift. I still meet Nat after work, but what was once every night and then waned to most nights has turned in to several nights a week, if that. She's been a good sport about not complaining. (We had the obligatory awkward lunch where the best friend meets the new boyfriend and they became fast friends in record time.)

In our fourth week on-air we get our first ratings announcement and the station is beyond excited. We're fourth overall, second in the desirable eighteen-to-thirty-five demographic, which tells you something about the fickle finger of most radio listeners in this area. I always default to the cautious—Nat would say the negative—but hitting our stride so quickly seems almost lucky. And speaking as one who knows, it's not lucky being that lucky.

The station immediately slaps a curse on us by committing to an even more sizable ad campaign than they'd originally promised. Billboards, bus benches, buildings—we're everywhere. The photo shoot is a study in the tired and true, and, no, I didn't mean "tried and true." Poses and concepts that were not used:

- Me balancing a pail on my head and Ryan dumping sand into it with a plastic shovel. "Fill your mornings with Riley and Lambert. Mornings on KKCR."
- Ryan and me standing in front of two cars that have collided at an intersection, obviously exasperated but

preciously so, which made it somehow more irritating for the L.A. drivers condemned to stare at it in rush-hour traffic. "Run into Riley and Lambert."

- Ryan with fingers poised above my nipples. Yes, you read that right. Me looking surprised. "Tune in to Riley and Lambert." (As a side note on this one: The reactions did not include the words "juvenile," "inappropriate," "sexist," or "disgusting." The station manager's question was, "Do you think they'll get what he's doing?")

- This one was odd—and maybe I'm paranoid (strike that: I'm definitely paranoid)—but at one point Ryan said, "How about the two of us dressed as clowns, with a headline like, 'Put some fun in your morning'?" Sarcastically. And the account executive's face went a little ashen, and she moved on, but the meeting wrapped up pretty quickly after that, and I could tell she'd skipped over one of the concepts on her agenda.

And our winner: Ryan and me, standing back-to-back, arms folded. Headline: "*Morning Mayhem.* It's So On. Riley and Lambert, Mornings." Eh. What it lacked in originality it more than made up for in predictability.

In week seven the ads started showing up on billboards and bus stops, and by our eighth week I had officially been defaced, defiled, and dick-ified. By that I mean someone had drawn a penis, inches from my mouth, on our poster at Sunset and La Brea. Mom would be so proud.

If it sounds like navigating the new show has been relatively problem-free, it has been. Until one morning when a particular caller gets under my skin, and for whatever reason, I don't laugh it off.

"So how many dates before you got down and dirty?" the caller asks.

"Okay, a) nobody said we slept together, and b) that's none of your business," I say, leaning into the mic, practically biting it off.

"What she means," Ryan jumps in, "is that she doesn't kiss and tell."

"No . . . What I meant is that it's none of your business."

"Sounds like you're a little uptight there, Berry," says the asshat. "Maybe you're not getting enough."

"Oh, you're 'that guy.' " I lean in again. "That friend that every guy has who every girlfriend hates. Your name is probably Steve or Mike or—"

"You know what?" the caller says. "I'll bet you're so frigid you haven't even done it yet. And it sounds like you seriously need to get laid, so maybe you should get on that."

Is this really happening live on the radio? All I can manage to do is toss it to Ryan, hoping he'll tell this guy where he can shove it.

"Ryan?"

"Bro, that's not cool," Ryan says. "And if you're this concerned with our love life, it sounds like you're the one who needs to get laid. Good luck with that. You'll need it."

This was what I'd been worried about all along, this inherent invasion of privacy. I know you give up a certain quantity of rights when you put yourself in the public eye, even at the radio level. Tabloid journalism is so popular these days, it's just something you have to accept. But when you're just a radio DJ with a modest following, should strangers be able to grill you on how many dates it took for you to get between the sheets?

Apparently, yes. I discover this later that night. Ryan and I are at Swingers, a restaurant that's open late for second-shift people like me and late-night eaters who must have really good metabolisms.

"You might need to lighten up a little," Ryan says, with a knowing, almost obnoxious shrug.

"You might need to consider that I don't want to broadcast when we first had sex on the radio."

"That's part of the deal," Ryan says.

"Not the part I signed up for! Ryan, we've talked about this. I know I have to be open about some things. But there are limits. I signed up to host a morning show, not to be your sidekick in *Ryan's Sexy-Time Show Part Deux.*"

I can tell he's stung. We sit in silence for much longer than is comfortable. I don't want to take it back, because it's true. But I just belittled his other show, something that I'd find infuriating and a little heartbreaking if Ryan had done it to me.

And the beat goes on. And by "beat," I mean Ryan tapping his foot aggressively, either trying to think of a comeback or trying not to say the one that's on the tip of his tongue.

Finally I speak, because the tapping is unbearable.

"Look, I don't want to fight with you—" I start.

"*Ryan's Sexy-Time Show?*" he interrupts.

"I'm sorry. I know it sounded demeaning. That's not what I meant."

"Okay, then what did you mean?"

"I meant to . . . I just meant . . . I just wanted to make it clear that I didn't want our show to be about sex and relationships . . . like your show is. I mean, isn't our show a morning show? Would you classify that as 'morning fodder'?" At this point, I can't stop my mouth from moving. "Is Regis asking Kelly about the last time Mark gave it to her good?"

"Slow down," Ryan says. "That's where we're having a disconnect here. I didn't ask you about your sex life. That was a caller. A caller I defended you from, by the way. Honestly, though, Berry, I shouldn't have had to do that. You punted to me, and I knew you were upset, but people can ask what they want. That's kind of how a morning show works. Occasionally you take calls, and occasionally the callers are assholes, but we can't censor them."

"We censor them all the time. That's what the screeners are for. And I really don't think they should be allowed to ask about our sex life!"

And again we sit in silence. Finally, Ryan opens his mouth, and I'm hoping he's going to say something that guides us to the making-up part of this argument, because I hate this, hate this, hate this.

"I'm going to the bathroom," he says. He leaves without even looking at me.

I sit there, shaking, waiting for him to return, wondering whether we'll find a way to agree on this when he returns. I don't know. Maybe this type of show just isn't for me. Maybe I just said yes to make Ryan happy. Sure, it's great exposure, but I'm not even sure I want exposure. I love music. I got into this business because I live and breathe music, and I thought, how cool would it be to be a DJ—to introduce people to new bands and sounds and to be the first person to say, "Here's the new unreleased song by so-and-so . . ."? Granted, I'm working at a classic-rock station, so there's not too much introduction happening, but that's why I got into radio. To turn people on to great music and to be a part of a sadly dying business but at least to be a part of it in some capacity while I still could. I wanted to expose people to music . . . not to me.

"That's heads up," a voice says from behind me. I turn and see a guy I don't know, pointing down toward my right foot. I look down and see a penny, heads up. "Heads up means it's lucky. You should pick it up."

He's telling me? I look back up at the guy—who, if we're being honest, happens to be pretty good-looking, not that I'm looking—and I notice he has a four-leaf clover tattooed on his wrist. *Are you kidding me?*

"I know it's good luck," I say. "I'm like a beacon of superstitious knowledge."

"Then you better get on that," he says, and nods to the penny. I pick it up, wincing when my fingers touch Swingers' potentially not very sanitary floor.

"Are you Irish?" I ask, motioning at his tattoo, hoping he'll say yes, and that's why he has the clover tattoo, because the last thing I need right now is a sign that I'm with the wrong guy, so maybe if this extremely good-looking person with deep brown eyes I could get lost in for three weeks is just Irish and not a proponent of luck or superstitions or anything I can relate to, he'll just go on his merry way and I can get back to fighting with my boyfriend—the one who is technically unlucky Guy Number Three in a string of Bad News Boys.

"Yeah," he says. "Plus, in college I somehow earned the nickname Lucky, and it stuck. . . ."

Fantastic. "Oh," I say. It's all I can muster.

Ryan saves me from having to say anything more. He returns to the table, his head cocked to the side, on his face a genuine look that says "I don't want to fight anymore."

"I know you're not used to this," he blurts. "I know your radio and my radio are two entirely different animals . . . and you're not used to the kinds of animals who call into my show."

"You can say that again."

"I know you're not used to this," he starts, repeating what he said, riffing off my "you can say that again," and it breaks the tension. We're back on track. I look up to see if Lucky Penny Guy has caught this moment of mature relationship conversation, but he's gone, so I focus back on Ryan and on making up.

U

Our show's third month is our best ever, ratings-wise, and I have to say, I've learned to lighten up . . . for the most part. I feel I'm growing comfortable with my private life being quasi-public as long as I'm in control of it. As long as the things we share are about the movie we saw last night or the restaurant we went to or how I nailed "Fergalicious" at karaoke. That's all fine.

Until Ryan, during a show, casually mentions my undergarments being strewn around my apartment.

"Now, I do think lingerie is important," he says to a caller, who is complaining that his girlfriend wears "ugly granny panties" and he wishes she would try a little harder. "But you should be talking to Berry here. She thinks lingerie is so important that it should be seen at all times, hence she leaves her bras and panties on the dresser, the bed, or the bathroom floor whenever she's done wearing them."

I'm stunned. I'm speechless. But only momentarily. I find my mouth moving before I can even stop it.

"Funny you mention that, Ryan," I say. "Mission accomplished."

He looks confused but rolls with it—he's got his "Dr. Love" face on. "I didn't know there was a mission. Want to enlighten us?"

"Well, folks," I say, "Ryan here is always in such a hurry to get to the 'good part' that he wouldn't know if I was wearing silk and lace or an ex-boyfriend's boxers. So, yes, occasionally I'll leave them on the dresser just so maybe he'll take a hint . . . like, oh, she wears sexy things under her clothes . . . perhaps I should take a moment when undressing her to actually notice."

He must hear the bite in my voice, because he pauses. And Ryan never pauses.

"I . . . I had no idea you felt so strongly about whether I noticed your underwear," he says, sounding genuinely uncomfortable.

A normal person would have ended it right there. But oh, no, not me. I'm out for blood. Ryan's pushed it too far. "Yeah, that's pretty clear," I say and everyone in the control booth laughs, egging me on . . . so I deliver. "There's a word for it. . . . What is it again? Oh, right, 'foreplay.' " On "fore-," I slam one hand down on the desk and use the other to shoot Ryan a nasty thumbs-up.

"Ouch," Ryan says under his breath. I notice him turning a little red, something I've never seen before. I immediately feel awful.

"You heard it here first," Ryan says into the mic, taking it on the chin. "Your trusted Dr. Love apparently has no idea what he's doing in the sack."

"That's not what I'm saying," I say, but the damage is done. Ryan's not letting me off the hook.

"Oh, don't backpedal now, Ber."

"I said nothing about your . . . lovemaking." I pause for a second, because I just said "lovemaking" on the radio, and I'm now actually actively participating in a discussion about my sex life, and this is spiraling into something really stupid. We're in this uncomfortable area between doing a bit and really digging into each other, and I'm not sure where this is going. I was genuinely pissed about the underwear comment, but this is taking on a life of its own. I try to make amends. "I was just teasing you because . . . some lingerie is just meant to be seen. Women spend ridiculous amounts of money on ridiculously tiny items that more often than not go completely unnoticed."

"Then why don't we put a photo collage of your regretfully unnoticed lingerie up on our website? Then everyone can see it."

"Yeah," I say. "I don't think so. And, hey, wonder of wonders, it's time for a commercial break. Stay tuned, folks. We'll be right back." My phone rings. *Mom. Great.* I have to take this one. I can practically see the disappointment on the caller ID.

I pick up the phone and walk out of the sound booth, glancing once back at Ryan to give him a dirty look. I've barely flipped the thing open before Mom starts.

"You're not exactly setting a good example here," she says. "You're kind of a role model now, Berry."

"Well, Mom," I say, "that may be. But good example versus bad example really depends on the role you want to play."

Be who you are and say what you feel because those who
mind don't matter and those who matter don't mind.

—DR. SEUSS

Chapter Sixteen

You don't know humiliation until your minor on-air tiff with your
boyfriend is reduced to a minute-and-forty-five-second MP3 that's
been shared, embedded, podcasted, and otherwise made viral by
D-list gossip sites and is spreading around the Internet like wildfire.
One minute you're Ryan and Berry, co-hosts of *Morning Mayhem,*
and the next you're "the girl who leaves her underwear all over the
apartment and her 'sexpert' boyfriend who thinks 'foreplay' is a
rock group from the eighties."

Mayhem indeed, especially when your sexpert hasn't said more
than six off-air words to you in three days.

My dad calls, which immediately snaps me out of my self-loathing, at least for the moment, when I see his name on my caller ID.

"My friend just forwarded me something on the email," he says. He calls it "the email," which is cute and anachronistic and incorrect. My dad may have his issues—many and varied—but at least he's too computer illiterate (and hopefully even if he wasn't, he would still not be compelled) to look at Asian-teen porn. I think he's going to tell me some stupid lawyer joke for a brief three seconds before he adds, "My little girl's all grown up . . . and wearing lingerie, apparently."

Never before now have I wished that I was on a bad cell that drops calls every three seconds until you're so frustrated you figure you'll just see that person within the next few months, anyway. But wish as I might that I could un-hear my father telling me that my underwear is a hot topic among his friends, this is what's become my life.

"I will say, Ber, that whether this guy appreciates it or not—and if he doesn't, good riddance to the louse—it's always a nice gesture to wear something sexy."

"Dad!" I shout. "I really don't want to talk about this with you."

"What, we're not friends? I'm your pal, Berry. If you can't talk about this stuff with me, then who can you talk about it with?"

"Wow, um, pretty much anyone else?" I reply. "This is not appropriate discussion for a father and a daughter."

"Appropriate, shmappropriate" is his comeback. "Your mother used to wear very sexy nighties."

"La, la, la," I interject. "I can't hear you, and when I stop talking, I want you to never say anything like that again and immediately change the subject or just hang up if you can't manage, because this is unbearable. One, two, three, new subject—"

"Can I stay at your place for a few days?" he says suddenly, definitely changing the subject.

"What—um, yeah, of course, but what's wrong with your place?"

"Nothing . . ." he says, much like a child who's just been caught doing something wrong but lies when you ask what's going on.

"Dad," I say, "let's be real here. You are welcome to stay with me, but what is it? Are you in trouble? Is someone after you?"

"Berry, come on. Do you think if I was in any kind of danger I would bring that danger straight to you?"

"No," I say, feeling guilty for even suggesting it. "Then what is it?"

"Can't a guy just want to spend time with his daughter?"

"Dad . . ."

"My electricity's turned off."

"Oh, Dad," I say, and sigh. "Give me your account number, I'll pay the bill."

"It's okay, honey. I got it. I just need a few days to get back on my feet."

"Dad, you're welcome to stay with me, but I want to get your electricity back on. I'm sure you have food in the fridge. . . ." Once I think about that, I'm pretty sure he doesn't, but regardless, he needs to have electricity.

"I don't feel right asking you to do that."

"You're not asking me. I'm offering. It's fine. I have two jobs right now. Really, it's no problem."

"My big girl. My big grown-up famous girl. My grown-up girl who wears lingerie—"

"Dad!" I interrupt. "We covered that already. We're not talking about that anymore, remember? Now, what's your account number?"

"That's ridiculous. No. I'm not—no."

"Dad."

"Now, Beryl, I won't hear of it." And the "Beryl," seldom heard, indicates serious business. "Don't even think about it."

"Dad, this is much easier. Really. What's the account number?"

And with barely a second's delay, he's spouting numbers at me. "Four eight seven, seven zero zero . . . Wait, there are three zeroes, and I don't know if they need this hyphen. . . ."

The number secure, I throw in casually, "And how much are you owing?"

"Uh, let me . . . Hmm. I had it, maybe on this page here." I hear shuffling. Too much shuffling. How many pages are in the average electric bill? "Okay, here it is. Five hundred eighty-nine sixty."

I gulp as quietly as I can manage. Sure, I could freak out, gasp in horror, repeat the number. But Dad and I are well beyond those histrionics. You can humiliate someone only so many times before it loses its charm. And at the same time, I'm guessing that this isn't exactly an ideal teaching moment. He's too far gone to be starting with Shame 101. Meanwhile, my doorbell rings.

I let Natalie in, wave to show her I'm on the phone and will be with her in a second, and then walk back to my desk to finish taking down my dad's information. Nat drops her bag on the floor and starts an über-competitive game of tug-of-war with Moose and his sock monkey. In case they don't turn his electricity on immediately, I tell Dad where he can find my spare key, but he assures me that Southern California Edison has an excellent response time. I hang up and file the conversation in my mental hard drive alongside the dozens—maybe hundreds—of others I wish I could drag into the little trash can.

"Would you like to permanently delete these umpty-million conversations?" Click "yes." And you're left with a pleasant emptiness—and no knowledge that you'd ever had a dad this helpless.

I turn to Nat, who has an understanding look on her face and has mercifully brought coffee.

"Dude," she says, "I know you must be freaking right now, but it's really not a huge deal."

"For me it kind of is," I say.

"I hear you," she says. "I do . . . but this, too, shall pass."

She hands me a coffee.

"Ryan asked me to have dinner with him tonight," I tell her.

"And that's different from . . . any other night how?"

"His asking felt weighty. Like maybe we're breaking up or something."

"No." Natalie waves my idea away like I just blew cigarette smoke in her face. "No way. He's nuts about you."

"I don't know," I say. "He *is* Guy Number Three. Maybe this is all signs of worse to come. Maybe I should just trust my instincts."

"Those aren't instincts. Instincts are when a guy you're seeing fast-whispers 'I gotta go' into the phone every time you walk up to him and slams his phone shut, and you think, *Abort mission.* That's instincts working for you. What you have is buggy-eyed crazies."

"Nat, I love you, but you can't call me crazy."

"I didn't. I called the rejection of this man crazy. You don't want to break up with him," she says. "Preemptively or not."

"How do you know?"

"Because I know you."

"We still haven't said I love you," I say, as if that means by extension that I don't love him.

She gives me a knowing look.

"Where are you guys going?" she asks.

"Loteria."

"I love Loteria!" she screeches. "Farmers Market?"

"Yes," I say. Loteria is technically not a restaurant but more of a food stand in the middle of Farmers Market in West Hollywood. That said, it's the best Mexican food I've had in L.A.

"Okay," she says. "First of all, nobody breaks up with someone at Farmers Market. It's just not done."

"Oh, really? Says who?"

"Come on! It's Farmers Market. Fresh food! Happiness!"

"Well, there's always a first for everything. . . ."

"Let's go, Ms. Half-Empty," she says, and then, the consonance of it having struck her, she sings: "Half-empty dempty sat on a wall; half-empty dempty anticipated a great fall; all the good girlfriends and all the good men couldn't convince half-empty to quit making herself miserable all the time."

"Catchy," I deadpan. "Where are we going?"

"Farmers Market," she says. "I need broccolini for service, and you need to get out of your head. It's perfect. You'll be there early and prepare yourself for impending doom . . . or tasty enchiladas. Or both."

"Fine," I say as I grab my bag, checking for my chewy Rolaids. You never can be too careful in the Book of Berry.

U

Natalie and I pretend that my relationship is not about to potentially end as we fondle fruits and vegetables. After a good amount of time discussing pineapple, when it's ripe, how you know it's ripe, and who the person was who did the extensive research to decide that pineapple supposedly makes semen taste better (this is a widely circulated and, at least in my own experience, totally untested rumor), we say our goodbyes. I'm left alone at the fountain in the middle of The Grove, still unfortunately contemplating the pineapple/semen thing, so I head into the Barnes & Noble to see what's on the "new" tables.

Turns out an awful lot is new, as always seems to be the case, so I'm quickly consumed, reading back-cover synopses, flopping open thick biographies I know I'll never finish.

I've just turned the first page of Cheever when I feel a pair of eyes burning into the side of my face, and I look up to catch a guy with about a three-day beard staring at me. This alone isn't remarkable; believe it or not, Berry gets her share of the lookie-loos. It's probably the combo studious co-ed/closet party girl thing I've got going on to this day. Wife-beater under a ratty Lakers T-shirt, designer jeans with carefully spaced rips on the thighs, low-slung woven Bottega purse with beater Adidas that are nonetheless clean. Not exactly Versace material, but a definite look. What's remarkable is that he doesn't pretend he wasn't staring and quickly redirect his glance. Instead, he casually but persistently makes his way to the pile directly across from me.

He smiles. I smile back and focus my attention on the table.

"Wanna hear a poem?" he says, so I have to look back up at him. Oh, boy. He's wearing sunglasses inside. The first sign of trouble. Guys, unless you're Stevie Wonder or the Terminator, sunglasses inside are never appropriate. And what's this about a poem? What do you say to that? Say no and you're rude. Say yes and you're opening the floodgates to God knows what. Some poems are pages and pages long. But he can't have pages and pages memorized. Or can he? *Beowulf* is a poem, for God's sake. What if he reads me *Beowulf*? That'll take all day. I'll never get to my breakup dinner—*oh, God, I just mentally called it a breakup dinner*—in time. Maybe it's just a haiku.

"Uh . . . sure."

"Looking back, life was pretty worth my while," he starts. "But in the end, turned out death was more my style."

He stops there.

"Is . . . that it?" I ask.

"That's it," he says.

"I . . . like it," I say, now confused and uncomfortable.

"It's a suicide note," he says.

Now I'm even more confused and uncomfortable.

"Uh . . ." I stammer. *What do I do now? Call a suicide hotline? Guide him to the self-help section? Run?*

"You like it?" he says. "You said you did, but do you really?"

"I really like it," I say. "It's just a poem, though, right? Not like a real suicide note?" And if not, is anyone else the recipient of this note? Or just lucky me?

"Just a poem," he says. "For now."

"Okay," I say, with an awkward smile. "Well, it's very interesting. Thank you for sharing it with me." I look down at my watch and see that I'm supposed to be about three hundred yards away with Ryan. Thankfully. "Well, I gotta run."

"That's cool," he says. "Nice chatting."

On that note, I exit and head back to Farmers Market to meet Ryan. Every step I take I think about Suicide Note Guy and wonder if that was some kind of omen. A precursor to the death of my relationship. I did tell Nat that maybe I should end things. Was that little encounter a sign that I should commit Relationship Suicide? In the end, death was more his style. I'm confused and upset, and now a laughingstock, so maybe it's not the worst idea to quit while I'm ahead . . . if this can even be classified as ahead.

When I get to Loteria, I spot Ryan immediately, and my heart starts beating faster. *Stop it, heart.* I can't tell if it's I Still Like You beating or I'm Panicking Because I'm About to Break Up with You beating, but before I can even determine which it is, I notice that he's standing next to two older people and they're talking. They seem to know one another. Ryan waves me over and then points at me as he says something to the couple that I can't make out because despite working daily with a producer who is behind Plexiglas, and despite my one very exciting helicopter ride, my lip-reading skills are not what they probably should be.

A crowd-witnessed breakup is not what I expected at all. I can't tell if I'm more nervous or less nervous.

"Hi," I say to the trio.

"Berry, this is my mom and dad," Ryan says. "Mom . . . Dad . . . this is Berry."

"Very nice to meet you," the mom person says.

"You, too," I say back. The dad just smiles and nods.

"Did you just bump into your parents here?" I ask. "Because that's a fun coincidence."

The parents look to Ryan, and it's clear from their look that this was a planned meeting, but I was the only one not in on the plan.

"No, I ambushed you," Ryan admits. "I wanted you to meet my parents, and I didn't want it to be awkward and stressful for you if I said, 'Do you want to meet my parents?' and I didn't want you to stress in the time leading up to the meeting of my parents, espe-cially since there's been some tension lately that I really want to get past, assuming when I asked you said, 'Yes, I'd love to meet your parents,' so I thought I'd just bring us all together. At a taco stand. Which in hindsight maybe wasn't the best idea because now there's no place to sit, but I did want you to meet. So here we are."

Ryan is rambling like he never does. He seems almost nervous. Totally out of character. I guess he wasn't breaking up with me. And I guess I'm not breaking up with him.

"We're really happy to finally meet you," the dad says. "I'm Robert, and this is Lily."

"It's very nice to meet you both," I say. Then add, "I love the name Lily." *Kiss ass.*

"Oh, you don't have to flatter me," she says. "I've been listening to you both on the radio since day one, and I'm already a fan."

"Thank you," I say, wondering if my complexion is mimicking my embarrassment. "But I swear, I really do love that name." I open my mouth and for some reason don't have the forethought to stop myself from the next sentence that comes bounding out like a runaway train. "If I got a dog and it was female, I was going to name her Lily. But my dog is a boy. Named Moose. He's super-handsome. But really, Lily is too pretty a name for a dog, anyway. Not that dogs aren't pretty, but, you know . . ." I trail off. Essentially I've just equated my boyfriend's mother not only to a dog but to a bitch dog.

Kill me.

"Okay! So I'm not the only one who's nervous!" Ryan says with a laugh.

I bury my head in his chest and try to momentarily hide my face, but when I think better of it and straighten up, everyone is still there and I'm not a child hiding in the safety of her mother's pants leg.

"Let's find a table and sit, shall we?" That's Robert. The person I haven't insulted. But there's still time.

Thankfully, once we order, there's a natural ease to our conversation. Ryan's parents already know way more about me than I'd like, yet I'm still trying to make a first impression. It's a bizarre dynamic. Lily couldn't be sweeter. She laughs at all of Ryan's jokes, good or bad, and I can see where he gets his lightheartedness from.

"You know," she says, "the last girl Ryan wanted us to meet was his prom date."

"Mom," Ryan says, but it's already out there. Nobody in his adult life has ever met his parents. This is a big deal. Much bigger than I'd realized.

"Wow," I say. "How do I compare?"

"Well, you don't have braces," Robert chimes in. "So that's a plus. I didn't know if he was more embarrassed of us or the girls he was dating, so either way, it's a good sign that we're all together tonight."

"It wasn't you, Dad," Ryan says. "How could it be you guys?" Then he turns to me. "I'm pretty lucky. I have the best parents on the planet. And they know it, so they say stuff like that just so I'll say stuff like this. Shameless."

I watch the easy camaraderie that they have, and while having two mature, happily married parents isn't something I can relate to, it's definitely something I can admire.

"We know it wasn't us, son," Robert goes on. "We just wanted Berry to know that this isn't a normal thing. That she's special."

"She knows," Ryan says.

It's not until our food comes that I notice Suicide Boy from the bookstore is hovering nearby. He catches my eye and nods at me. And here I thought he was just some random extra in my life who had already fulfilled his purpose. There he is again. Ryan notices me noticing him.

"You know that guy?" he asks.

"No," I say. "I met him in the bookstore about an hour ago. I didn't meet him, really. He came up to me and told me a—" I stop myself, because I don't want to go into detail. It seems almost too bizarre.

"He told you a what?"

"A poem," I say. "He walked up to me and asked if I wanted to hear a poem."

"Sounds like you've got some competition," Robert teases his son.

"Hardly," I say. "He was creepy."

"She's taken," Ryan announces to no one in particular. He puts his arm around me. His parents smile proudly, and I have to admit it feels good.

○

Later, when Lily and Robert have headed back to Encino, Ryan and I walk to The Coffee Bean, get a couple hot teas, and sit outside.

"Sorry about the ambush," he says.

"Your parents are great," I say. "I was thrilled to meet them. Although, yes, being able to make sure I looked presentable would have been nice, too."

"You always look presentable."

"Ten points for that one."

"So . . . as they said, I don't bring girls to meet my parents," he says. "And it's true, I don't usually have relationships past the three-month mark. Ever."

If you include the helicopter ride and Chuck E. Cheese's, Ryan and I have been dating for four months. I've broken his personal record.

"Is that by choice?" I ask.

"I guess it is in a way, but it's not like I watch a calendar and when their three months are up I kick 'em to the curb. I guess I just never like anyone enough to stick it out. That's part of it, anyway. The other part is, if we want to get all psychological about it, I guess I have a fear of commitment."

"Huh," I say, surprised that he's opening up this way and also that he has this fear, since I've just met his perfect parents and you'd expect that type of fear to come from a person from a broken home. A person like me. But I guess not.

"What I'm saying is that I'm happy you've made it past the three-month mark."

"I am, too," I say.

"And now I feel all vulnerable and stupid, so your turn. Share something with me."

"Okay," I say. "Well, you know how I have a few superstitions. . . ."

"I have noticed, yes."

"It goes beyond that," I admit. "I mean, it can be almost crippling. I have certain . . . things . . ."

"I enjoy your things very much," he says, teasing.

"Hey . . ." I say. "You opened up about being a total commitment-phobe . . . I'm trying to open up to you, too, here. So shut it."

"Shut," he says, pursing his lips and reaching up to zip them shut and turn the key, showing me he's locking his mouth.

"Thank you. Where was I? Oh, well . . . things. I don't like even numbers—you know that. That's whatever. Here's more you don't know: If I hit too many yellow lights on my way to one place, that's a bad omen. So much so that I'll reschedule whatever it is, even if I push it to an hour later if possible."

Ryan nods but says nothing.

"If I'm going to get a manicure and they don't have the color I want, it's going to be a bad week. If I have something important, like a job interview or a first date—not that I'm having those currently—I have to wear a color called It's in the Bag. I've bought seven bottles of it, and it's proven its worth. Mostly. If for some reason I forget to bring it to the salon and they don't have it and I get another color, the job is as good as lost. I may as well not even go to the interview."

Ryan nods again and raises his eyebrows as if to say, "What else?"

"I am afraid of black cats. I know it's cliché, but I am, I just am. I will get into a car accident to avoid a black cat crossing my path.

If I have a friend who has a black cat, I won't go to their house—ever. I'm also afraid of William Shatner. He did a spoken-word record, and it's haunted me to this day. I felt like if you played it backward, there'd be a secret message in there, like an even creepier 'Revolution Nine.' So every time I see him on a Priceline commercial or one of his TV shows it gives me a chill. I feel like something bad is going to happen and often it does. Shatner. Something's up with that guy."

Ryan's smiling, and he probably thinks I'm crazy, but I go on. "If I sneeze and nobody says 'Bless you,' I'll bless myself, and on occasion I'll call my mom and tell her I sneezed so she can bless me. If someone else sneezes and I don't bless them, I feel like bad things will happen to them or me or both. I always bless a stranger. That's why I get so incensed when nobody blesses me."

Ryan raises his hand.

"Yes? You can speak now."

"You're crazy," he says. "Truly."

"Thanks for that."

"And I am crazy about you," he adds. "In fact, I am sixty-four percent more crazy about you after that diatribe than I was before you started. You're adorable."

I know I'm blushing. I force out a thank-you, and try to keep my smile about the size of a normal person's so I'm not a beaming idiot on the outside like I am on the inside.

It's funny how a few hours ago I thought maybe this wasn't right, and now . . . maybe I was wrong. Maybe this is for real. Maybe it just took three guys to get it right. . . .

Yeah, but so what? Everybody's weird.
—CHRIS CHAMBERS, IN *STAND BY ME*

Chapter Seventeen

On a major high after my meet-the-parents ambush, and thrilled to be absolutely, positively not broken up, I walk into my apartment to find Moose looking up at me expectantly. I assume that even though the dog walker took him out earlier, he may want an extra walk, and I'm in too good a mood to say no to my boy, so I grab his leash and we head downstairs.

Moose doesn't seem to need to do any of his business and after our third lap around the block, I'm pooped—even though he hasn't. We head back upstairs, and once I'm home I do a quick change into my PJs, brush my teeth, pull my bedcovers back, and nestle in. I start on my left side. Left arm outstretched under my head, under the pillow, right knee up and over my left leg. Then I flip. Right side, right arm outstretched under my head, under the pillow, left knee up and over my right leg. Repeat. Always the same, night after night.

I realize this sounds obsessive, maybe even has tinges of OCD. But it's comforting, and I've been doing it since I was a little kid. Puts me to sleep every time. Tonight, though, on the third go-round, my left knee pushes forward and meets . . .

What.

Is.

That??!?

A body? A large, broad, slightly flabby male body. I scream and jump out of my bed, run out the door, down the hall, into the elevator, and out on the street.

I'm waving my arms and screaming and crying, my heart's going a mile a minute, and a guy walking his dog rushes over to me.

"Are you okay?" he asks.

"No!" I shout. "Call the police! There's a man in my apartment, *in my bed,* and I just got in it and I was in my apartment for at least twenty minutes not even knowing he was in there and he's in my bed, *he is in my bed*!"

"Okay," he says as he pulls out his cellphone and dials 911. "Calm down. You're okay. You are okay, right? He didn't . . . touch you?"

"His back touched my *kneeeeee*," I cry, the word "knee" drawn out into heaves and sobs.

"It's okay," the guy says. "You'll be okay."

I look down at his dog, an English bulldog who's looking up at me, head cocked sideways, one snaggletooth sticking out to greet me.

"Hello," I say to the dog, and I kneel down to pet him and then just sit on the concrete and start sobbing into the poor dog.

Then I sit up with a start. "Moose!" I exclaim.

"I . . . I don't know what that means," the stranger says.

"My dog, Moose, is in there. What if he's hurting him?" I wail.

When the police show up, I'm still hysterical. So much so that the kind stranger with the dog I've soaked with my tears has to explain what happened while I nod and confirm that what he says is true.

"Ma'am, what apartment is it?" the policeman asks.

"That building," I say, pointing to the apartment building across the street. "Apartment four-D. And my dog is in there! Make sure he's okay!"

"Some guard dog," the cop scoffs.

"Stay here while we go in," the other one orders. "Look, I don't mean to worry you, but there has been a rapist in this neighborhood recently. He's been targeting single women about your age. Actually, pretty much women with your build and hair color."

I gasp. I reflexively touch my hair and decide I'm going to dye it red or blond. Or buy a wig. Or shave it off. Or move.

The policemen radio for backup and enter my building while I continue to freak out.

"Oh my God!" I say. "I have to move. I'm moving. I'm moving tomorrow."

"Well, if this is the guy, the rapist guy, then you're fine now— they caught him," the Good Samaritan says.

"My apartment will never be the same," I say.

I pace and pace, and then hide behind a tree because I don't want the rapist to see me and know that I fingered him in his rapist bust and then come after me in a few years when he gets out on good behavior or because of overcrowding. I'll never be able to sleep peacefully. I'll have to keep tabs on his jail time and hope he shanks someone and gets locked up for good. But if he doesn't and he gets out, I'll never be free.

"They're coming out," my new friend says.

I hear yelling and peek around the tree to see two cops pushing a handcuffed man out the door. A handcuffed man whose name was the first word I spoke at six months of age: "Daddy."

Oops.

I step out from behind the tree. "Daddy, what are you doing?"

"You told me I could stay with you!" he shouts. "You told me where the extra key was!"

"But I paid your bill! I didn't think you would come if you had electricity at your own apartment!" I exclaim, relieved and embarrassed.

"This is your father, ma'am?" the police officer asks, and it's only when he ma'ams me that I make the connection: This is the same officer who almost arrested me for breaking and entering into Nat's apartment.

I send up a silent prayer to the big guy upstairs. *Please don't let them recognize me. Please don't let them remember me. I've already had a bad enough night. Please?*

"Yes," I say. "That would be my father." I don't even look at my dad when I say it, and really he's done nothing wrong—I told him he could stay, I told him where my hide-a-key was. Yet I feel a little violated. I guess because of the complete and sheer terror I felt when my knee inched up to find its comfortable place and instead found a suspiciously pointy vertebra. And the fact that my dad thought it was totally fine to just crawl into my bed? What is that? Aren't dads supposed to sleep on the sofa?

"Wait," Officer Ma'am says. "Aren't you that woman who was painting her friend's apartment a few months ago?"

Thanks for nothing, Lord Almighty.

"No," I say, standing up into my lie a little straighter. "I don't be-lieve so. I'm terribly sorry for this inconvenience. May I go back up-stairs now?"

"We'll still need to fill out a report," he says. "You know the drill. *Same as last time.*"

Damn it.

When all is said and done, my dad follows me back into my apartment, and I make eye contact with him for the first time since I ID'd him.

"Dad, I really wish you would have told me you were coming."

"I thought that was implied in the me asking you if I could stay with you and you saying yes."

"But then I said I was paying your bill," I say, a little higher-pitched than normal.

"Well, the lights weren't back on, and I wanted to watch TV."

"Fine," I say. "It's fine that you came. I was just surprised . . . to find you in my bed. Didn't Moose bark when you came in?"

"Not that little guy. He was asleep before me. I'm sorry, honey. I'm sure I scared the shit out of you."

I make a mental note to look into getting Moose some guard-dog training ASAP. "Yes." I nod. "You did."

"I couldn't get the remote to work in the living room, so I came into your bedroom to watch the *SVU.*" Again with the "the" in front of things that don't have or require it. "I was lying on top of the covers, and then I fell asleep with the TV on. I woke up at some point and turned it off, and I guess I forgot where I was and just got under the covers."

"Yes, I guess you did."

"I'm sorry, baby."

I can't stay mad at him. He didn't mean to terrify the living shit out of me.

"It's okay, Dad," I say.

"You want me to go?"

"No, of course not. Especially not now that I know there's a rapist out there."

"There is?"

"Yes, and I'm his type!"

"You're everybody's type," my dad says in that dad way that somehow makes you feel better and reminds you that no matter who breaks your heart, you'll always be Daddy's girl.

But then I snap out of it and remember the rapist. I don't want to be the rapist's type. I imagine him having a thin mustache like a fourteen-year-old boy or a smarmy Frenchman. Only menacing and fat. With a stocking over his head, but I know that mustache is underneath. And I hate him all the more for it. What kind of asshole wears a mustache like that? A rapist, that's who.

I pull out my laptop and start Googling recent rapes in the area. My dad sets himself up on the couch, and when nothing of note turns up, I vow to get myself a police scanner tomorrow.

U

They say there are no accidents. Everything happens for a reason, blah, blah, blah. I'm not sure I believe it. I mean, of course I believe it, but I also believe that you can cherry-pick which things you want to attach that theory to. So when a week after I've decided in my mind that Ryan is not the enemy, and I've exhaled for the first time because I can finally put my pesky fear that everything bad happens in threes to rest, I notice Clover Boy, "Lucky," the guy who told me to pick up the penny at Swingers that day, I decide to chalk it up to an accident. The elevator doors are closing on him, and I see him lunge forward to stop them, but it's too late. That, I think, is what was meant to happen. He was meant to miss the "open doors" button, because I belong with Ryan. Then Ryan proves me wrong.

We're in the middle of a live show and some woman is on the phone, telling Ryan that she has a fear of the unknown, when he announces that "everybody has a fear of the unknown."

"It's natural," Ryan says. "Don't beat yourself up about it. It's not like you have some irrational fear of William Shatner." He winks at me as if this is okay. As if he didn't just totally betray me right then. Does he think this is something to joke about? Doesn't he get it? Yes, it's an irrational fear. But it's my fear. My private fear.

"That's silly," the woman says. "Who would have a fear of William Shatner? Nobody has a fear of William Shatner."

"Au contraire, mon frère," he says in his best betraying-me French. "Berry here is terrified of Shatner."

"That's not exactly true," I say, and the look I give Ryan could melt the skin off his face. He should know what's in bounds and out of bounds by now, but he doesn't seem to look at all apologetic. He needs to stop before this gets out of hand.

"It's absolutely true," Ryan says. "Berry has about a bazillion superstitions. . . . That's just the tip of the iceberg."

"Ryan," I say, in that way that you say someone's name instead of saying "stop."

"Are you going to deny it?" he asks me.

I press the mute button and hiss through my teeth, "What are you doing?"

Ryan completely ignores this and un-mutes us. "Berry doesn't want me to talk about this. But I think it's good for her to talk about it. Isn't admitting the problem the first step to getting better? Isn't that step one of Shatner-phobes Anonymous?"

"You're an ass," I say, and at this point I don't care who hears it.

"Note she's not denying it, folks."

There are "ooohs" and "oh, no, he didn'ts" coming from the control room.

"Yes," I finally say into the mic. "I jokingly told Ryan that I had a fear of William Shatner one night when I felt bad for him because of . . . well, we don't need to get into details, but let's just say he was feeling a bit vulnerable. . . ."

The caller laughs the understanding laugh of a woman who gets what I'm hinting at. "Say no more," she says. "We've all been there. You tell him, 'It's okay. . . . It happens to everybody. . . . We can try again later. . . . Let's just cuddle.' "

"Exactly," I agree. "Only in my case, I knew just coddling him and saying it would all be okay wouldn't be enough, so I tried to put the focus on me, and I made up a stupid story about being afraid of William Shatner."

"Nice." Ryan laughs. "Well played."

"And he bought it?" The woman laughs, too.

"Men are idiots," I say, but I'm not laughing. I'm looking straight through Ryan when I say it. Yet he's got a smile plastered on his face. Clearly he doesn't get the severity of this indiscretion. He doesn't get that he's just totally betrayed my trust. But he should know by now. He should know this isn't some cute quirk he can use for a bit. This matters to me, and that should matter to him.

As soon as we wrap the show I get up, throw my headphones down, and storm out, replaying everything that led up to this. Clover Boy. Maybe he was a warning sign. Maybe I misread everything. Ryan comes after me, perhaps only now realizing how truly pissed I am.

"Wait up, Ber. You're not seriously mad about this, are you?"

"Yes, Ryan," I say. "I seriously am."

"It was no big deal."

"It was a big deal to me."

"C'mon," he says, and tries to reach for me, but I recoil. "Really? You're really gonna get that mad over this?"

"Ryan, I told you that in private. I was sharing with you. That was between us."

"I didn't realize it was that big a deal. I thought we were just jousting out there. It was good radio. If I can let our entire listening audience think I can't get it up, I think you can be okay with them knowing you have some silly fear."

"It was not 'good radio,' " I say. "It was my personal business. Not everything is about 'good radio,' Ryan. Some things are sacred."

"Your fear of William Shatner is sacred?"

"You don't get it," I say.

"No, I guess I don't."

"Wow," I say, shaking my head at myself. "You were the third asshole."

"I don't know what that means."

"It means . . . this shouldn't have gone as far as it did. It means I should have listened to the facts—to what I knew to be true the minute I met you. It means . . . we're done."

"Yeah?" He steps back, shaking his head in disbelief. "Over this? Then you really are crazy."

"Whatever, Ryan. Then I'm crazy." I make air quotes when I say the word "crazy." "But I'll tell you what: I'm not crazy enough to waste any more time on you."

"That's great, Berry. Except we have a show together."

"And that's really unfortunate."

"Unlucky, you might say."

We stand there facing each other, and I'm shaking like a leaf. I can't believe it's come to this. I can't believe I let myself like him as much as I did. And now this.

"I did this for you," I say. "I never wanted to do a talk show."

"Yeah. Well, I guess I should have listened to you, then. I guess I should have paid closer attention to your bad vibes and your sixth sense and the twelve yellow lights on your way to work this morning."

I don't say anything back, because I'm about to start crying and he doesn't deserve to see my tears. And because once I start crying, I won't be able to stop.

I turn around and walk away. I know he's just standing there, watching me go, but I don't look back, I can't look back.

"Your relationship ended because of William Shatner?" Natalie says, when I call her from behind closed doors in my office.

"Didn't you hear that? If we're breaking it down, yes."

"You'll make up."

"I don't want to make up," I tell her. "If he's that clueless that I was sharing something with him—something that wasn't for public consumption—and he can go and announce it to millions of listeners—"

"Let's not get carried away about the size of your audience, there, chief."

"I don't care if we had an audience of five people. Even if nobody was listening, it doesn't change the fact that he would do that."

"I get it, I do. . . . It's just . . . you could be a little sensitive about this in a way that he doesn't understand. Did you explain it to him?"

"I shouldn't have to. And you're supposed to be on my side, so just be on my side."

"Okay." She exhales. "I'm on your side."

"Can you meet me now?" I ask.

"I'm already at the restaurant. I got here early, but I can meet you and still be back before dinner. I just had to be here when nobody else was here. I'm laying a crap out for Victor."

"I'm sorry, what?"

"Victor!" she says, in the same hushed tone she just, I think, told me she's doing something involving feces that I don't quite understand. "The one who's been stealing."

"Is it fake?" I ask. I'm hoping it is, because if she's just dropping trou and taking a dump in her kitchen to show that guy who's boss, there's a good chance they'll shut her restaurant down.

"Is what fake?"

"I mean, is it like fake dog poo that you can buy on the Internet or something?"

"What the hell are you talking about, Berry?"

"I was going to ask you the same question!" I shout. "Did you not just say you're laying a crap?"

"A trap," she says. "Trap. *T-R-A-P.* I'm leaving out food to see if he . . . You know." She's still talking out the side of her mouth from what it sounds like, but at least now I get it. And I'm relieved.

"Got it," I say. "It was hard to understand you in your top secret, probably-very-obvious-to-everyone-around-you voice."

"Nobody's here," she says.

"Oh, then you talking in that crazed, hushed, incoherent mumble makes even more sense."

"See you in fifteen," she says, and I hang up and stare at the wall for a good ten of those fifteen minutes. Finally I get up, grab my things, and get in the elevator.

When the doors open, I'm face-to-face once again with Clover Boy. Maybe I was wrong about things happening for a reason.

"Look who it is again," he says. "Twice in a matter of hours. Must really be my lucky day. So I gotta ask how's that penny working out for you?"

"Awful," I say. "Are you sure it wasn't tails-up when you saw it and you accidentally kicked it to turn heads-up or something?"

"Why would I do that?" he says with a smile. "You think I don't know that a tails-up penny is bad news?"

"Well," I say, looking down and kicking at the floor. "It's nice that someone understands. What are you doing here?"

He spins around to show me the guitar strapped to his back.

"We're doing a session," he says. "I . . . play guitar."

"Oh, I didn't know that," I say. "You didn't say before."

"Yeah, you were in a hurry. And how could you know? I'm just the random maybe dangerous guy who flips pennies under pretty girls' tables to have an excuse to talk to them."

He said I was pretty. In any other circumstance this might lift my mood, but I'm too angry right now to even take in the compliment.

"Sorry I couldn't save the elevator for you this morning."

"Oh, that's okay," I say. "It was pretty much an indicator of how my day was about to go."

"Well, it was cool to bump into you. And even better this time. Third time's the charm, they say. I'm Brendan."

"Berry," I say. "What's your band called? And forgive me for not knowing. Should I know you guys?"

"Well, my band and who I'm here playing with are two completely different animals. I'm here today as a session guy. I'm a hired gun for a certain teen sensation who's playing today to commemorate her new album dropping tonight at midnight."

"Nice," I say.

"It's a gig. I'd rather be playing to commemorate my album dropping."

"I'm sure you will someday," I say.

"Well, you should come," he says. "Studio twenty-two."

"I would," I say, "but I'm fifteen minutes post-breakup, and late to meet my best friend to have an anger powwow."

"You just broke up with your dude?" he asks.

"I think I did, yup."

"That's awful," he says with a wide grin.

"Yes," I say. "You look crushed."

"I'm crushed if you're crushed," he says. "But if my crush isn't crushed by her breakup . . . then I see me bumping into you right now as a very good omen."

"I'm crushed," I admit.

"How crushed?" he asks. "Like a crumpled-up piece of paper that can be straightened out and still resemble paper in a week or so, when some guy with impeccable timing calls you?"

"I'm sorry," I say. "I'm really flattered, and you're very cute, and you have the whole clover-tattoo thing that bodes well for you, I'll give you that, but I literally just broke up with my boyfriend like thirty seconds ago. I can't even think about dating someone else."

"Just so we're clear, you did say I'm very cute just now, right?"

I can't help but smile at his persistence, and it feels good to take my mind off my reality for a minute. "Yes, I did say you were cute."

"Very cute, I believe it was."

"Your point?"

"Just making sure we both have all the facts," he says. He is charming, I'll give him that.

"I think we're clear," I say.

"What are you doing here, by the way?" he asks.

"Oh . . . I work here."

"Really? That's awesome. What do you do?"

"I'm a DJ," I say. Then add, "And a talk-show host as of late, but that's not really my thing."

"No?"

"The DJ part, yes. The music part is why I do what I do. But then my . . . now ex-boyfriend coerced me into doing a morning show with him, which I never should have done, and now I'm stuck, or maybe I'm not. . . . I don't know. He really wants the show. I really . . . might not. I don't know. Anyway, blah, blah, blah, that's what I do."

"I love that you're into music," he says. "You should definitely see my band one of these days. I know that sounds lame, but we're actually pretty good."

"What are you called?"

"Magically Delicious."

"Really?"

He holds out his wrist to show me his clover tattoo. "You know," he says. "The Lucky Charms commercials. It's their tagline."

"Oh, I know," I say. "It was the only cereal I'd eat as a kid. Partially because I liked those little marshmallows, but also because it was all my dad would buy. We have a thing with luck . . . and superstitions. Me personally—I could do without the leprechaun on the front, but the fact that 'lucky' was in the brand name made it tolerable. I'm very superstitious. In fact, since you're so gung-ho about going on a date with me, you should know that I'm crazy. Apparently. I have too many superstitious . . . beliefs. I'm extremely superstitious—that's my thing. And I have about eleventy billion crazy little things that I believe or do or don't do, and that's me."

"You done?" he asks.

"Yes," I say. "But I reserve the right to an addendum. Where I can further disparage myself. Oh, and even though I just told you all about my superstitious nature and I barely know you, you may not give me shit about it. . . . Well, maybe just a tiny bit. Within reason."

"Noted."

"Now I'm done."

"Good," he says. "I . . . the person you are looking at—who already thinks you're great—also happen to be extremely superstitious. I have a freakin' four-leaf clover tattooed on my wrist, for Christ's sake. So not only do I think that anyone who would fault you for that is a gigantic idiot, I think that what you just disclosed does not only make you adorable . . . it may very well make you my soul mate."

"Wow, we just went from a maybe first date sometime in the future to being soul mates? You move fast."

"What can I say? I believe in fate. Do you?"

U

I must say it was a nice momentary distraction, but the timing couldn't have been worse. Yes, he's cute, and, yes, he's got that tattoo, and, yes, he just said those things that sounded kind of incredible . . . but he's just some random cute guy with a clover tattoo who may or may not be my twin. Emphasis on random. They say timing is everything. Unfortunately, his timing stinks.

I'm ten minutes late meeting Natalie because of my Clover Boy interlude, and she's tapping her foot and looking at her watch when I walk in.

"Late much?" she asks.

"Sorry, I was being wooed."

"He wooed you? Did he grovel? Was he on his knees? And if he was, I don't need the gory details of your sex life, so keep them to yourself."

"No, no, no, and wrong guy. It wasn't Ryan."

"Wow. You move fast."

"He moves fast, and I didn't agree to anything, even though he could potentially be my soul mate."

"Hold the wedding toast," she says. "Some other guy who I haven't heard of is potentially your soul mate."

"So he says."

"And you and Ryan are broken up."

"Correct."

"And you have a show in a few hours, so you probably don't want to get drunk right now."

"Also correct." I nod.

"But you'll watch me down a couple, because Victor is totally stealing from me and I have to fire him if when I get back that pumpernickel bread is gone."

"Absolutely."

"And I'll need to hear all about the Ryan fiasco—in full detail—and apparently about your new soul mate, whom I've somehow never heard of. But Ryan first."

I order a latte, and Nat orders a vodka gimlet, her new "signature drink." I don't question it. I download all the pertinent information to Natalie, and as soon as I finish she pulls out a penny, a piece of paper, and a pen. She rips the paper in half and writes "Ryan" on one piece and "Clover" on the other. She places the penny down on the table and makes me pick a hand.

"Pick a hand for heads," she says.

"What do you mean?"

"Ryan is in one and Clover is in the other. I know you won't willingly assign tails to someone, so pick a hand."

"First of all," I say, "Clover has a name—it's Brendan."

"Too bad. You never told me his name, and I already wrote Clover."

"Second of all, Ryan is out. He's done. We're over."

"Humor me," she says.

"Fine," I say, with a roll of the eyes so big I think I just saw my ear. "The right one."

"That's deep," she says. "Works on many levels."

She pulls out her right hand and unfolds the piece of paper. "Ryan." I make her show me what's in the left hand to make sure she wasn't double-Ryan-ing out of some misguided loyalty to the familiar vs. the unknown. Sure enough, it says "Clover." She was being fair.

"So Ryan is heads, Clover is tails."

"Brendan," I say.

"Whatever. You wanna flip, or you want me to?"

"I'll do it," I say, and I swipe the penny from the table.

I shake my head to reiterate that I don't even know the point of all this, and then I toss the penny in the air.

Blues is easy to play but hard to feel.

—JIMI HENDRIX

Chapter Eighteen

Nobody who ever wanted to get into talk radio was a good person. I mean, think about it: When's the last time someone who wasn't a completely narcissistic egomaniac decided to get into talk? I'll tell you when: never. Sure, there are varying degrees, but aren't all of these people more or less blowhards who are basically just in love with the sound of their own voices?

You've got Howard Stern and his legion of wannabes. Howard may be a nice guy underneath his shock-jock exterior, and *Private Parts* was surprisingly moving, but he's more than earned his shock-jock title, and while, yes, I admit he can be funny, and, yes, I may be genuinely curious if Lay Down Sally is actually going to have sex with five hundred men, I wouldn't say he's doing anything to further our society. And he's certainly not doing the world a favor by celebrating his minions every time they manage to crash some unsuspecting event, spew nonsense, and then make sure it's known that they did it in the name of *The Howard Stern Show* by saying that one magical phrase: "Baba Booey." Never have four syllables summed up idiocy so perfectly.

There are the pompous Rush Limbaughs of the world who are so caught up in their own self-importance that they forget they're there only to comment on political issues and instead spew rhetoric as if they are actually elected government officials.

Dr. Laura? That woman has single-handedly set the women's movement back about fifty years. Thank God she went away.

And the list goes on. All of these people have one thing in common: They are their own biggest fans. So why did I not think about this when I got involved with Ryan?

Because I'm an idiot, that's why. Because not only did I not listen to my gut . . . I ignored simple common sense.

When I get back to the station for my night shift, I completely disregard the scheduled playlist and instead opt for a wide selection of songs about heartache and betrayal.

I punctuate each song with commentary that, were it to be scrutinized—and I'm pretending it's not—would be deemed bitter, angry, and teetering on the fence of bunny boiling.

I've had no time to cry between getting hit on by Lucky McBandmember, meeting Nat, and doing my show, so as soon as I take my headphones off at the end of the night, I make up for lost time. I'm sobbing by the time I get to the parking lot, and I have no idea how I even make it back to my apartment. My head feels like a dingy smoke-filled dive bar full of miserable people who drink during the day. When I get home, I don't even wash my face or brush my teeth—I just get into my pajamas, and I cry on my way to bed. A soon as I'm about to turn back the covers, I think better of the teeth-brushing thing and go into the bathroom. I floss like the good girl I am, brush my teeth, and then look at myself in the mirror to see how sad I look on a scale of one to pathetic.

I don't need to wash the makeup off because my tears have done it for me, leaving an artistic streak of mascara down my right cheek. So artistic, in fact, that I grab my iPhone and take pictures of myself in the mirror so I'll have a record of my misery. I take one of my whole face—no smile, obviously. One of just the right side. One close-up of the eye . . . which comes out blurry, so I then take a series of miserable, right-eye close-ups to get the angle just right and the despondency properly captured. When I'm pleased with my selection, I start firing them off to Nat, not even to say "I'm so sad," but more because I'm quite proud of my work. I could do an exhibit of My Sad Self and call it just that.

Seconds later my iPhone chimes with an email from Natalie.

To: Berry.Lambert@kkcr.com
From: NatalieSaysSo@gmail.com
Subject: Go to bed.
Seriously. Get out of your bathroom and go to bed.
—Nat
p.s. I fired Victor.
p.p.s. I rehired him because I felt guilty. I left $5s, $10s, and $20s around the kitchen and he didn't take a dime. I even left a dime. He didn't touch it. I can't fire him if he's literally stealing food because he's hungry. Don't tell anyone I have a heart.
p.p.p.s. I told him if he ever steals so much as a shallot again I will mince his balls, sauté them in a white wine and garlic reduction, and force-feed them to him.

I walk into work wearing dark Jackie O sunglasses, and it looks like I'm trying to be fashionable and aloof, but the truth is I got a total of about eleven minutes of sleep, my eyes are bloodshot, and I look like crap. My first post-breakup show with Ryan. How are we going to deal with this? Do we pretend everything's fine? Do we make some big announcement?

I'm self-conscious as I walk down the halls. I wonder if people know, if they'll act differently. I feel like I'm in high school all over again . . . and I used to be half of "the most popular couple" but now we broke up and everyone's going to be whispering about it.

Then I see him. He's standing over the coffee machine, talking to Brad Stevens, our sports guy. Big Brad Stevens, who moonlights as a traffic guy, the secret I know only because Ryan told me. How would Ryan feel if I told Brad I know he does traffic? My ears start to ring a little, and then a lot, and things get a little fuzzy and I feel like I might faint, so I steady myself against the wall and try to take a few breaths.

This is all I need, I think. I'm going to pass out perfectly positioned in the direct sightline of Ryan and Moonlighting Brad. I'm going to faint right here, and they'll think it's because I'm so distraught over my breakup, and sure, partially it is, but they're also not taking other factors into consideration: general anxiety; stress; zero sleep last night; Talouse, my fat mustachioed French rapist. These are all major factors.

But somehow I pull it together. I decide that it's bad karma for me to even be thinking about telling Brad I was aware of his scheme. That's just not who I am. Which is why it hurt so much when Ryan couldn't respect those sacred boundaries.

When I'm certain that I'm not going to face-plant, I walk over to the coffee machine because I need coffee, too, and Ryan doesn't own the coffee machine. We both need to caffeinate before our show—Lord knows I do.

When he sees me his mouth tightens, then forms into a polite smile but certainly not a warm one. I smile back and simultaneously feel like I'm going to throw up. He doesn't say anything, so I don't say anything. I'm not going to be the first one to say something. He owes me an apology, really, and at no point did he acknowledge that he did betray my trust. Plus, we're broken up, and it's not exactly like he was fighting for me, so to hell with him.

I punch the buttons on the machine to make me a below-average "Starbucks" cappuccino, and by the time it starts brewing, Ryan is long gone. *Good. Fine by me.* We can speak on the radio and only on the radio.

I decide I'm not going to announce to our listening audience that we are no longer a "we," because what's the point? If it comes out, it will happen organically. We can still bullshit with each other on-air and talk about hot topics and do what we do that for whatever reason people want to hear. I'm definitely not going to make a big deal out of the breakup. It's nobody's business.

∪

"Ryan and I are no longer a couple," I find myself saying as soon as our intro music finishes. "Might as well get it out there right up front. We broke up. So while the tagline for our show is 'It's so on,' I'm somewhat sorry to report that our relationship is definitely off."

So much for nobody's business.

But at least I took the bull by the horns. What's that they say in public relations about "shaping the conversation"? Well, I just shaped the conversation before Ryan could. I wonder how he'll respond.

"I wondered how we were going to navigate this one," Ryan says into his mic, "but thank you, Berry, for so succinctly taking the lead."

Can't read much from that. Wonder when the other shoe will drop.

Of course, the phone lines immediately light up. I look through the glass to see Bill's reaction. Clearly Ryan hadn't let the cat out of the bag around the office, either, because Bill's turning red and maybe even slightly purple. He's waving his arms and trying to mouth something, and I'm pretty sure I get the gist.

Ryan punches a line. "Caller, you're on the air."

"Who broke up with whom?" the girl asks.

"That's none of your business," I answer.

"Berry broke up with me," Ryan says. *Oh, so that's how he's gonna play it.* I steel myself for an interesting show.

"Are you really broken up, or are you Eminem-and-Kim broken up?"

Ryan looks at me, and we hold each other's gaze for a moment. I speak first. "We're really broken up."

"Why'd you break up with him?" the caller asks.

"We're only taking one question at a time, and you already got yours answered," I say, and then disconnect her.

I know I can't deflect this forever. I knew this was coming. But damn it, I'm not giving in without a fight.

Ryan punches in another caller. "You're live with Ryan and Berry. . . ."

"You can't just leave us hanging," a male voice says. "Was it the fact that foreplay wasn't his forte?"

I don't have the strength to be cute about this.

"You know, that was a misleading day," I say. "Things were mis-stated and blown out of proportion." I wonder, *Why am I protect-*

ing him? "I'm not going to bring our sex life into this. That's what Ryan's nighttime show is for. Let's move on to the news."

"You guys are the news," says Patrick, our board operator, and the rest of the morning crew laugh.

"Caller, you're on the air," Ryan says.

"Can I talk to Berry?" a male voice asks.

"You are," I chime in. "What none-of-your-business question would you like to ask me?"

"Well," he says, "I was wondering if you reconsidered going out with me?"

"Brendan?" I ask.

"Who's Brendan?" Ryan says, his head cocked backward like he's truly perplexed.

"He's nobody," I say.

"I'll try not to be offended by that," Brendan says.

"This isn't a good time," I say. "Thanks for your call, Brendan."

"Hold up," Ryan says. "Hi, Brendan." When he says Brendan's name, he looks like he's smelling a fart.

"Hey, man," Brendan says. "Sorry about your breakup."

"Yeah, you seem real sorry," Ryan says. "Tell me, dear Brendan, what made you think now would be a good time to ask Berry out?"

"Well," Patrick chimes in, "you asked her out live on the radio, too, Ryan."

"Not helping, Patrick," Ryan says.

"She's single, isn't she?" Brendan asks.

Ryan looks at me for a long beat. I'm not saying a thing. This is beyond awkward. Ryan can handle it.

"Yeah, bro. She's single."

Stay little Valentine stay
Each day is Valentine's Day.

—LORENZ HART

Chapter Nineteen

If you took a poll of how many people get engaged on Valentine's Day and how many people break up on Valentine's Day, I think you'd have an even split. Yes, it's a nice excuse to show the person you love that you love them, even if it is a Hallmark holiday. But it's also an opportunity to show the person you love that you are an insensitive asshole who thinks only about himself. Or herself.

I remember one Valentine's Day when I was dating a total egomaniac. His mother had treated him as if the sun rose and set around him, so in typical spoiled-mama's-boy fashion he expected everyone around him to jump when he called, greet him at the door like a panting puppy dog, and cater to his every whim. But would the gestures be returned? Not so much. What his mother failed to teach him was that to inspire this kind of warmth you needed to also be a warm person. And sadly, this guy pretty much had ice water running through his veins, pumping into a makeshift contraption that was somehow functioning to keep him alive.

For whatever reason, I kept convincing myself that there was good in him even though every single one of my friends would (correctly) tell me he was a textbook narcissist. I refused to believe it. They'd ask me what I liked about him, and I couldn't put it into words because the truth was—there wasn't much to like. I just had this illogical crazy connection to him, and I couldn't let it go. Even he would ask me, "Why me? What makes you so sure I'm the one you want to be with?" And every time he asked, I tried my best to convince both of us that I believed whatever I could pull out of thin air. I was just dumbstruck in love. It was magical. It was chemical. It was a disaster.

Weeks before our first Valentine's Day, I became obsessed with getting him the perfect gift. I wound up getting him several things: some cute (prescription pills, which were actually Red Hots candy in a real prescription bottle with his name professionally inscribed as the "lovesick patient"), some touching and sweet (I won't go into detail, because it's so sweet you'll get a cavity), some other little trinkets, and then his main present—an engraved silver key ring from Tiffany & Co. that he could keep with him always.

A couple days before Valentine's Day, he finally brought up the fact that Valentine's Day was coming up. I, of course, couldn't contain my smile.

"Oh," he said, somewhat surprised. "Is that something you celebrate?"

"Well," I said, " I think it's something every girl who's in a relationship celebrates."

"That's not necessarily true," he said.

"Is it something you don't celebrate?"

"Doesn't mean anything to me, but if it means something to you, then I guess we can celebrate it," he generously offered. Nothing like being made to feel like someone's doing you a favor by celebrating Valentine's Day. *Quelle romance!*

Come V-Day—or D-Day, as it were—I showed up at his place when instructed and was delightfully telling him about the cute "pajama-gram" that my grandmother had sent me for Valentine's Day when he finally got it.

"We're not exchanging gifts today, are we?"

What I thought: *I guess I'll be having edible panties and salad for dinner tonight.*

What I said: "I guess not . . . although I did pick up a couple trinkets for you."

I gave him the less-expensive gifts and saved the really nice one for later because I wasn't certain at that point that it wasn't just a game—him pretending not to have bought me a gift when, really, he'd done something mind-blowingly special that was going to be a surprise.

The surprise was there was no gift. And bonus: He complained throughout our entire dinner about everything he possibly could. I remember him glancing up from his menu and saying, "Next year we're staying home." And I so vividly remember thinking, *Next year? There isn't even going to be a "next week" for you and me.*

Two days later, he went on Yelp.com to give the restaurant a bad review. Talk about a miserable human being. And know this: It's not like I was expecting more bling than Lil Wayne's teeth. I'd have been happy with some tiny token of thoughtfulness. Even a sweet card would have made my day. But the lack of effort was almost inspired.

I ended the relationship a week later. I loved him. I truly did. For whatever unexplainable reason. With all my heart and soul. But not nearly as much as he loved himself. And with both of us being so head-over-heels in love with him, there was nobody actually loving me.

So that was a bad example, and of course there are the good examples of what lovers do for each other, and I've absolutely had my share of good ones, too. That's how I know the difference. But good or bad, celebrated or not, Valentine's Day is a pressure cooker.

And walking into work to do a live radio show with my recent ex on Valentine's Day feels like a death march to a pressure cooker. Bad enough that when I was reading myself to sleep last night my book had a missing page in it. Not a torn-out page . . . a missing page. It's bad luck to skip a page in a book. And there I was, reading myself wide awake with the notion that there was nothing I could do to remedy this one. Best shot I had was stopping at that page so I wasn't "skipping the page." At least that's what I talked myself down with as I tried to get to sleep, but then when I did fall asleep and woke up this morning, I noticed a heads-down penny on the floor, staring at me. All signs were pointing to a very bad day.

"Good morning, Berry," Ryan says as I walk into our studio. "Happy Valentine's Day."

"Heh." I muster a pseudo half-chuckle. "Yeah, happy Valentine's Day to you, too."

As we set up for the show, I don't look at Ryan, but I can feel his eyes burning into me. Still, I don't look up. Because if I do, I'll get lost in his eyes and forget that he's just not right for me. We don't value the same things.

But *gah*! It's really fucking hard to make myself remember this when I'm two feet away from him. What I need is a distraction.

"You kids getting back together today?" Bill says as he saunters into the studio, clueless as ever.

Ryan looks up at me and lets me answer.

"Not so much, Bill," I say.

"Good," he says. Not at all what I was expecting. "Because there's someone who seems to have it bad for you, and I didn't want this to get awkward."

Someone has it bad for whom? For me? For Ryan? Who?

"I'm not sure what you mean by that," I say, trying to play it cool.

"You will soon," Bill says, wiping his comb-over out of the way, punctuating his cryptic message with that much more annoyance. I wonder what Crazy Helicopter Guy would think if he ever hovered over Bill's head. Hell, he'd easily have room for a landing.

"Bill," Ryan says finally. "What's the deal? We don't need any surprises."

"The surprise isn't for you, Ryan," Bill replies pointedly.

"Well, I hate surprises, so I don't need one, either," I say.

"She does," Ryan says with world-weary authority. "She hates surprises."

"She'll like this one."

"Says who?" I ask.

"Says me and anyone with a heart on Valentine's Day," Bill says, now puffed up with pride.

What the hell is going on?

"Bill," I say, now more serious than ever. "What is it? I really don't like surprises. And I don't celebrate Valentine's Day."

"Really?" Ryan says. "That doesn't seem like you. I'd think you love Valentine's Day. I think if you hadn't dumped me we'd be doing something special tonight. I know I'd have been planning for that."

This isn't a conversation I want to get into with Ryan. This isn't a conversation I want to get into with anyone in front of Bill. But when the barn door's already open . . .

"I mean, I don't celebrate it if I don't have anyone to celebrate with. Single people don't celebrate Valentine's Day. Single people hate Valentine's Day. They have anti–Valentine's Day parties. Or they sit at home on the couch feeling sorry for themselves with a carton of ice cream and perhaps another carton of ice cream. Or they pretend it's just a Hallmark holiday that doesn't matter. They would rather celebrate Arbor Day than Valentine's Day. They make it a point to note that Valentine's Day's initials are the same as those for venereal disease."

The men both stare at me.

"O-kay," Ryan says.

"Right," I say, clearing my throat, realizing I may have gone a bit overboard.

"Well, too bad," Bill says. "Because you get a surprise today." Bill winks at Clark, our producer.

Just then, someone I don't know walks into the studio with an electrical cord, plugs it into the wall, and walks out. It's not attached to anything. *What the hell?*

"And, three . . . two . . . one," Clark counts us in.

"Good morning, and happy Valentine's Day," Ryan says into the mic, looking directly at me.

"Happy Valentine's Day to you, too, Ryan," I say. "And to all of you people out there who are celebrating."

"I know we're celebrating here," Clark says, uncharacteristically chiming into his mic.

"We've been getting teased about some special Valentine's Day surprise," Ryan says. "None of us here know what it is. Well, some of us do, but not those of us who actually host this show."

"Which," I interrupt, "is a bit unnerving. And annoying."

"No need to wait any longer," Clark says. "We have a special guest on the show today. Some of you locals may know this guy from his band, Magically Delicious. Some of you may know this guy from when he called in and asked Berry out over the air."

Oh, no. "That guy?" Ryan says. "He's here?"

"He's nothing if not persistent," Clark goes on. "And he's got it bad for our little Berry. Please welcome Brendan Scott to our studio."

I watch as Brendan walks in, his guitar strapped across his chest. Ryan turns to finally get a look at the "mystery caller." Brendan won't meet his gaze, smiles at me, and plugs his guitar into the dangling electrical cord.

"Happy Valentine's Day, Berry," he says. Then adds, "You, too, Ryan."

I open my mouth to say something, but nothing comes out. This is beyond awkward.

"I thought I'd play you a song as a Valentine's gesture. See if maybe this will help change your mind."

"Really?" Ryan says, shaking his head in a healthy combination of disgust and disbelief. "Seriously, dude?"

"Totally, 'dude,' " Brendan says, and the two of them have a staring contest that is making everyone—or maybe it's just me—in the studio crawl out of their skin. Brendan starts to play the familiar bass line to "Superstition" by Stevie Wonder. He's changed the words just a tiny bit.

"Berry superstitious," he sings. "Writing's on the wall . . ."

How clever. He's changed the lyrics to include my name. Cute. If I wasn't so completely freaked out by the awkwardness of the moment, I might be a little charmed. Even though the song debunks superstition, we'll hold that against Stevie, not Brendan.

Ryan rolls his eyes. "Wow, I'm swooning."

"Berry superstitious . . ." Brendan sings on. "Careful you might fall . . . for me . . ."

He's really making a go at this wooing thing.

"Now I'm gagging," Ryan says.

"Try not to choke," Clark says. "On your jealousy."

Everyone in the studio laughs. Except me. And Ryan. This really is an odd situation.

"Jealous?" Ryan recoils. "I'm embarrassed for the dude. And for Berry."

"Don't be embarrassed for me," I say, feeling bad for talking over Brendan's crooning. "Or him. He's a pretty good singer."

Ryan grunts, then says in his best girl voice, "Oh, em, gee! Isn't this romantic? He is positively dreamy. You should go over there and give him a big, sloppy Valentine's kiss."

"I can't do this anymore," I say, looking over at poor Brendan, who is still singing, his face contorted into what I can only describe as "forced sexy."

"Finally!" Ryan says. "Berry's heard enough. Pull the plug on this clown!"

"No, Ryan," I say, standing up, yanking my headphones off, letting them drop to my desk. "I'm done with this. This show, with you. With everything. I can't do it. It's over."

I start to walk out, realizing that Brendan is still singing, following me with his eyes.

"Berry superstitious . . . Is it cool if I still call . . . ?"

The studio laughs at his impromptu last attempt. I might, too, if a million emotions weren't surging through me. I manage to mouth the words "I'm sorry" to Brendan as I storm out.

I head straight for Bill's office, but he's already bounding down the hall toward me.

"What do you think you're doing?" he shouts.

"I'm done, Bill," I say. "I can't do it anymore."

"Sure you can," Bill says. "Act like a professional."

"I am a professional, Bill. I'm a professional DJ. I never wanted to do this to begin with. I'm sorry. I'm done. I'll see you later when I come to play music. Like I used to."

And with that I walk out, wondering what the hell I just did.

Take a chance on me.

—ABBA

Chapter Twenty

"What did I do?" I ask Natalie as I pace her restaurant kitchen.

"Sounds like you quit."

"I quit. I totally just quit. I quit."

"Yes, that's what I said."

"Oh my God. I quit."

"Sit down," she says. "You're wearing a path in my floor. And I think I just saw you step on a crack."

"Did not," I say.

"Sit."

I take a seat but only because I'm starting to get dizzy from all of my pacing and circling.

"What did I do?" I say, head now in my hands.

"We covered this."

"Did I make a mistake?"

"Do you want to do the show?" she asks pointedly.

I take a minute to think about it. It's just me and Nat. Nobody else can hear me.

"No," I say. "I really don't. I really never did."

"I know," she says. "You did it for him. And I bullied you into it because I thought you'd get over the whole invasion-of-privacy thing, because it sounded so cool. . . ."

"Having your privacy invaded sounds cool?"

"No, but having a morning show does. Being on billboards does."

"Being defaced on billboards?" I interrupt. "Because for every ten billboards I was on, there were at least seven that had additional 'artwork' scrawled across them."

"The price of fame."

"A kind of fame I never wanted."

"Then be happy."

"I am," I say. "I'm . . ." the tears start forming in my eyes, even though I'm not crying. "I'm happy. I am. Really. I've never been happier." And now the waterworks are in full effect. I'm sobbing, my shoulders are heaving, and I can't catch my breath.

"I know, honey," Nat says, petting my hair. "You're happy."

We both laugh for a second, but as quickly as I start to laugh I resume my crying. Like a maniac. This is what I've been driven to. I'm going crazy.

"Can I ask you something?" she says softly.

I look up and try to sniff the escaping mucus back into my nose, to no avail.

"Are you crying over the show? Over Ryan? What are you the most upset about?"

I don't say anything because I need to think that one over. I'm just feeling overwhelmed. The end of the relationship and the end of the show . . . Both happened so abruptly. And I tell Natalie as much when I catch my breath again.

"Those things didn't 'happen abruptly,' " she says. "Just so we're clear. You ended that relationship—"

"Because he proved I couldn't trust him!"

"And you walked off the show."

"I know."

"That's all I'm saying. That maybe . . . just maybe . . . you over-reacted a little bit. In both situations."

"I hear you."

"And what do you think about that?"

"I think," I say, sniffing back more relentless tears. "I think that you should go back to preparing your soup of the day, and I'll get out of your hair."

"You're not in my hair, but nice avoidance."

"Thanks," I say, and I make my way out of the kitchen.

U

I'm in the car, halfway home, when my cellphone rings. I don't recognize the number, but I answer it on speaker anyway.

"Hello?" I say.

"I'm sorry, Berry," says the voice, and I recognize it instantly. "It's Brendan. I guess that wasn't cool. It was one of those things that would either be really romantic or really stalkery, and I guess it came across to you as the latter."

"No," I say. "Brendan, you were just fine. I liked it, I did. I'm sorry to have left in the middle of . . . your performance. I know that was really rude, but with the whole thing with Ryan, it was just so . . ."

"Awkward," he finishes for me. "I get it."

"It was very sweet of you," I say.

"Have dinner with me tonight."

"I . . . uh . . ."

"Stop thinking. Just go with your gut. Say yes. Berry, it's Valentine's Day. Maybe my little song wasn't the best way to get a date . . . but can I get an A for effort? I'll even take a B."

"I have my show tonight," I say.

"How about between now and then?"

"I don't know."

"That's not a no," he says. "Well, technically, phonetically, there's a no in there, but without closed captioning I'm going to assume it wasn't an 'I don't' followed by a completely separate no. Like a snap decision made midsentence. You know what I mean? No?"

I giggle. Silly. Very silly. But he is creative. And he obviously really wants this date.

"You're quick," I say.

"Like a ninja. I will steal that heart of yours before you even—"

"No, I see it coming," I interrupt.

"Then it's working. My evil plan is working. Muaahahaha . . ."

"Are you a ninja or Count Chocula?"

"Ninja!" he says, with the cuteness of a little boy proudly announcing his Halloween costume.

U

Forty-five minutes later, Brendan is at my door, announcing that we're going on a picnic. This is something I haven't done in a while, and it's sweet and romantic, I suppose, as long as there's no ant rebellion.

The conversation in the car is easy. The food smells amazing, and he won't tell me where he got it from, but I'm ravenous by the time we get to Will Rogers State Park.

U

We pull up to the park, and Brendan lays out our blanket and pulls out three gigantic bags of food.

"Roscoe's House of Chicken and Waffles!" he exclaims proudly. "Ever been?"

"I've always wanted to," I say. "But I've never made it."

"Then allow me to Roscoe's devirginize you."

"Is it gonna hurt?"

"Only when it's gone," he says, and I think to myself how true that is. My mind goes to Ryan, but the scent of fried goodness quickly pulls me back to the present. I take in the scene, the trees, the couple with their new puppy, the family with their new baby, the dirty hippies who for some reason still haven't received the memo that tie-dye is just not okay. I look back to Brendan, who's dishing out our food.

"That really smells unreal," I say.

"Now, I picked Roscoe's not just because it's awesome," he says, "but because they pack one hell of a lucky lunch."

"Really . . ." I reply, my curiosity piqued.

"Hell, yes. You are about to have the luckiest meal of your life."

"That's quite the proclamation."

"Behold . . ." he says as he waves his hand over a container. "Black-eyed peas." It's true. Black-eyed peas are supposed to be lucky, especially on New Year's Day; they'll bring good fortune for the new year. As he pulls out different containers, it seems he's put more thought into this picnic than I'd realized. It's really sweet and quite charming.

"We have collard greens," he says. "Known to be lucky, as they resemble folded money. Corn bread, which represents wealth because of its golden color. Chicken . . . which is not necessarily lucky for us, certainly not lucky for the chickens, but is undeniably delicious. Circular foods represent coming full circle and living a full life—we have two of these represented by exhibit A, the waffles, and exhibit B, the sweet-potato pie."

"You're too much," I say as I marvel at the feast before us and all of the good-luck blessings that he's gone so out of his way to bestow upon us. While I don't like surprises in general, this meal really is a surprise, both in content and in the character of my date. He definitely gets brownie points for this. Or sweet-potato points, as it were.

"That smells really good," someone says, and I look up to see that one of the hippies has sauntered over. His jeans are longer than his leg span and, were I to take a wild guess, haven't been washed since Jerry Garcia died.

"It does indeed," I say, trying to be polite.

"Looks like you have a lot of food," the hippie girl now chimes in.

It almost seems like they want some of our food, but we haven't even started eating yet. "We're big eaters," Brendan says, and we make eye contact and share a smile.

"Yeah . . ." the hippie guy says. "Man, that chicken smells good."

"Yeah, it does, bro," Brendan says, in a way that would signal to a normal person that the conversation was over. But we don't seem to be dealing with normal people. These are hungry, hungry hippies.

"Is that corn bread?" the guy asks.

It doesn't seem as though these people are going away. Neither of us wants to be rude, but this is awkward—two full-on grown people hovering like vultures.

"Yes," Brendan says. "It's corn bread."

"If you don't like dark meat, I don't mind it," Hippie Boy says.

"Tell you what," Brendan says. "We do have a lot of food, but we're also trying to have a date here, so I'm gonna give you a couple drumsticks . . ."

I know what Brendan was going for. Had he been able to finish his sentence, he'd have said something to the effect of "and you two can be on your merry way." But that's not what happens. They sit down on our blanket.

"Thanks, man," Hippie Boy says as he plops down next to us.

"Yeah," Hippie Girl says. "Thanks a lot. Really cool of you to share."

Now we're screwed.

Brendan and I exchange entire conversations with our eyes as we eat our "lucky" meal. Our hippie friends eat like it's their last supper, even though that wasn't exactly what Brendan meant when he offered the drumsticks.

But that's not what makes this date memorable. Brendan shifts his body closer to me so we can ignore them. He does such a good job that it's about fifteen minutes before it comes to our attention that our hippie friends are enjoying their own company as well. A lot.

"I'm afraid to turn around," I say to Brendan. "But is there something going on behind me?"

The look on Brendan's face tells me that yes, yes, there is indeed something going on behind me. Our lucky meal is working wonders, so much so that our hippie friends are getting lucky right this second. Right beside us. In public. On our blanket.

"This is new," Brendan says.

"Oh my God," I say, while I stifle a laugh and am simultaneously in awe and repulsed by their nerve.

"Dude—" Brendan says, shielding his eyes as he turns around. "What are you doing?"

Hippie Boy barely looks up from whatever he's nuzzling. "I'm loving my lady, man."

"You just lost your corn-bread privileges" is all Brendan can think to say, and we both burst out in a fit of laughter.

"Should we . . . leave?" I ask.

"Oh, yeah," Brendan says. "I think picnic time is over."

"It's been a most memorable date," I say as we stand up and survey the situation.

"We'll just let them keep the blanket," Brendan says. Then he calls out to them, "Happy Valentine's Day . . . you freaks!"

I can barely catch my breath, I'm laughing so hard on our way back to the car.

"Should I take you home or back to the station?" he asks.

I look at the clock and realize that time did get away from us. "You should probably just take me to the station. I'll have my friend Nat pick me up when my shift is over."

"Or I can," he offers.

"That's okay," I say.

"I want to," he says. "I want to hear about your show . . . or shows?"

"Show," I correct. "I'm not doing the show with Ryan anymore."

"But you're still gonna do nighttime, right?"

"Oh, yeah," I say. "That's never going to change."

"Good."

"Why good?"

"Because music is my life," he says. "And I like that it's a big part of yours, too."

"I like that you like that."

"There's a lot that I like about you. And not just the fact that you're almost exactly like me."

"You think?"

"Yeah," he says. "I do. I think we're more alike than you even realize."

Life is a shipwreck but we must not forget to sing in the lifeboats.

—VOLTAIRE

Chapter Twenty-one

Brendan and I spend the next three weeks together, really together, almost inseparable. We don't have sex, because for some reason I'm not ready to go there yet, and he doesn't push me, which makes getting to know him easier. That said, we kiss and grope like teenagers—something about how eerily similar we are really does it for me. It's like he read a diary that I don't have and then created himself just for me. And things are great. Until Ryan calls one night when Brendan and I are curled up on the couch, ignoring a movie.

I'm not even entirely sure why I answer the phone. Curious, I guess. We've been avoiding each other at the station and certainly haven't spoken since Valentine's Day.

"Are you alone?" Ryan asks.

"Yes," I lie. "Are you okay?"

"No," he says. "Can you come over?"

This is obviously unexpected. But so is the shakiness in his voice. It doesn't sound like the Ryan I remember. And there must be something big going on for him to break through the wall of silence after all this time and ask me to come over practically in the same breath.

"Of course," I say. "I'll be there in twenty."

I hang up the phone and tell Brendan that Natalie is having an emergency, my head spinning with why I lied to Brendan, why I lied to Ryan, and why my car can't go fast enough to get me to him.

Ryan opens the door, and he doesn't have to say anything for me to see how much pain he's in. His eyes are completely bloodshot, he's shaking, and he looks like he's about to crumble into a heap of himself.

"I'm sorry," he says. "I didn't know who else to call."

"It's okay," I say. "I'm glad you called."

"That's not true. It's not that I didn't know who else to call . . . more like there was nobody else I wanted to call."

"Either way," I say. "What's going on?"

"Come in," he says, opening the door for me. The pictures of us are still up in his living room, exactly where they were when I was last here. I wonder if my pajamas are still in "my" drawer? We sit on the couch, and Ryan shakes his head back and forth as he tries to find his words.

I take his hand in mine and squeeze it. "Whatever it is, we'll get you through it."

"It's my mom," he says. "They found a lump in her breast. They're doing a biopsy tomorrow morning."

"Oh my God," I say. "I'm sorry. That's terrifying."

I think back to our impromptu "fancy meeting you here" dinner at Farmers Market and how lovely and genuinely warm Lily was. What a shame it is that Ryan and I broke up before I got to know her and Robert better. I bet they'd be fantastic in-laws. Having met her, however, makes me feel more connected to him right now—especially since she made a point to tell me they never met his girlfriends. I send up my own prayer to the powers that be. *Please don't let Lily have cancer. Please.*

"Yeah," he says, his eyes welling up. "It is. She can't have cancer. I can't lose her."

"Ryan, I know you're worried. I would be, too. This actually is fairly common. Lots and lots of women have lumps. It could very well be benign."

"What if it isn't?" he asks desperately.

"We'll cross that bridge when we get to it. One thing at a time. Let her have the biopsy first."

"I know," he says. "You're right. I need to think positive."

"You absolutely do."

"Thanks for coming over."

"I think I ran almost every red light."

"Okay, don't do that," he says angrily. "I don't want to worry about both of you."

"You don't have to worry about me. I'm an excellent driver when I'm not worrying about you."

Ryan's anger fades as quickly as it arrives, and his face falls again. "What if my mom has cancer?"

"We'll deal with it," I say. "I know it's scary, but right now we don't know that."

"I know," he says. "I just get sick every time I think of the possibility."

"When did you find out?"

"About three seconds before I called you."

"I'm glad you called."

"I know you hate me," he says. "Thanks for coming."

"You've already thanked me like five times. All of which were unnecessary. And I don't hate you."

"I hate me."

"You don't hate you, either."

"Well, someone hates me."

"Probably," I say, and manage a soft smile. "But nobody in this room."

"I screwed us up," he says. "I betrayed your confidence."

I bite my lip. Yes . . . he did. But now's not the time to make him feel bad for it. "It happens."

"It happens?"

"I'm trying to be nice."

This gets a smile. I smile back, and he shakes his head. "I promise you, I hate me more than you hate me."

"Stop with the hating you. Nobody hates you."

"I'm so worried about my mom," he says.

"I know," I say. "What time is her biopsy?"

"Nine a.m. My dad and I are both going."

"Just stay positive until we know anything else. Right now it's a lump. Just a lump. Can you do that?"

"I don't know."

"Yes, you can," I say. "I'll stay with you tonight. I'll stay until you have to go take her. We'll stay positive together. One minute at a time."

"I'm sorry I screwed us up," he says, and I know he means it.

"It's okay," I say. "You didn't mean to."

We sit in silence for a long time. He leans into me, and I run my fingers through his hair. He rests his head on my shoulder, and when he blinks, a tear falls from his eye onto my arm. It breaks my heart. I hate to see him worry. I hate that there's nothing I can do to help. I hope to God that his mom is okay and that this is just a scare. I know the odds. Terrifying. If not her, it could be my mom. Or me.

I pretend not to notice the tiny drop of water on my arm, but then another falls . . . and another. He turns and wipes his face on his shoulder and looks up at me with a shrug.

"I know," I say. "I get it."

I can feel his stare like a magnet, pulling toward me, pulling me toward him. Before I know what's happening, our lips meet and we kiss like our lives depend on it. I find tears welling up in my eyes, too, so I keep them closed so they don't sneak out. He's the one who pulls away.

"I'm sorry," he says. "Was that not okay?"

"Did it feel not okay?"

"It felt very okay," he says. "It felt amazing."

"Agreed," I say.

"Should we talk about this?" he asks.

"No," I say, uncharacteristically. "No talking, no thinking."

"I can get on board with that," he says, and we're pulled back together, kissing hungrily.

I feel things I don't want to feel. My mind is awash in contradictions. "I love you so freakin' much" wants to come flying out of my mouth, but thankfully my mouth is occupied, because we're just having a moment. He's afraid for his mom, and he trusts me, and this is just a moment. At least that's what I tell myself.

But Ryan's touch feels like home. I imagine that's what I feel like to him, too. We're lost in each other yet somehow found. So even if this is all it is, a moment, one night . . . it feels right.

Before we know it, it's five a.m. and Ryan has to get ready for his—formerly our—show. He's skipping the last hour of on-air to take Lily to the doctor. I think he should take the whole morning off, but he wants to keep busy, and I can understand that, too. I gather my things and pull him to me for a goodbye hug.

"I'm gonna get out of your hair so you can get ready," I say. "But call me whenever you want, and definitely call me as soon as you hear anything about your mom."

"Okay," he says. "I will. And . . . thanks."

"Of course," I say, without looking at him.

I pass a black cat when I'm walking back to my car. I skirt it to avoid giving it any opportunity to cross my path and breathe a sigh of relief. Lily doesn't need a black cat right now, even if I'm not entirely sure that bad luck is transferable.

I pull out my cellphone and see four missed calls from Brendan. I quickly dial his number, but I get his voicemail.

"It's me," I say. "Sorry I missed your calls. My ringer was off and Nat . . . was just having a really bad night. Her favorite chef has been stealing, and she's very upset, and it's really odd because he steals things like Gouda cheese and . . . I don't know . . . bread—anyway, so she was upset." At this point I realize I'm rambling, and I speed up my speech to record speed. "So, yeah, just call me whenever and we'll talk. Okay, bye."

The guilt.

The guilt!

Should I feel guilty?

I check myself out in my rearview mirror, and wow—my hair looks like it could turn you to stone. Lovely. This is what Ryan was looking at. Medusa on steroids. I shake off my morning humiliation and pull away from the curb. As soon as I do, that idiot black cat runs in front of my car and shoots me a look that says, "That's right, bitch—I'm crossing your path, and there's nothing you can do about it." When technically, yes, there is something I could do. I could run the damn thing over in hopes that a deceased black cat can no longer ooze bad luck, but then I'll have the whole karma thing to deal with, and of course I would never run over a cat, so this is all a moot point except for the fact that this cat has just totally ruined my morning.

Three yellow lights in a row aren't making a strong case for the rest of the day. I've said it before and I'll say it again. Too many yellow lights are a warning sign. Something bad is brewing. It's when I near my fourth yellow light that it hits me: These are all warning signs. Here I have this nice guy who gets me and relates to me, and I lie to him and jump the second my ex calls. Maybe these signs are saying I just made a mistake. Maybe they're saying I should stay away from Ryan. Maybe I'm being pulled over by a fucking cop right now.

Fuck.

"License and registration, please," he says as I roll down my window and smile.

"Certainly, Officer," I say as sweetly as I can muster. "But may I ask why I was pulled over?"

"You ran a red," he says.

"It was yellow," I counter. "I mean, it was really yellow. It was the fourth one I've passed in five minutes, so I think I know what yellow looks like."

"If you think that was a yellow light, you've just admitted to running four red lights in a row."

"Yellow," I say. "They were all yellow."

I'm starting to miss Officer Ma'am. At least he doesn't give me tickets. Now this guy's gone back to his car to run my license or call his mom or eat a doughnut—whatever the hell they do when they walk away with your stuff.

"I don't suppose you'll let me off with a warning?" I call out to him, but he ignores me.

Damn it.

I pull out my cellphone and listen to the rest of my missed messages. There are two from Bill; both say it's urgent that I call him. At first, I think he knows about Ryan's mom and he's gonna use this as an angle to make me feel sorry for him and do the morning show again, but that ship has sailed, and when I think a little more clearheadedly I realize that of course Bill doesn't know about Ryan's mom. Nobody knows about Ryan's mom except for Ryan. And me.

I think about Ryan and text him:

Just got pulled over for running a red light. It was YELLOW, I swear. Anyway, since you yelled at me for running them last night, I thought you'd enjoy my karmic ass-biting.

A minute later he texts back:

Please drive safely! What did I tell you about making me worry?

I text him immediately:

A little pity here? I'm getting a ticket!

He responds:

Sorry. No pity here. Drive safely and I'll pity you for other reasons. Already do. HA!

Well, at least he's obviously feeling better. A little Berry boning works wonders on the emotionally fragile, I guess. I respond:

Glad to see you have your sense of humor this morning. I'll just be here GETTING THIS TICKET! SOB!

When Officer Red Light Liar returns, we share very little small talk. He hands me the ticket and tells me that unless it is unsafe to stop, I should probably slow down and try to stop whenever I see yellow lights.

"Mainly because it would appear that you're color-blind," he says.

Oh, he's a joker now? Fulfilling his ticket quota puts him in a good mood?

"The light was yellow," I say.

"Have a nice day, ma'am."

Just when I thought I was at least getting away without a "ma'am," he hits me. There needs to be an equivalent comeback to "ma'am." But what would it be? All that comes to mind is "saggy balls," and that's hardly appropriate, since "ma'am," for all of its faults, is a pseudo-attempt toward politeness. Even though to me it's just the equivalent of a Southerner saying "Bless your heart" when what they really mean is "Fuck you."

After a quick shower I change to go to the station—I don't really have to be there for a few more hours to prep for my show, but the truth is I want to be there just in case Ryan gets upset while he's on the air or after and he needs me. When I pull into my parking spot, it's oddly missing my nameplate.

Okay, that's very strange. And very worrisome. Bill can't be that upset about my quitting the show. Could he?

There's a sinking feeling settling in my stomach, and it doesn't improve when I walk up to the elevator. Jed and Daryl are carrying packed crates out of the building. *Oh my God,* I think to myself. They finally crossed a line and got fired.

"This is bullshit," Daryl says.

"Guys, what happened?"

They look at each other. Jed responds, "What do you care? You never liked us. The way you just up and quit things . . . You don't even like your job."

"Hold it," I say. "I quit the talk job. And I understand you're emotional right now, so I won't take that personally, but I do care about my job. That's why I worked my ass off to get this job, and that is the job I still care about."

"Yeah, you seem all broken up," Daryl says, and pushes past me.

"Is that a breakup pun?" I ask Jed.

"Whatever," Jed says. "I'm sure you'll be back on your morning show in no time."

"No, I won't."

"Well, good luck. Whatever you do."

"Thanks," I say, mildly confused. "But seriously, what happened?"

Daryl looks at me with what almost seems like a touch of actual empathy and shakes his head.

"You'll see, Berry."

I don't recognize anything when the elevator door opens. *Shit.* I'm so frazzled I got off on the wrong floor.

Wait. I am on the right floor. What the hell's going on?

It's like I left for college and returned home to find my childhood bedroom was rented out to Jeff Foxworthy. The hall posters that once featured the Doors and the Stones and Jimi Hendrix and Led Zeppelin have been replaced with Toby Keith and Tim McGraw and Kenny Chesney and Brad Paisley. *This can't be good.* The sinking feeling in my stomach has turned into the *Titanic.*

There are people I don't recognize and cowboy hats everywhere. It's like a nightmare in which I wake up and tell people, "I had the weirdest dream! I walked into work Monday morning and our station had turned into a country music station!" It's baffling. Are we having a party? And who are these people scurrying about like they work here?

∪

"There you are." I turn to see where the voice is coming from and find Bill . . . wearing a cowboy hat. Sadly, he's one of the few people whose looks are markedly improved by one. "Uh," I say, trying to sound calm, but I am so not calm. "Bill, I didn't get the memo. Is it dress-up day? Are we having a hoedown? What's going on?"

"I called you twice, Berry," he says. "Most people didn't even get the courtesy call."

"Huh?" is all I can muster. I still don't know for certain, but I'm suddenly getting quick flashes of my recent past, like in the *Lost* finale. Daryl and Jed walking out with their things, people staring at me ominously as I pushed the button for the elevator, the sawdust, the new framed posters, swapped out like the old ones were never there.

Oh.

My.

God.

It's not a joke.

We've gone country.

The station format has changed. We're now . . .

"L.A.'s new home for new country, baby!" Bill says as he tips his hat for effect. "Yeehaw!"

I swallow back my panic.

"What does this mean?" I ask as calmly as I can muster. "I mean . . . I know what it means, but . . . is there still a rock show on weeknights from seven to midnight, or am I out of a job?"

"There's no rock show, Berry."

"No rock show," I repeat. "So I have no job."

Bill switches his "yeehaw" face to an "I guess I need to actually show some sensitivity now" face.

"I'm sorry, Berry."

"But you're staying? You still have a job?"

"I love country."

"Since when?"

Bill looks at his watch. "Since about five hours ago."

I can't help but smile a little, even as I feel the weight of unemployment pressing on my shoulders. "Right," I say. "Well. I guess . . . I guess I'll go clean out my office."

"Berry, hold on," he says. "Actually, there is one thing I can offer you." He's looking sideways, upward, around, behind, and pretty much anywhere that's not my eyes.

"What is it?"

"You might consider it a lateral move. . . ."

"Lateral?"

"You can take overnights," he says.

"Graveyard," I say as I try to wrap my head around the notion that he is suggesting this with a straight face.

"Yes," he answers. He's serious.

"Bill, lateral, by definition, means sideways: one way or the other. But overnights? That's not lateral. That's a definitive step backward. You do graveyard when you're starting out . . . paying your dues . . . desperate for anything."

"I know."

"Well, I'm not starting out," I say. "And I've paid my dues."

"So I guess the question becomes: Are you desperate for anything? Because I'm offering you this time slot to be nice. But there are about fifty eager DJs who would jump at that offer."

"I'm sure there are," I say knowingly.

"You have until eleven p.m. tonight," he says. "If you take the job, you start now. But you'll be limited to a specific playlist that features only two kinds of music: country and western. Think about it."

"Okay," I say, but the word gets caught in my throat and I choke on my own saliva. I start to cough, but I wave him away to say "I'm fine. Thanks for the offer. I'll think about it."

"Good luck, Berry," he says. I don't say anything back. *Good luck?* A confusing night with my ex. A ticket on my way to work—where, as it turns out, I no longer work. No, this is not what I'd call "good luck."

Don't worry about the world coming to an end today. It is already tomorrow in Australia.

—CHARLES M. SCHULZ

Chapter Twenty-two

When things go wrong, you tend to think, *What have I done to deserve this?* At least you do if you're me. You'll track back your every move, retrace every last step to find the wrong turn. Surely I can't be being punished by the universe for being there for Ryan—even if he was a boyfriend, and even if he was the last in my bad-luck trio, and even if I lied to my current beau in an effort not to hurt his feelings. It was nothing. I know that Ryan and I aren't right for each other. Even if we did accidentally hook up.

Right?

Is Ryan such bad luck that my minor backslide changed the format of the entire radio station? If I come clean to Brendan, will that make things go back to normal? If the luck I've created by being with Ryan is X (or R) and I do Y (tell Brendan the truth), then Z (Will I negate the bad luck and reverse the negative effects of it?). Maybe? If nothing else, it will make me feel like less of a liar, so I decide that's what I'll do.

I call Brendan and ask if he'll meet me.

"Absofuckinlutely," he says. "Are you at the station getting ready for your show?"

"Not exactly," I say.

"What do you mean?"

"There's been a . . . disaster," I say.

"Are you okay?" he asks.

"I'm fine," I say. "Well, I'm physically fine."

"Where are you?" he asks.

"I'm driving," I say. "And I need to be careful, because I got a ticket this morning. So can you meet me?"

"Um . . ."

"Um . . . ?" I question. "What happened to absofuckinlutely?"

He sighs. I'm starting to wonder if he somehow already knows I spent the night with Ryan.

"Fine. I'll meet you wherever. Just say where."

"Coffee Bean?" I suggest.

"See you there."

He hangs up without saying goodbye, which is odd, but I convince myself it's my own guilty conscience that's making me question every breath he takes.

I pull up to The Coffee Bean on Sunset Boulevard, and he's there when I arrive.

"Hey," he says, and puts one arm around me to give me a half-hug.

"Hey," I say, overthinking the half-hug. But as weird as he was on the phone . . .

Once we get our iced, whipped, caffeinated calorie injections, we sit together at a table outside. I look around us, and everything I see looks like a flashing neon bad sign. The girl sitting across from me is wearing a football jersey with the number twenty-two on it. I hate the number twenty-two. Always a bad sign. Three guys to the left of us are smoking cigars. There's a girl with a small poodle with dyed pink hair. *Really, lady? You need to be punched in the baby-maker.*

"So is everything okay?" I ask, mostly because I just need reassurance.

"No," he says. "Not according to you. There's been a disaster. So what happened?"

"The station's gone country," I say. "Country!"

"Seriously?"

"Yes."

"And your show?"

"My show is no longer."

"Seriously?"

"Seriously," I say. "So you can see why I'm freaking out."

"So you have no show at all?"

"Well . . ." I get confused and frustrated just thinking about it. "I don't know. I mean, my show, my rock show . . . doesn't exist."

"How come?" he asks, still not getting it.

"Because despite the fact that my ex-boss is likely blaring the Osmonds' creepy anthem at this very moment, there is not even a little bit of rock and roll in this now-country station."

"That sucks."

"Yes, it does. So if I still want a job, I can have overnights. Playing country."

"That really sucks."

"Yes, it does."

We know it sucks. It obviously sucks. But where's my hug? Where's my "it'll be okay"? This is awkward and not in the least bit comforting. Everything just feels off. And I didn't think it could feel any worse, yet here we are.

"So country, huh?"

"Can you believe it?" I say. "I mean, don't get me wrong. I like some of the old stuff. Johnny Cash? Patsy Cline? Love it. But day in, day out country? Who can take all that whining?"

"I hear ya," he says as he takes a sip of his drink and looks around. "Will you try to get another job at another station?"

"I don't know." I find myself tapping my foot nervously, trying to psych myself up for my confession. "Also, I wanted to tell you that I went to Ryan's last night."

"Ryan's? Thought you two were at odds."

"We were. But he was having a crisis. And he needed a friend. And I lied to you when I said I was going to Natalie's. And I'm sorry."

"You're allowed to have friends," he says.

"I know. But I'm sorry for lying. And I can't help but think that maybe that was the first thing that caused this . . . this awful chain reaction. Do you think that's possible?" Telling him I saw Ryan is one thing. Telling him we slept together is another. I'm not going there. And honestly, it doesn't even seem like he'd care all that much. Maybe he's having a bad day, but this is not the sweet, supportive "boyfriend" one needs in times like this. Granted, I may not karmically deserve that boyfriend today, but he's not even a semi-reasonable facsimile.

"No."

"No?" I prod. "Just no?"

Brendan stretches and stares up at the sun. When he turns back to me, his expression is unreadable. "Honestly, Berry, I don't buy into all of your superstitious stuff as much as I might have led you to believe."

"Oh," I say, a bit taken aback. "Well . . . what does that mean exactly?"

"It means I thought it was cute that you had all those quirks at first, but I really didn't think you believed *all* of it. I know I humor you, but the truth is that I can't take that stuff seriously. Frankly, I find it hard to believe that someone as together as you puts so much faith in that garbage."

"You were the one who pointed out the lucky penny," I say, shocked, embarrassed, and pretty much mortified. But it just gets worse.

"I didn't know I was poking the bear, though. It was just innocent flirting with the cute DJ I recognized. I was taking the opportunity to talk to you while your man went to the bathroom."

"Wait—you already knew who I was?" This is getting worse by the minute.

"Dude, you're on billboards."

"Sorry, dude. I didn't think you'd pretend not to know me."

"No harm no foul, right?"

No harm no foul? Yes, harm! Yes, foul, in fact! I find it hard to believe this is happening. Can he be that much of an asshole? I may have put a little extra faith in making him what I needed to believe he was, but I didn't make up all of it. He is here, sitting before me, clover tattoo mocking me from his wrist.

"You have a lucky-clover tattoo."

"I'm Irish," he says. "Not stupid."

"I have no comeback to that," I say. "Except ouch."

I let this settle for a second. Wow, did he run a game on me. This is not the quasi-perfect, tailor-made-for-me guy I thought I knew. This is a world-class lying, using asshole.

"Sorry," he says. "Look, if nobody in your life cares enough about you to tell you, then at least let me be the one. All your superstitions, it's all a load of crap. You liked me because I wasn't the 'third guy' in some made-up string of bad-luck dudes when you clearly weren't even looking hard enough to see that I was really just trying to have a good time and maybe get my band on the radio in the deal."

"If you're finished," I say, getting up, "I'm just gonna go."

"I know it must feel bad," he says.

"How does being a smug jackass feel?"

"Liberating," he says.

U

Tears form in my eyes as soon as I'm back in the car and dialing my dad's number. Funny how when you know you're calling someone safe you get even more emotional.

"There's my lucky girl," he says. "Just the one I wanted to talk to. You must be psychic."

"Psychotic," I correct. "That would be the term. Stupidly psychotic and superstitious."

"Never," he says. "Listen, baby. Can I borrow four hundred bucks? Just for the next week . . ."

"Really, Dad?" I say, defeated. And then I just start crying.

"Aw, come on, cookie?" he says. "I'll pay it back. Really. I promise."

"Man, am I ever stupid," I say. "Why did I think turning to you was the way to go? Because I'm stupid, apparently."

"Whoa, hang on, sweetie," my dad says. "What's wrong?"

"I just feel stupid. The guy I was dating is a complete asshole who was only using me, and I was so blinded by wanting him to be the one—simply by virtue of the fact that he wasn't Ryan—that I didn't see it."

"Well, screw that guy," he says. "At least you found out now."

"Only because my show was canceled so he felt the freedom to be a complete asshole."

"Your show was canceled? Oh, honey, I'm sorry."

"Yeah," I say. "Me, too."

"Sweetie, I really am sorry. You'll land on your feet, though. And I just . . . well . . . I'm sorry, but I really need that four hundred dollars."

The guttural "ugh" that I emit is like something I've been holding in since before I was able to form words. But this time, there's nothing after it. Only emptiness. No offer to drop everything and drive across the desert to pick him up and carry him home.

U

In times of crisis, people turn to safe harbors, and having pretty much exhausted mine, I'm driven to do something wild. Something I haven't done in more than four years.

Go see my brother.

Yes, my older brother, Peter Lambert, is what you might call estranged, but I don't think of him that way, not in the classical sense. It's sadder and simpler than a dark divide, in our case. I don't call him. He doesn't call me. Our parents—the one thing we have in common—don't connect us. Peter's thirteen years older (mind you, I was no mistake, my mom always assured me—just a late blessing), so maybe it's the age difference, maybe it's because to start over now would be too uncomfortable, maybe we associate each other with exhausting times. Whatever it is, we simply avoid each other. Except now, when a little distance might help my sanity.

I take Moose to the kennel—which is more dog spa than kennel, if we're being honest, but I feel too guilty if I don't put him in a comfortable setting—and fly to Chicago three days after Peter invites me. He was overjoyed to hear from me, which would under normal circumstances send me into a spiral of second-guessing but right now just feels like the most welcome thing on earth.

Knowing only that he's a trader with a small but growing finance firm of his own, I'm not sure what to expect. I never understood that world, so in my brain and with my family background, I just carried around the popular shorthand: high-stakes gambling.

On a warm day I wander tentatively along the Chicago River, looking for his building. After a few false starts and contradictory directions from fellow travelers, I find the place. His office is high in a glass fortress that gleams in the sun. It's auspicious. As depressed as I am, you could almost say I'm feeling fortunate.

"Berry!" he says, arms outstretched, as he strides up to greet me in the lobby. I can see my father's lean face on him but my mother's big dark eyes. His thick hair is longer than I might have assumed, and it seems oddly out of place framing his clean-shaven face and topping the tall, suited figure of a man in obvious control.

"Carolyn, this is my sister, Berry."

The receptionist smiles.

"Pleased to meet you," she says. "I'd tell you I've heard all about you—but he never even mentioned that he had a sister."

"Carolyn is one of our more annoying employees, as you'll discover," Peter says. "Actually, there are many annoying people here, but she has an awful habit of saying what's on her mind and being honest. It's amazing we've found any use for her at all."

"And Peter is a great man. You're lucky to have him as a brother."

"On second thought, we're doubling your salary," he says. The phone rings, ending what I'm certain would have gone on all afternoon. The place is already making me a little happier.

"Come with me. We'll do a walking lunch."

Peter takes me to the kitchen—which is far nicer than mine, with its stainless-steel everything and mounds of fresh fruit and snacks on tables along the walls. He opens the refrigerator and says, "Banana-strawberry or kiwi-mango?"

"Uh, well, um, banana—no, kiwi."

"I should have pegged you for a berry." He hands me a fruit smoothie. Then he shoots into the hallway as though sucked out of a plane at altitude.

We move down a long open corridor, behind employees intent on their flashing screens. And it's a sea of screens. An ocean. The perfect calling for anyone with serious ADD.

"G-man, how goes the battle?" Peter asks a very young man with auburn hair and freckles who looks a little like Howdy Doody.

"Not good," says Howdy, not looking up from the garden wall of monitors arrayed in front of him but waving at them dismissively. "All day I'm short where I should be long and long where I should be short."

"Keep at it," my brother says, slapping him smartly on the shoulder. "But not too long, or you're fired." G-man looks straight ahead without smiling. I'm not even positive it was a joke.

"And am I to understand that all this madness is making you rich?"

"Rich and poor. Depends on which day you ask," he replied. "No, we're doing okay. You can't get tied up in the ebb and flow. You'll go nuts."

"I've been here about thirty minutes and I feel I'm already nuts."

Peter guides me into his office. "You started nuts, Berry," he says, pointing three fingers at me. "That's different. Seriously, growing up like we did, what we went through, you're bound to be a little cautious. I happen to think you've taken it up a notch, at least from what I hear, but it's a free country. They can't arrest you for being nuts."

"They certainly can," I shoot back. I had that one on good authority. The timing is off sometimes, but they catch up with nuts every day and take them out of circulation.

"Not our kind of nuts."

"From what I hear." *Our kind of nuts.* The implication that he has a dossier on me is a little unsettling. "Peter, respectfully, how the hell do you know anything about me? And what do you know?"

"Only what Mom tells me."

"You talk to Mom?"

"Not enough. But, yeah, a few times a year. It's hard."

He pauses, and for the first time, the charging bull is a little nonplussed.

"What do you talk about?" I ask.

"Things. Her. The dimwit." He winds his finger round and round in a circle, then points. "But a lot of times, we talk about you. Because she's concerned, all the time. She wants happiness for you."

"I'm happy. Usually. Sometimes. It's been a tough few weeks."

"She told me some things that I could have guessed."

"Guessed what? What did she tell you?"

He cocks his head to one side like a bird does when it's sizing you up. "I want to show you something."

He crosses the floor of the sparse but fairly large office to a filing cabinet. With effort, he dislodges the lowest drawer and hoists it onto a round table.

"Okay, what do you want first? Let's do key chains."

From a plastic quart container, he pours out a mound of key chains that would be the envy of any valet.

"NASA. Notre Dame. Seattle Space Needle. Waffle World. Yellowstone Park."

"Quite a collection," I say.

"Not a collection," he corrects. "Protection."

Then he pulls out a plastic container of coins and shakes it.

"I won't pour these out. Too much of a mess."

"What is it?"

"Every coin I ever found. Every one lucky. Time was I'd nearly kill myself retrieving them. I was hit by a train once going after a penny."

"Oh, God," I say, thinking that was really a lucky penny.

"It was a kiddie train at the mall," he says. "I was fine, but the conductor had security escort me out."

Peter takes out four more containers, each brimming with odds and ends that I recognize all too well by type and kind. Rabbits' feet, shiny charms, amulets—the stuff of our superstitions—my dream treasure chest. I'm fascinated.

"What's this one?" I ask, peering into a box of sticks.

"Lucky sticks," he says. Believe it or not, that's one I've never contemplated. Secretly, I'm wondering how much he'll take for the whole lot. But he slams the drawer back into place. "What did you see?"

"Well," I say, wondering what he wants me to say, because I suddenly want a closer relationship with this person and fear I might blow it if I answer honestly, "I think you're being careful. I know. I'm careful, too."

"Careful," he says. "Let me ask you: Did you ever fall and hurt yourself?"

"Maybe when I was little," I reply, without any clue where he's going with this. "But not for a long time."

"Well, you should. I wish you would."

"Thanks, Pete. And I hope your hair falls out."

"Berry, all that trash I just showed you was an obsession. It took me years to figure out it didn't matter. I used to rub a lucky alligator I had in my pocket before I'd make a trade, and I couldn't buy or sell anything that had the letters X and T next to each other in the symbol, and if anyone walked behind me while I was executing the trade, I knew it was going to be a loser, so I stole some velvet ropes from a nightclub and made people walk around the long way."

"But it worked. Look at you now."

"Actually, one day my boss tripped over the ropes and chipped a tooth on my cubicle wall, and I got fired."

"Oh. But see, he walked behind you. You were right."

Peter walks to the window. The sky is pure blue, and against the backdrop, he looks like a comic-book superhero standing tall, fists clenched.

"I was a wreck. I couldn't function. Finally I started swimming long distances. I did it in the ocean. I'd go right to the edge of the current and come back. I did extreme helicopter skiing. I rock-climbed without ropes. I walked right up to the prettiest woman I'd ever seen and told her I didn't like her dress, but it didn't matter, because she still made it look beautiful."

"And?"

"And she half smiled at me, turned back to her friends, and I never saw her again."

The story would have been better if he'd married her, but I was still enjoying the ride. And at least it meant he wasn't bullshitting me. Which right now I could not abide.

"Berry, we're both equal and opposite reactions to the same force. You run from risk. I run to it, make love to it, and stick by it even when I learn it's found somebody else and has cleaned out all my bank accounts."

Peter's phone chirps, and he presses a few buttons.

"Oh, shit. Oh, well," he says, then looks back at me and resumes his cheery tone. "We're two extremes, you and me. Neither is probably appropriate all the time, but I'm thinking my side of it is more fun. Anyway, you don't have to be like me. Maybe just a little more like me."

He waves me over to stand beside him in front of an enormous computer monitor. "Here," he says, pointing to a chart that rises and falls, falls some more, and then rises again. "I'm about to place a bet on this stock. Our software is giving me a few scenarios, and I honestly don't know which way I think it's going. So you look at this list of eight trades, and you pick one."

"Pick one?"

"Just one. Tell me which one you think will work best."

"How am I supposed to know?"

"That's just it. You don't know. You can't know. According to our trading software—which is very sophisticated, by the way—they have approximately the same probability of success."

"How do you know which one to choose?"

"You don't. That would destroy the whole system. But do it quickly, because in about five more seconds, everything changes, and the deal probably goes away."

"Oh, God, oh . . . then . . . number five."

"Five it is," he says, and he clicks a line on the screen, then punches a button before tapping his chin and spinning back to face me.

"So now we wait," I say, still looking at the screen.

"It won't take long," he replies.

"For what?"

"For us to know which way the wind blows, and whether we do a Dorothy and get swept away to Oz."

"And that number, that 547, that's the five hundred forty-seven dollars. So what's the worst—"

"Those are in thousands."

"But it says five—whoa. You mean five hundred thousand?"

"Yeppity."

Yeppity. I don't even know what that means. In this moment, I'm too much in shock to understand whether this is more of my brother's argot and a positive or somehow a negative that I'm just not getting. It can't be five hundred thousand. Even a novice, non-investor type like me recognizes that the prospect of losing five hundred thousand dollars is completely and utterly terrifying.

"But you have some sort of protection, right? You didn't gamble the whole amount?"

"Correct," he says. "We are hedged up to our ass—armpits, sorry. So let's see."

Under the sleek, soft caramel of his desk hutch, between stacks of paper and reports piled neatly if innumerably around him, smaller screens flash like a checkerboard of heart monitors. And in my imagination, we are watching heart monitors. Six, eight, maybe sixteen patients all lying there, counting on him and his people to keep them from dropping into cardiac arrest at any moment. Maybe all at the same moment.

My brother bites his upper lip and exhales. He taps his mouse with his middle finger, waiting for something.

Waiting. Waiting.

"All right," he says, clicking the mouse emphatically and then turning to me with a smile that opens into a laugh. "See? That wasn't so hard. You did fantastic!"

"We won?" I look at the screens, but I can't even tell which one he's been working on, let alone what happened. "I mean, it's over? It worked?"

"Well, it always works, in a sense. We lost sixty thousand dollars."

The deed to my condo passes before my eyes. I've ruined my brother. Let's see, my charm collection, value two hundred fifty dollars or so (the amethyst monkey paw alone cost me two hundred dollars). And my car must have some equity; I've been paying off the damn thing for something like five years. Maybe my Cabbage Patch collection? I think that's still in Mom's attic.

I choke back tears. "My God, Peter, I'm so sorry."

He stands swiftly, takes my hands in his. "No, no, no, no. Berry, it's fine. Don't worry about it. By the time I walk out on the floor, we'll have made it back. Or lost ten times as much. It's the work we do. You take your best shot, consider every option, try to increase your odds, mix a million bits of news with . . . I don't know, instinct, experience, feeling, not luck, but not always a perfect, foolproof plan. If every plan were foolproof, we'd have fewer fools in charge of everything."

My heart feels like it's returned to its proper place in my chest. I sigh, smile up at him, and see something I hadn't before: a scar on his forehead, slightly curved, arcing away from his left eye.

"Peter, this is going to sound a little out of bounds, but . . . what happened to your forehead there?"

"The scar?" He touches it and looks to the side. "I hit a tree skiing. Never did find out why they let that tree get on skis."

"How many times have you told that one?"

"Few hundred."

"But you could have been killed."

"I was lucky. Always have been, even when I wasn't."

I stare at him. "What's that even mean?"

"I've got a meeting, Berry," he says. "But let's have dinner tonight. We'll solve the world's problems."

I walk to the elevator with him and say goodbye for now. He walks away confidently, and already I feel better about the Lambert genes I'm wearing.

Life is the art of drawing without an eraser.

—JOHN W. GARDNER

Chapter Twenty-three

Standing at the airport newsstand with a four-dollar bottle of Smartwater in my hand. (I know—how "smart" is it to pay four dollars for water? It's ridiculous. But it's my favorite brand, and they gouge you at the airport regardless. If it's good enough for Jennifer Aniston—then again, her taste in things, certainly men, may be questionable. Looks aside, I mean. Who'd turn down any of the guys she's dated? Certainly not me.) I'm debating between *Us Weekly* and *Star* to thumb through on my trip home when I feel a buzz in my handbag. I pull the phone out and see that it's Ryan calling.

"Hey," I say. "How are you?"

"I'm okay," he says. "I'm good. My mom's test came back, and it's benign. She's fine."

"That's so great," I say, hugely relieved.

"Yeah, I knew you'd want to know immediately, and I feel like a total baby for having you come over that night."

"Please," I say. "I'd be there . . . always . . ."

"Yeah," he says, and I detect a sadness in his voice and a distance between us once again. Any closeness that we regained that night has disappeared in the light of a new day and a clean bill of health. "Anyway, Ber, I'm sorry, we're coming back from commercial— I gotta run. But I wanted to let you know and say thanks again."

"I'm really happy for you, Ryan. That's great news."

"Take care, Berry," he says, and although he hangs up, I find my-self holding the phone to my ear for an extra moment, wishing he was still on the other end.

◡

"With all due respect," Natalie says, "your dad's a loser."

"I know," I say, now back on familiar ground, back across from Natalie, who now sounds different to me, though she hasn't changed at all.

"So you basing your entire belief system on his messed-up shit is . . ."

"I know . . . I get it."

"Loserish," she continues.

"Enough with the name-calling."

"The point is, you're better than that. You're better than him."

Even though I know she's right, I find myself feeling protective of my dad. As angry as I am . . . as much as he lets me down . . . he's still my dad. The only one I have. I'm not about to bring up her dad's porn habit, but come on . . . it's not like her dad's Captain Perfect, either. Still, she's right. I've based so much of my life on being afraid. What's worse . . . all of my fears have been based on completely unfounded, silly, made-up hypotheticals. An existence based on fear of "what ifs."

"He has his demons," I admit. "But you're right. I need to distance myself from his way of thinking."

Natalie exhales a gigantic breath. "I gotta admit, I never thought I'd see the day. I'm proud of you."

"Okay, come on."

"I'm serious, Ber," she says. "You've been like an emotional cripple."

"That's a little extreme."

"I was putting it nicely."

"Thank you?"

"Look," she goes on. "This is good. This is growth. The first step is admitting you have a problem. Isn't that what they say?"

"If I was an alcoholic," I say.

"You're a something-ic."

"I'm something ick?"

"You know what I meant."

"Yeah, yeah."

"This is big," she says, with an encouraging smile. "I sense a change in you. A real one."

"Yeah, so now what?" I ask.

"Now you be opposite Berry."

"Bizarro Berry," I offer.

"Yes."

"I don't even know what that means," I say.

"It means take charge. Do things you're afraid of. Take your life back."

"Yeah, I don't need to do a bunch of shit that's just tempting fate."

"You're not tempting fate," she says. "You're trusting yourself. You're not living in fear."

Her words are taking root. A self-confident, self-reliant me? I can almost picture it.

"That would be nice," I admit.

"What's your biggest fear?" Nat asks.

"That's kind of a heavy question. You mean my biggest fear based on superstition, or . . ."

"Whatever—just your biggest fear."

"What's your biggest fear?" I ask her, eager to get out from under the microscope.

"Easy," she says. "I fear that I will one day be hospitalized and unable to use my arms, or worse, in a coma and nobody will be there to pluck hairs out of my face."

"Oh, I know," I say. "I'm in the mirror, tweezing my freakin' eyebrows like every single morning."

"No," she says with a grave look as she grabs my arm. "This goes beyond eyebrows. I grow hair in my mustache area like a wildebeest. And on my chin I have about seven hairs that require plucking at various times."

"I had no idea."

"It's an albatross," she goes on. "When I was young I was afraid of heights . . . and spiders . . . and my parents dying. Now I would eat a tarantula on top of the Empire State Building while my parents swan-dive off the deck in exchange for no facial hair."

"That's not true," I say.

"It would be a toss-up," she says.

"Look, let's not talk about tarantulas and swan dives."

"If I'm ever in a coma, will you pluck the hair from my face?"

"Yes," I say.

"Every day?"

"If you require it, yes."

"I require it!" she says vehemently.

"Then I will."

"Can I get that in writing?" Nat asks, completely serious. "I mean, at some point this was going to need to come up, like a living will or something. I need to know that I can count on you."

"Wow, did we just switch bodies?" I tease. "I thought I was the crazy one."

"You're the superstitious one. I am an ape descendant—the missing link. One is a mental case—I mean a choice—the other is an unfortunate existence."

"Got it," I say. "And calling me a mental case? Not gonna bode well when you're in a coma."

"Don't go there," she says.

"I'm just sayin' . . . do me wrong and you could wake up with a goatee."

"I will cut you."

Nat's right. It's time for me to take my life back. But back from when? I've been this way since I was born. Now I have to start over? Learn to not be afraid? Not think I'm jinxing myself if I do this, that, or the other thing? I don't even know what a life like that looks like.

We make a list of my fears and basically create tasks that will force me to face them. I start sweating at the thought of it, but Nat calms me down and assures me that nothing bad will happen. And that once I start and see that the sun still rises and sets, it will be freeing.

"We're gonna test this right now," Natalie says triumphantly.

"How so?"

"Go get an umbrella," she says.

"Don't be stupid."

"I'm serious," she says.

"You're going to make me open an umbrella in my house?"

"Yes."

"No."

"You have to," she says.

"Come on, Nat," I whine, even though I know she's right about me getting past this stuff. But it's still terrifying.

She ignores my whine and goes on. "You have to do an about-face, Berry. Open an umbrella indoors, break a mirror, adopt a black cat, and see that nothing bad will happen, and if it does, realize that it has nothing to do with the cat or the umbrella or the mirror."

"I'm a dog person," I say. "And besides, I don't think Moose would appreciate sharing his space with a cat."

"Go get an umbrella," she repeats.

I sigh as I get up and walk to my closet. I know this is supposed to be a meaningful ritual. I know I have to take these steps. But I'm not a hundred percent ready to do this. Hell, I'm not fifty percent ready.

I take the umbrella out of my closet and walk over to Natalie. I know I can't think about it for another second or it'll never happen. I'll just stay locked in my patterns.

So I just open it. And . . . it feels good. I feel relieved.

"Ta-da," I say, twirling the umbrella.

"And look," she says. "The sky isn't falling."

"It's not like every bad reaction happens immediately."

"Bad shit is gonna happen," she says. "Whether you open umbrellas indoors or not."

"I know."

"But it's not gonna happen because you opened the umbrella indoors."

"Says you," I tease.

"Well, we're testing the theory."

◡

One week and three tests with Natalie later, nothing bad has happened. In fact, I get a job offer at another station without getting a manicure in my lucky color. I'm still wearing my horseshoe necklace because . . . some things are sacred, but all in all, I feel liberated. It's a process, damn it. They don't make heroin addicts go cold turkey. It could kill them. Or something like that. I don't know, it's been a while since I tuned in to *Dr. Drew.*

I don't want to complain, because I know compared to most I've lived a very fortunate life. I have two parents who love me, a brother who's now back in my life, and a roof over my head. I was raised in a loving household. For all of my dad's issues, he cared for me. There was no abuse, and my parents did love each other the best they knew how. I had a good childhood. I was loved and nurtured. I was safe. I was protected.

But beyond all of my safety precautions was a cage. An impenetrable wall that was, yes, meant to keep me safe from harm but also keep me safe from life experience. I wasn't taught to trust, I was taught to be on guard—always. From the most benign to the most intrinsic life experiences, all would come with consequence if *A* plus *B* didn't equal *C.* If I did this wrong thing, said this wrong phrase, knocked on wood this many times instead of that many times . . . something would break, someone would leave, someone would die.

◡

Being with my brother somehow put everything in perspective, brought it all home, and when I think about it, it all comes down to one moment—the root of it all—the thing that made me believe if I didn't do some random thing, nothing would work out right. A silly little girl, watching my mother pack up our suitcases in Vegas as I cried and begged her to stay so we could be a family, I betrayed my father's habit of tapping the door frame twice whenever leaving a room for good. We were leaving, but my hands were occupied and my mom was upset and I wanted to touch the wall to make things right. I thought if I could touch the wall like my dad taught me then we'd turn around and check back in, that my mom and dad would make up, that we'd stay a family intact.

But I didn't tap the door frame. And my parents barely spoke from that day on. And I never stopped wondering if things would be different had I done that. If I had just tapped that wall two times. Was that superstition? Obsessive-compulsion? Maybe a combination of both, so deeply ingrained into my psyche from my father and his frightened way of life that while safe from harm, I lived a life that was entirely too safe.

There were no carefree moments; there was no living on the edge. Everything I did was calculated and measured and with the implicit understanding that for every action there is a reaction. My father may as well have been Isaac Newton, and I was his prize pupil. Except in place of physics was fear. And in place of logic was insanity.

Why did it take me so long to wake up?

∪

"Had I been more aggressive in pointing this stuff out to you," my mother says as she sips her tea, "you would have thought I was pitting you against your father."

"I know," I say.

"And I knew you'd ultimately figure it out."

"I blew it so bad with Ryan," I say.

"I don't think so, honey."

"I did. He made a mistake. He teased me for something that anyone in their right mind would find ridiculous. And I was defensive and cold and freaked out, and I blew it. . . . I totally blew it. He even sort of apologized the last time I saw him and did I say anything back? No . . ."

"Have you tried telling him any of this?"

"No," I say.

"Maybe you should."

"I don't see what difference it would make."

"That's not a very good attitude. You won't know until you try. . . ."

"Spoken like a true mom."

"Isn't that what I am?" she asks.

"Yes." I nod. "You are indeed that."

"Well, as your mom, I am responsible for at least fifty percent of your DNA. So if you've spent the first twentysomething years of your life mimicking your father, maybe you can try it my way for the next twentysomething."

U

I'm listening to Ryan's "Dr. Love" show. They do a "mailbag" segment, where a handful of emails get chosen to be read on-air. Sometimes they're genuine questions, but usually they're complaints and hate mail. There's an abundance of crazy rants, too. I'm listening to Ryan read a furious missive from someone whose girlfriend refuses to shave her armpits when I get an idea: I'll write him a thinly veiled email to gauge his feelings. It'll be up to fate whether or not it gets picked.

The following Thursday, Ryan's reading my email out loud. I'm driving in my car, and as soon as he starts, I pull over and roll my windows up. I'm clutching the steering wheel like a panicked fifteen-year-old about to take her driver's ed test, hands locked at ten and two. Or nine and three. Whatever the rules are these days. And this had better go better than that did, considering poor Mr. McElhenny had to retire after I took out two stop signs and made his airbag deploy.

Hearing my words read in his voice . . . Well, it's hot. It's just hot. Not my words per se, but his voice. God, I miss that voice. Not that I can't hear it on the radio whenever I want to, but who wants to listen to their ex on the radio with no hope of reconciling? Hearing him read my letter makes me think there's a chance. Even if he has no idea that he's reading my words. He chose my letter. They get lots of letters and choose only a few. He chose mine. That's gotta be a sign. He reads aloud:

> Dear Ryan,
> I made a mistake with my boyfriend. Actually, he made a mistake first, but I overreacted and ended things. If someone did this to you and then realized that they'd screwed up . . . that maybe they were being unreasonable and they were sorry . . . would you consider giving them a second chance? And if you would, what would it take to get you back?
> Signed,
> Screwed Up and Sorry

"Did you hear that, callers?" Ryan asks. "That was the sound of me rolling my eyes. Don't get me wrong—I don't roll my eyes because I think all women are crazy . . . I roll them because—wait, I take it back: You are all crazy. But . . . maybe that's why we love you? You need a little bit of the crazy to keep things fun. Note: I said a little. What do you think, callers?" Ryan asks, and suddenly my heart is in my throat. "I don't know. I mean, I can relate to the guy in this situation all too well. Heck, I think every man has been through this one."

Okay, so far, so . . . I don't know what to think. Does he know? Did he figure it out?

"Look, Screwed Up: Of course you're screwed up. We're all a little screwed up, some more than others. But you kicked this guy to the curb because of something minor and just now you think you overreacted? Guys get hurt, too, babe. How do you think he's been feeling all this time?"

Okay, that's all fair. Maybe he's projecting a bit? Does that mean he was really hurt by our breakup? That makes me feel wonderful and horrible, all at the same time.

"Hey, it's great you can recognize your mistake after overreacting. But maybe if you'd take the time to think things over first, you wouldn't be in the position of having to write in to someone on the radio."

Duh.

"But yeah, if you're asking me? Of course I'd give you a second chance. Because I'm only human, and so are you. People make mistakes. . . . And what separates us from monkeys is our ability to give second chances."

"Is that what separates us from monkeys?" someone from the studio peanut gallery chimes in.

"That and not flinging poop," Ryan says.

Enough with the jokes, Ryan. Back to the good stuff.

He refocuses. "As for how you can get him to take you back, that's a good question. We're not exactly used to women admitting they made a mistake, so part of me thinks I've stumbled upon a letter from a mythical being. But, hey, that makes it all the more special when you do. Just talk to the guy. Do you have an inside joke or some kind of white flag you can wave? Try that. If it works, great. If he doesn't take you back, hell, pop on over to the studio. We love women who can admit they were wrong. It keeps us from having to do it. Anyway, good luck. I hope it works out."

With a little luck, we can help it out.
We can make this whole damn thing work out.

—PAUL MCCARTNEY

Chapter Twenty-four

The morning I'm set to do a walk-through at Indie 108, the station where I'm about to start my new gig, does not kick off the way you'd hope at a new job. Granted, today is just a "get acquainted" day, but I still want to put my best foot forward.

And as Murphy's Law would have it, my alarm clock doesn't go off when it's supposed to and I cut myself shaving in the shower. My ankle, right on the bone. It's the same place I always cut myself, so you'd think I'd be careful, but I'm bleeding like the shower scene from *Psycho* even though it's just a tiny cut, but it's a full-color cut, damn it, and when I step out of the shower and reach for my towel, I remember I didn't take my laundry out of the washing machine last night. *Awesome.* So I will not only have to rewash everything in order to de-mildew it, I won't have time to do it right now because I'm running late, thanks to my alarm-clock fail.

I tiptoe into my kitchen—why I'm tiptoeing, I have no idea—and commence towel drying from head to toe via . . . Brawny. Half a roll of paper towels later, I get dressed and go downstairs into my laundry room to find that not only did I not move my clothes from the washer to the dryer . . . every towel, sock, and white shirt I own is now a lovely shade of pink—my least favorite color.

I let out a guttural roar and fling garments out of the washer one by one, trying to find the asshole red piece of clothing that somehow got mixed in with my whites. Lo and behold, I find it.

Underwear.

Red underwear.

Red men's underwear.

Red men's underwear that do not even belong to me.

My blood is boiling, racing through my veins. I feel it throbbing in my head, and I half expect it to come spraying out of my poor wounded ankle like a fucking fire hydrant. *Whose red underwear are these?* sounds in my head like "No wire hangers!" as I stomp back up the stairs with my wet pink towels. I make a mental note to myself that I'll need to go to Bed Bath & Beyond—or as I call it, due to the state of my wallet every time I leave the store, Bloodbath and Beyond.

Oh, and by the way, Bed Bath & Beyond: Beyond? Really? Beyond? There is no Beyond! There's Kitchen! Beyond is Kitchen! You're Bed Bath & Kitchen! That's what you are! I don't give a crap if it's not alliterative!

Back upstairs, I get dressed and go to the beyond—ahem, the kitchen—to pour my cup of coffee. (Thank God for coffeemakers with timers.) Now, though, I'll have to take it in my travel mug due to time constraints. But when I move my favorite ceramic mug with the frog face and buggy eyes aside, I push a little too forcefully, and the next thing you know there are green shards of frog scattered all over my kitchen. It looks like Leatherface just wiped out Kermit's entire family in here.

However, I take one good thing away from this: that that was Bad Thing Number Three. I cut my leg, my laundry was ruined, and I broke my mug. Now my day can turn around. (What? Old habits die hard. Like heroin. Okay, so I have been watching a little more *Celebrity Rehab*.)

I get in my car and make a conscious decision not to listen to Ryan on my way to work. Turning our old morning show on will only depress me, and this day is turning around. But of course, running late, I end up stopped at a very long red at the very first traffic light.

Which is exactly when the universe declares:

Not so fast, Berry.

Wham! I feel a car slam into my rear bumper, rocketing me forward into my steering wheel.

Okay, "rocketing" is a bit much. But I feel it. I step out to discover some girl in a BMW who just nailed me from behind. Which is not how I'm going to describe this to Natalie, because I'll never hear the end of it.

"I'm so sorry," the bleached blonde says as we both inspect our cars for damage. My car has a minor scratch, not enough to freak out over. Her outfit, however, is. She's wearing a half-shirt, jean shorts, and what I'd guess to be six-inch heels. How does she drive with those? No wonder she hit me. She's one of those skinny-skinny girls with a comparatively oversized head. She looks like a lollipop.

"It's okay," I say. "Accidents happen."

"Ugh," she says. "I was texting. My boyfriend always tells me not to text when I'm driving, and I did and stupid me . . . Are you okay? Is your car okay?"

Bad enough that she rear-ends me because she's texting while driving—and she's dumb enough to admit it—but she gets to have a boyfriend, while I'm single and miserable?

"My car's fine," I say. "But your boyfriend's right. You shouldn't text and drive."

"I know," she says. "Bad habit."

"Dangerous one," I say. "Anyway, no point in us both getting our insurance rates raised over a scratch."

"Really?" she squeals. "You're so cool; thanks so much. I'm really sorry!"

She clops back to her car in those heels, and as I get to my car door, oddly enough, I find the door is locked. I reach for my keys, but . . . That's weird. Where did they go? They're not in my hand, and holy shit, no! I've locked my keys in my car.

"Are you kidding me?" I shout at no one in particular. I reach for my phone, and you guessed it, that's in the car, too. This is so uncool. I spin around to catch Bleach Blonde, but she's already starting to drive away. I catch her eye and wave to her, but she just idiotically waves back like we're old buddies. *Bye-bye, very nice lady who's about to get fired on her first day.*

I scream her name—okay, I don't actually know her name, so I alternately scream *Blonde Girl, Hey, Blondie,* and *Get Back Here, You Stupid Blond Lollipop,* but she's cranking techno at a volume of approximately "this one goes to eleven" and she can't hear me and she's gone.

Fuck.

If I just curl into a fetal position now, will some kind soul take pity on me, take me home, and feed me warm broth and a balanced meal, then . . . um . . . throw me into a pit and tell me to put the lotion in the basket?

Yeah. I'd better fight through this.

I walk to the corner and convince a guy to let me borrow his phone to call Triple A. And while I wait for them to show up, I think about my morning and realize that the mug breaking wasn't number three; I'd forgotten to count the alarm not going off. So essentially this has been bad thing after bad thing in no particular order.

♘

When I finally get back in my car, I have three missed calls from my dad.

I dial his number, and a stranger answers.

"Who's this?" I ask.

"This is Lenny," the voice says. "I'm a friend of your dad's."

"Is he okay?" I ask, panicked, my heart speeding up to DefCon 5 mode.

"Your dad got arrested. He gave me his phone and told me to call you. He needs bail money."

"Slow down—arrested for what?" I ask, my head now spinning.

"I—uh . . . he had a bench warrant for a ticket. He needs five hundred dollars."

"So . . . okay, where is he?"

"I can just meet you and you give me the money and I'll go to the bail bondsman and get him out. He doesn't want to take up too much of your time."

"It's fine," I say, thinking at this point I should now call Indie 108 and ask if I can do my walk-through tomorrow. I got rear-ended, for Pete's sake. I have . . . Well, there's a scratch on the bumper. Maybe they'll understand. "Look, um . . . Lenny, right? Where's my dad?"

"I'll just meet you," he says again.

"What jail is my father in?" I ask, and I hear rustling.

"I don't know," he says.

That doesn't sound right.

"Lenny, how are you going to bail him out of jail if you don't know what jail he's in?"

"I have it written down on a piece of paper somewhere."

"Then get the paper and give me the info," I say, losing my patience.

Silence.

"Hello?" I notice the call was dropped. I call back, but the guy just lets it ring through to voicemail.

So someone's trying to put one over on me, and it sure as hell appears to be my dad. Really bad day to try that. *Think I'm that dumb, Dad? Really? Let's test it out.* I drive to a pay phone and call my dad's cell . . . and, yep, my father answers.

"Dad?"

He says nothing for a few seconds. It worked. He didn't expect it to be me calling, because my cellphone number would have shown up.

I've never been more disappointed to be right.

"Hi, baby," he says, trying and failing to sound natural. He knows I know.

"Did you just have your friend lie to me to get five hundred dollars?"

"Baby . . . I'm so sorry. I . . . I knew I couldn't just ask. I know how upset you were last time, and I felt like a loser."

I'm seething. He lied to me, tried to get me to give money to a stranger because I thought he was in jail?

"You felt like a loser? Really, Dad? And you thought the appearance of being in jail was somehow less loserish?"

"Cookie, I'm sorry," he says. "I really am. Look, I'm going to pay you back this time. I just need it today. I woke up at eleven-eleven. You know what that means. And when I looked in the papers I saw that there's a horse running today named Make a Wish. If that's not a sign, I don't know what is. Sweetie, you know how this works. It's golden. Everything's lined up, and that horse is gonna win. And then I'll be able to pay you back big. It's just that—"

"Dad," I interrupt. "Stop."

"Sweetie, look, I know that—"

"No. Just stop. I need to say this."

He waits. I take a deep breath.

"Dad, I love you. I love you so much. And Dad, I cannot do this. I will not do this. This ends right now. I can't keep taking care of you. It's over."

Silence. I take another deep breath and continue.

"And Dad, this stuff . . . all of it, it isn't true, this ridiculous, childish way of thinking. I've had the worst morning I've had in as long as I can remember, and it wasn't because I did something I shouldn't or I forgot to touch the wall when I left or took my lucky necklace off. You know why I've had this morning?"

"Why?"

"Because sometimes shit happens."

He doesn't say anything for a long while. And I don't say anything, either. I'm standing at a disgusting pay phone that I had to use to trap my own father into answering his phone.

And this is all a lot to take in, and it hurts in places I didn't think existed. But at the same time, on some level, it's unbelievably freeing.

He speaks first. "You're right."

Daddy, I love you, but you're not getting off that easy. Not this time. I find myself screaming into this nasty germ-encrusted phone, "The guy who can't get himself out of bed and go to a real job and has his friends call me up and scare me half to death thinking he's dead at first but then reassuring me that no, he's not dead, he's just in jail . . . which is a total lie, because he really just needs to borrow money and doesn't want to ask for it. Again. And I base everything I do on wisdom passed down from this guy?"

"I know," he says. And the words come slowly, heavily, and I can hear his throat tightening up, I can tell he's starting to cry. "You're right. You're one hundred percent right. Baby, I don't want you to be like me. Don't. Don't ever be like me. I don't know what happened to me, and I'm not gonna change. But you can."

I don't know what to say. I feel so sad for him. But there's only one thing I can say, for both of our sakes.

"Dad, I'm sorry. And I do love you. But I'm not giving you the money."

"I know, baby," he says, and he actually sounds relieved. He's really crying now, and it's breaking my heart. "I don't want you to. I want you to be better than me. Which isn't hard, I know. I love you, cookie."

"Goodbye, Dad," I say, and hang up.

In a few minutes I'll call the station and tell them I'm running late but I'm on my way. I'm not going to rearrange my life because of bad omens and bullshit reasoning.

But first I take five, lean back against my car, and feel myself calming down, getting it together. I can handle this.

That was excruciating. That was amazing.

That was the best worst thing I've ever done in my life.

The Indie 108 folks couldn't be nicer. They show me the break room and take me to the kitchen. They warn me about the bad coffee, and it's pretty much like every other radio station in the world in that they all feel like home to me.

Only one other place feels like home, come to think, and that's with Ryan. Sending that email was a chickenshit move. Ryan reading my letter, saying he'd give the girl a second chance. That's great, but would he give me one? I mean, it was nice to hear that he'd be forgiving in some hypothetical situation, but I'm not a hypothetical. This is me, and I want him back.

U

As soon as I sign my contracts and leave Indie 108, I find myself driving to KKRL.

He's still on the air. I have my phone out as I walk to the lobby. I wait to dial so my call doesn't get dropped in the elevator, but once the doors open on his floor, I hit the speed dial. I tell Randy, the board op, to patch me through but not to tell Ryan it's me. Randy, always up for some fresh drama, doesn't hesitate.

"This is Ryan. You're on the air," he says, and I take a deep breath.

"So about that letter you read with the girl asking about second chances," I say. I'm peeking into the booth, staying out of his view. For now.

"Um . . . yeah?" he replies. "I think . . . Screwed Up, right? A little while ago?"

"Right. You believe in second chances, even after some seriously obnoxious behavior?"

How can he not recognize my voice? "Well . . ." he says. "How obnoxious are we talking?"

"I'm talking really obnoxious," I say. "Like headache-inducing.

Like doubt-inspiring. Like relationship-killing. Like calling someone's baby uglier than a pug to her face. That level of obnoxious."

Is that a tiny smirk on his face? The cat's maybe out of the bag. It's hard to tell with me not yet ready to be seen. I'm still gauging his response.

"That's . . . Yeah, that's pretty obnoxious."

I go on. "Believing in the tooth fairy, but being afraid that if she leaves an even number of bills under your pillow you'll die in your sleep. That sort of thing. Do you think you know where I'm coming from?"

He doesn't yet know where I'm coming from. Or he does, but he's not sure what I'm getting at.

"Well, caller, I'm starting to get a vague idea. But I really think it depends on the person. I mean, there's obnoxious and then there's obnoxious. And Lord knows I've dealt with someone who could be like that at times."

"That's fair, but what if Queen Obnoxious wanted a second chance? And she swears she'll be less obnoxious?"

"How do I know she won't be obnoxious again? I mean, she's really good at it."

"You'd have to take her word. You have to take into consideration that this very private person is calling into a radio station to publicly grovel. That's gotta count for something."

"Well, technically . . . being a voice on the radio isn't exactly outing herself."

Oh, fine, you bastard. Want to flip it on me like that?

I tap on the window, and he nearly falls out of his chair.

"Gurrrk" is his on-air reply, which is mighty impressive from the "Doctor." But his face lights up. He smiles. God, I missed that smile.

"Ladies and gentlemen," he says, recovering impressively, motioning for me to take a seat in the guest chair. "We have here for you now, in the studio, in the flesh—well, in the flesh but wearing clothes, I assure you . . . the one and only Berry Lambert!"

I sit but keep talking into the phone. We're locking eyes, and I'm not sure how this is going to turn out but, man, I'm glad I'm doing this.

"So," I continue, "what if this girl is willing to admit that she only ended things because she believed that everything happened in threes? And because you were Guy Number Three in a string of bad dating experiences . . . Much as it pains her to admit this, and admit it publicly . . . she thought you couldn't possibly be Mr. Right."

Ryan cocks an eyebrow. "Um . . . wow. Well, I guess I'd say that was far and away the dumbest reason to end a relationship ever."

"You'd be right."

"Okay," he says. "We finally agree on something."

"So if this girl realized that she was being silly . . . and wanted a second chance . . . on a scale of one to 'she drove me crazy,' where would you fall on getting back together?"

"Oh, she definitely drove me crazy," he says.

"She wasn't all bad, was she?"

"No," he admits. "She was pretty awesome. Actually, she was the most awesome woman I've ever met. I mean, when she wasn't being insane."

"Okay. We can definitely work with awesome. Talk to me. Ratio of awesome to insane."

"Okay . . . sixty-forty awesome."

"Sixty-forty!"

"Fine . . . fifty-fifty," he says, and I choke on my own spit.

"That's worse!"

"Seventy-thirty?"

"Okay." I nod. "Seventy percent is pretty good."

"Yeah," he says. "It is. But what's to say that this girl won't find a penny on the ground and take it as a sign to delete everything on my DVR?"

"She would never."

"That's one small check in her pros column, I suppose."

"So what's holding you back?" I ask, trying to be cool, trying to look cool, trying to act cool, heart jammed somewhere between my esophagus and my tonsils.

He's serious now. He looks me straight in the eyes and says, "Being lumped in with the two yokels that you dated before me, among other things."

"I'm sorry for that," I say. "You told Screwed Up you wanted to see a girl in the flesh who knew how to say she was sorry. Well, there you go. Witness: I. Am. Sorry."

"Thank you," he says, and can't hold back his devilish grin. "Because I demand to be treated like the unique snowflake I am."

Now we're both smiling, and I feel a little better, but I want more. Off-air.

"Can we get a coffee when your shift is over?" I ask.

"Fine," he says. "But you're paying."

"That's fine," I say.

"And I want a doughnut," he adds.

"You got it," I say.

"Will you guys just kiss and make up already?" Wendell says.

"We are private people," Ryan replies. "Mind your own business."

U

Ryan knows his doughnuts and the doughnuts at Stan's in Westwood are always fresh out of the fryer. He gets the peanut-butter-chocolate doughnut, and I opt for the classic glazed. At the register, Ryan won't let me pay even though he insisted I do over the air. We get back in the car and don't stop until we get to the ocean.

Sitting together in the sand, I can feel Ryan's hesitation. He doesn't want to live on eggshells, worrying about which superstition he's crossing, and I don't blame him. But I've been making a lot of progress. I know I'm the one in control of my destiny.

And I am damn well gonna fight for him.

"You want to know the secret to shopping smart?" I ask.

"Sure," he says, not sure where I'm going with this.

"When you find something you think you want to buy . . . you leave the store."

"I suppose that's one way to save your money."

"I'm not finished," I say.

"By all means," he replies with a bemused grin.

"If you can't stop thinking about it . . . then you go back and get it. And if you don't find yourself obsessing over it . . . then obviously you can live without it."

"But what if somebody else buys it when you're figuring out if you can't live without it?"

"You put it on hold before you leave."

"Ah," he says. "You left that part out."

"You can't put people on hold, though," I say. "That's where the metaphor kind of falls apart."

"The whole setting-something-free thing to see if it comes back to you?"

"Exactly. Except my version would be the more proactive version. Setting it free to see if you can't live without it. And not seeing if it comes back to you, but rather, going back and getting it."

"Your version also isn't so much 'setting it free' as 'kicking it to the curb based on superstitious manias.' "

"Come with me," I say, and I stand and brush the sand from my jeans.

When we get to where the tide comes in, I reach around my neck and unclasp my lucky horseshoe necklace. Strange thing is, I can almost still feel it there around my neck, getting tighter, even, almost choking me. It's fear. Fear of letting go. Fear of the unknown. A few deep breaths and the clarity kicks in. I swallow and shake it off. Ryan is none the wiser to my brief moment of panic.

"See this?" I say, holding my hand out before him, the necklace catching a light beam from the moonlight, glistening almost as if on cue.

"I know it well," he says. "The sacred lucky horseshoe."

"Exactly," I say. "You know what it means to me."

"I do."

"And you know what you mean to me?" I ask, eyebrows raised, hoping for a yes.

"You know, I think I do," he says. "Actually, yes, now I know I do. I'm saying a lot of 'I do's' here."

"Good thing there are no witnesses," I tease.

"No kidding," he says, but he's smiling wide, and it feels like he's warming up to me.

"Witness this!" I say, and I take off into the water, my shoes sloshing into the shallow tide, the cold water shocking my ankles.

"What are you doing, you nut?" Ryan shouts as he runs after me.

"Making sure I do it right," I say. "Making sure it gets a proper send-off."

Before I can think too hard about what I'm doing, I reach my hand up and cock my arm back, holding it behind me for a brief moment before I squeeze my eyes shut as tight as I can and thrust the necklace forward, out of my grasp, into the now escaping tide.

"Berry, don't!" he says, too late. "You love that thing."

I'd be lying if I didn't admit there was a gigantic gravitational pull urging me to run into the water after my necklace and dive around in a desperate attempt to find it. But the pull to Ryan is just that much stronger. I swallow hard, my eyes stinging with sudden tears as the horseshoe disappears beneath the waves. My heart races, and I have a million and one thoughts in about a moment's time. I open my eyes and turn to him.

"I love this thing," I say, motioning between the two of us. "I love what we have . . . or had before I screwed it up. I wish I could say, 'I wasn't always this way,' but this is exactly how I've always been."

"And I was a fan," he says.

"You're talking in past tense," I point out.

"So were you. I'm saying, the way you have always been . . . that's what drew me in. It was just the whole 'having to walk on eggshells or else the sky would fall' was a bit much. And even then, I was sticking it out. Look, I know I made fun of your silly habits, largely because . . . well, because they were silly. And I could have been more sensitive, I know. But you were the one who cut the cord."

"I know. I was afraid. I'm done with that."

And the beauty of the moment is I'm standing around a veritable potpourri of forbidden curses and danger zones. But where I once saw trip hazards, driftwood that might wash up at any moment and impale you, beach-buggy tread tracks that could swallow a person whole or at the very least cause a nasty ankle twist when navigating the beach in the dark, water teeming with stinging nettle seaweed that could entangle and drown an Olympic champion, runners and Rollerbladers whose crack-stepping qualified them for ten lifetimes of bad luck, I now see giant pillows of forgiving sand, a gentle ocean that washes over the tiny toes of intrepid little girls in frilly bathing suits, the crisscrossing of happy people out soaking it all in, like Ryan and me, right now.

The ball's in his court, of course. I've got the Clash's "Should I Stay or Should I Go" in my head. "If you say that you are mine, I'll be here 'til the end of time."

We walk back to dry sand, and I plunk myself down where our stuff is. Ryan sits beside me, and neither of us speaks. I reach into the doughnut bag and pull out a napkin, tearing it up out of nervousness. Before I know it, I've made a triangle. Then I take the straw from my iced coffee and stick it through the little makeshift fabric shape I've torn. Once in and then out so it looks like a tiny flag. I wave it before him.

"Is that your white flag?" he says, charmed by my pathetic impromptu arts and crafts.

I smile, guilty as charged.

"So you surrender?" he asks pointedly.

"I do," I say.

We were only just beginning when I screwed everything up, but I know I'm not living in fear anymore, and I want us to give this thing another chance. He takes the flag from my hand.

"What if I want to get a black cat?"

"We'll name him Lionel," I reply.

"Why Lionel?"

"You don't find many Lionels these days."

"True, true," he says.

"I'm cured," I insist. "I'm a new woman."

"I'm not so sure," Ryan says. "Perhaps we need a baptism."

"That water was cold," I say, dreading what's coming next.

Ryan stands up and reaches out for me.

"Uh-uh," I say, shaking my head. "No way." But Ryan leans down and scoops me up.

"It'll be fun," he says as I squirm and squeal. "Refreshing."

"Ryan," I say. "So help me, if you throw me in that water . . ."

"Then what?" he asks.

"On second thought," I say, "what are the odds we find my damn necklace? Because if you throw me in there, we are not getting out of that water until we find it."

"Oh, man," Ryan says as he surprisingly puts me back down.

But my smile tells him I'm kidding. I'm happy to let the necklace go, along with everything it stood for. And who knows? Maybe it'll wash ashore and bring someone else some comfort.

As for me, I'm looking forward to the unknown. Maybe knowing isn't what it's all about. Being "safe" sure hasn't kept me or my heart out of harm's way.

"Race ya," I say, and Ryan's eyes widen.

We take off toward the water, but at the last moment I stop short. He dives in, fully clothed, and comes up sputtering.

"You tease!" he shouts. "Don't you dare tell me you didn't want to get your lucky camisole wet!"

I smile, not cured maybe, but better. Far better than I have been in a long time.

"These are two-hundred-dollar jeans," I say. "And not to bring attention to something that might seriously bum you out right now . . . but would your cellphone happen to be in your pocket? Immersed in water?"

Without a word, he reaches into the water, retrieves his phone, shakes it, and looks for signs of life. Nothin' doin'. He looks back up to me and shrugs. No matter. He doesn't need it. The only person he wants to talk to right now is already here, shaking her head at the impetuous fool she loves.

Acknowledgments

Once you have three books under your belt, you also have three sets of acknowledgments under your belt. That means the obligatory "I'd better mention them" thing has been done. Probably all three times.

My fourth time around, I'm going to use these pages to give credit to the people who have *really* been my support system—my rocks—because without these people, this book wouldn't be in your hands.

My mom. First and always. Your unwavering support keeps me going when I'm running out of steam. I think back to you reading me *The Little Engine That Could*, and while it's no *Poky Little Puppy* . . . it's certainly been inspirational when it comes to me finishing every project I start. I love and adore you.

My grandma. You feisty vixen, you. Thank you for the intentional and unintentional laughs you provide. Thank you for your love. I know it doesn't come easy. Especially when I hang around with no-good, filthy louses and crooks. I love you dearly.

My stepmom. Thank you for loving my dad until he had had enough of this shithole. You made him happy, and that is everything. Thank you for always being proud of me and for flying in from San Francisco for my Los Angeles readings. Having my family at important events means *the world* to me. Sometimes it's the only time I get to see you, so . . . I guess I'll have to keep writing books.

My dog, Max. So handsome. So wise. So loyal. I could write a whole book on how much I love this dog. And perhaps when I run out of material I will, but for now I'll just say he's the best little guy in the world.

David Vanker. My dear, dear friend, happily married with a baby, *always* frenzied with work, yet still takes the time to listen to my occasional rant and does his damnedest to help me when I'm in need. David, you've been my hero countless times, and even if you follow through on your threat to move to Pakistan to avoid my calls, I know you'd still be there, and I cherish you for it.

Missy Peregrym. The exception to the rule. Real in a town full of fakes, more beautiful inside than out, although I'm not sure that's possible, because—just look at her. A true best friend. Someone I can count on to laugh with and cry with (and often both at once). Thank you for always pushing me to be better and stronger.

My Chicago writer girls: Jen Lancaster and Stacey Ballis. How many times did I freak out and say I wouldn't be able to finish this book? Before I'd even started writing it, no less? Don't answer that. Your talking me off a ledge each time made me believe I could do it. And I guess I did. I love you guys.

My New York writer girls: Karyn Bosnak, Gitty Daneshvari, and Sarah Grace McCandless. I always wondered what it would be like to have a cool group of girls to have regular dinners with and talk shop and talk boys and be silly with and to be surrounded by people who "get it." Girls who aren't backstabbing hos. Or at least not backstabbing ones. *Ha!*

My Los Angeles writer girl: Allison Schroeder. We've been through wars together and both came out relatively unscathed . . . or at least alive. I think. Unless M. Night is pulling a fast one on us. Thank you for always brainstorming when needed and listening when needed and going house-hunting when needed and being awesome pretty much always. I'm so proud of you and everything you've done this year.

My Los Angeles writer boy: Neal Brennan. I can't believe how long we've known each other. I *know* we're not that old, so someone has made a mathematical error. Just go with it. You are brilliant and hilarious, and I'm glad people recognize that. Thank you for being able to make me laugh when I'm pretty sure it would otherwise be impossible. I couldn't be happier to run into an ex every day at my local coffee shop. Seeing you is *always* a bright spot.

My bicoastal brother and sister in the fight for animal rights: Glen E. Friedman and Simone Reyes. Our time together, on whichever coast, is always comforting. Even if we get busy starring in reality shows (Simone) or balancing a great family with an already legendary photography career (Glen), just knowing that you are in the same city with me makes me feel better.

My L.A. homegirls: Jacqueline Lord, Christina Mcnown, and Abigail Spencer. Love, love, and love. Thank you, girls, for always being there when it counts.

My Breakfast Club: Stephen Hanks and Leslie Jordan. I love you both even more than I love my oatmeal, and that says everything.

The Gores. My family away from my family. You guys are simply the best. And the craziest. Which, I guess, is why I fit right in.

My two best Internet buddies, Peter DeWolf and Jason Logue, who absolutely make my life better. You're the best friends I've never met.

Additionally, this bunch of amazing friends who are too tricky to even classify: Jeremy Armstrong, Rick Biolsi, Adam Carl, Kim Falconnet, Gilly Garrett, U-Jung Jung, Devon Kellgren, Nez Mandel, Makyla Oakley, Jeff Schneider, Amanda Voelker, Fran Warner, and Harley Zinker. Man, I'm lucky.

You all make this world livable.

Never forget to thank your agent: thank you, Alanna Ramirez, and everyone at Trident. Thank you for working so hard on my behalf. Rob Goldman and Jeff Frankel should get in here, too, because they're the best lawyers on the planet.

And to my patient editor Kerri Buckley, who took my hysterical call in which I declared, "Guess what, I'm not gonna write this book!" And then the very next day took the call where I said, "Disregard everything I said yesterday." Kerri, you are the best and the coolest, and I'm so grateful to you for all your hard work, and thank you, too, Margaret Benton, production editor extraordinaire. Last but not least, a huge thank-you to Jane von Mehren, for giving me a home at Random House Trade Paperbacks.

About the Author

CAPRICE CRANE is the RT Readers' Choice Award–winning author of the novels *Stupid and Contagious, Forget About It,* and *Family Affair.* She has also written for film and television, including seven years at MTV and the first seasons of the new *90210* and *Melrose Place.* She divides her time between New York and Los Angeles, and her first original screenplay, *Love, Wedding, Marriage,* starring Mandy Moore and Kellan Lutz, will hit theaters in 2011.